SYDNEY NOIR

EDITED BY JOHN DALE

BROOKLYN, NEW YORK, USA
BALLYDEHOB, CO. CORK, IRELAND

Published by Akashic Books
©2019 Akashic Books

Series concept by Tim McLoughlin and Johnny Temple
Sydney map by Sohrab Habibion

Paperback ISBN: 978-1-61775-581-1
Hardcover ISBN: 978-1-61775-737-2
Library of Congress Control Number: 2018931222

Akashic Books
Brooklyn, New York, USA
Ballydehob, Co. Cork, Ireland
Twitter: @AkashicBooks
Facebook: AkashicBooks
E-mail: info@akashicbooks.com
Website: www.akashicbooks.com

ALSO IN THE AKASHIC NOIR SERIES

SYDNEY

PARRAMATTA

M4

BANKSTOWN

M5

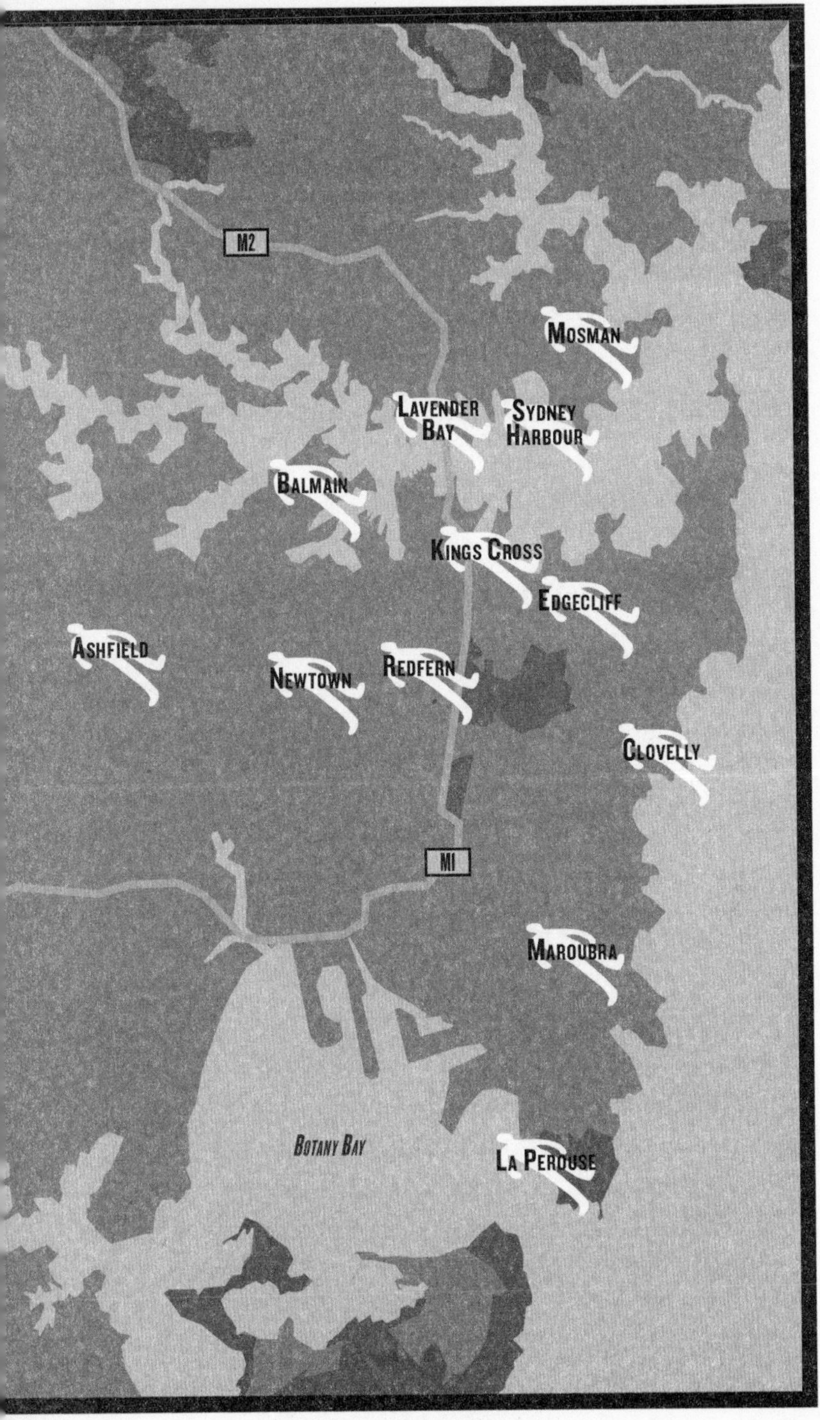
M2
Mosman
Lavender Bay
Sydney Harbour
Balmain
Kings Cross
Edgecliff
Ashfield
Newtown
Redfern
Clovelly
M1
Maroubra
Botany Bay
La Perouse

TABLE OF CONTENTS

PART III: CRIMINAL JUSTICE

INTRODUCTION
CITY OF CHANGE

Sydney has a long and distinguished criminal history. From the arrival of 756 convicts in 1788 through to the postwar waves of ethnic crime gangs, this city of five million people has more unsolved murders than any other Australian city, as well as more drive-by shootings and more jailed politicians. Noir is as much a part of Sydney's character as frangipanis and cockroaches, rusted iron lace and sandstone terraces, torrential rain and potholed roads.

A subgenre of crime fiction, noir is the most democratic of genres in that it includes people from all walks of life and in all kinds of trouble. The protagonists are not private eyes and implausible police detectives from central casting, but ordinary people caught up in crime and violence, the kind of people you pass in the street or sit next to on overcrowded buses and trains.

In the early 1980s, I was working in a rundown bar in Darlinghurst that was a popular watering hole for the notorious 21 Division, a flying squad of the city's hardest detectives. On Friday and Saturday nights, a couple of middle-aged women from the western suburbs would sit out on kitchen chairs on Riley Street soliciting for customers. On the other side of the street was a flea-ridden hostel for alcoholic men, and farther down the road was a tow truck business with criminal connections, while upstairs, the publican, a capable older woman, had shacked up with a Maori biker.

The bar was unlike any I had been to in Hobart, where I grew up. On busy nights cops, bikers, would-be actors, rock-and-rollers, trannies, small-time celebrities, and general riff-raff turned up in that Darlinghurst pub to drink to excess and hatch their plans while complying with the unspoken rule that no actual drug exchanges were to be undertaken on the premises.

The 21 Division detectives, chosen specifically for their size, congregated in the doorways so that everyone had to squeeze past them to get served. The old diggers from the hostel drank at the front bar perched on their stools like babies in high chairs. The sex workers were a friendly lot and ordered a sherry or gin and tonic after their shift, waiting in the lounge bar for their partners to pick them up for the long drive home. Sex and drugs and money and booze all came together in this seedy pub situated in the hollow between the central business district and the Cross. That old, rough-neck, Anglo-aboriginal inner Sydney is mostly gone now, modernized and corporatized, but the pub still stands and its clientele park their Audis and BMWs outside while they dine at the rooftop restaurant.

Nothing lasts in Sydney, especially good fortune: lives are upturned, shops are sold, roads dug up, trees and houses knocked down, premiers discarded, and entire communities relocated in the name of that economic mantra—growth and progress. Just when you think the traffic can't get any worse and the screech of the 747s descending over your roof can't get any louder and the pavements can't get any dirtier, along comes a wild electrical storm that batters the buildings and shakes the power lines and washes the garbage off the streets and you stand, sheltered under your broken brolly in the center of Sydney, admiring this big beautiful city.

What never changes, though, is the hustle on the street. My father was a detective in the vice squad shortly after the Second World War, and he told stories of busting SP bookies in Paddington and Surry Hills, collaring cockatoos stationed in the laneways of South Sydney, and arresting sly-groggers. Policing back then was hands-on for the poor and hands-off for the rich. Crime and Sydney have always been inseparable: a deep vein of corruption runs beneath the surface of even its most respectable suburbs.

These brand-new stories from some of Australia's best writers deal with men and women who work in finance or serve in Liquorland, drive cabs or beat-up utes; they might be architects or struggling students, athletes or aboriginal liaison officers, retired coppers or contract laborers, patternmakers or photographers, philosophy lecturers or drug dealers. Some are desperate for revenge or money and fame; others are simply caught up in circumstances beyond their control or in a sexual relationship gone wrong. These fourteen stories take us from Kings Cross to La Perouse, from Balmain to Parramatta, Redfern to Maroubra, Clovelly to Bankstown, Sydney Harbour to Edgecliff, Newtown to Ashfield, and Lavender Bay to Mosman. There are no safe spaces in this collection. What *Sydney Noir* does best is to provide a window onto the street.

So sit back and enjoy the view.

John Dale
Sydney, Australia
November 2018

PART I

FAMILY MATTERS

THE PASSENGER

BY KIRSTEN TRANTER

Balmain

S kye kept one hand on the front door, looked me over, and gave a sort of laugh. I wasn't sure if she would even remember me, but right away she said, "Rob," in a low drawl, "you used to seem so tall." She stood with one bare foot on top of the other. Her toenails were painted glittery pink. A teenager now.

"Hello, Skye," I said.

"Oh, hello yourself." She opened the door wide enough to let me in. "Virginia's here somewhere," she said, and gestured with a sloppy wave.

The back of the house was crowded with people; it was Fred's sixtieth. I'd been invited to the party but had come really for Virginia, Skye's older sister. Afternoon sun spilled in through the open doors leading out to the deck. The house—an enormous 1970s monstrosity—was perched at the east end of the Balmain peninsula. Ugly from the street, but you forgot about that ugliness as soon as you stepped inside. It was all redeemed by the view through the wall of glass that looked over the harbor toward the bridge. There was a mooring for the family's aging sailboat below.

Houses around them had been renovated or torn down and replaced with designer mansions since the last time I had visited, but nothing had changed at the Dawson house. The Berber carpet was worn through practically to the boards and the wood paneling was scratched; the durable Scandinavian modernist furniture had been recuperated by fashion and was cool again. I caught sight of Fred out on the deck, a bottle in his hand, his white linen shirt open at the neck by one button too many. I looked for Virginia. Everyone else at the party was about Fred's age: women with hair dyed orangey henna red and spectacles with brightly colored frames, men wearing Hawaiian shirts and smoking cigarettes. I recognized the local member of parliament in his shorts and Blundstone boots, beer in hand, arguing with a woman drinking from a can. It was old Balmain, aging bohemians, the generation who had bought workers' cottages down the street from the housing commission flats and derelict Victorian terraces by the water in the seventies and eighties when it was cheap, and were now sitting on millions of dollars of real estate. Writers and teachers and social workers and artists, and some of them, like Fred, men who dealt in money. I never knew exactly what his work entailed: he just said "finance," and grimaced. He was the money and his wife, Maureen, was the artist, a playwright. At university, one of her plays had been on the list of readings for an English course I'd taken, although I never actually read it. Virginia would change the subject if it ever came up.

Maureen waved at me from across the room and made her way over, voluptuous and perfumed and wearing a dress that seemed to be made of a hundred silk scarves sewn haphazardly together. She kissed me and I could feel the trace of lipstick on my cheek, the corner of my mouth. Her eyes were sharp and dark. She winked. "Robert," she said, "we've missed you." She squeezed my hand, her rings pressing uncomfortably against my fingers.

Virginia sidled up to us. "Here you are," she said. She was wearing a man's mirrored sunglasses, metal rimmed, oversized, and narrow trousers that showed how thin she had become. Maureen let me go and drifted away. "Why don't you have a drink?" Virginia said, in an accusing way, as though she were scolding me for being so empty-handed.

I had been sober for several days after the kind of hangover that makes you think about giving up drinking, but I wasn't that committed to the idea. She led me to the kitchen and elbowed people aside to get to the fridge, and pulled out a bottle of Riesling. "The wine out there is terrible," she said, nodding toward the deck. "Someone brought a *cask*." She pushed the fridge door closed. "Dad told me he'd run into you."

I had gone to Circular Quay the day after I flew in to Sydney with the idea of riding a ferry to Manly, wanting to get out of the city as soon as I arrived, but the ferry to Birchgrove had been about to leave, and I gave in to the idea, knowing it would take me by her house. Fred was on his way home; he had seen me just a minute before his stop, and shook my hand for too long. He'd invited me to this party. "It will be really good to see you," he'd said, beguilingly sincere, in that way he had of making you believe every commonplace he uttered.

I had thought about calling Virginia or sending her a message letting her know I would be there, but didn't. The last e-mail had been two years earlier, and she hadn't written back. It had been one of those e-mails I read the day after with another one of those hangovers and found it hard to remember actually writing, and regretted sending. I had written things that I probably shouldn't have, and I gave myself a hard time about it for a while, and wrote an apology and then deleted it. I heard that she went through with it, got married, and I wrote another message congratulating her and deleted that too. There had been others composed and trashed since then, most recently in the weeks before I decided to come back.

She pushed the wine bottle into my hand and I followed her upstairs to her old bedroom. The smell in the hallway was the same: the piney scent of Radox bath salts, a note of mildew from the water, the dusty smell of the carpet. Her room had a small balcony and we sat there on wooden boards hot from the day's sun. She had collected a couple of glasses on the way and held one out for me to fill. I hadn't seen Julian. I felt sure that he wasn't here, although I knew that this was just me projecting what I wanted to be true. But then she swallowed a big mouthful of her drink and gestured loosely toward the balcony doors, to the room inside. "I'm back here for the moment," she said, and I looked back inside and saw what I hadn't noticed, the thing she was explaining. The bed half made, the clothes draped on the armchair, and things strewn on the dresser, a lipstick, a book. "Julian's away for work. I hate being at the flat on my own."

Someone at the party on the deck below shrieked with laughter, probably Maureen, and there was the sound of glass breaking. Virginia pushed the sunglasses up the bridge of her nose.

"So, tell me about London. What the fuck are you doing back home?"

I started to tell her a bit about it, leaving out the reasons for returning.

"Virginia?" Skye was standing in the doorway of the bedroom. "Mum asked me to get you. Speech time."

"Are you making a speech?" I asked.

"No," Virginia said. "Maureen."

Maureen was tapping a champagne flute with a fork when we arrived downstairs. It seemed rude to leave, so I stayed, standing at the back of the crowd. There was singing and toasts, a cake, a huge pavlova. I looked for Virginia, wanting to say goodbye. Fred pulled me aside and handed me a bottle of beer and a paper plate with a slice of pavlova on it. Strawberries drowned in clots of meringue and cream.

"There you go," he said. "Pavlova and beer in hand, water view, you're back in Sydney alright." He smelled of beer and expensive aftershave, a perfumer's idea of the beach. "You found Virginia?"

I said that I had.

"She's moved back in for a while," Fred told me. "Doing some renovations on that flat of theirs."

I nodded at what was obviously a lie.

"You were friends with Julian, right?" He used the past tense, and I thought it was probably because the friendship was in the past, but it made it sound as though Julian himself was in the past, as though he were dead. The idea didn't bother me as much as it should have. "Heard any news of him?" he asked, and took a long swig of his beer, looking away from me.

"No, I haven't been back that long." The idea of a conversation with Fred about Virginia's relationship was about as appealing as the thought of a swim in the polluted waters of the harbor below. But I felt sorry for Fred, who seemed to be on the verge of saying something more, a worried expression on his face. "What's the story?" I asked.

"It's been five weeks," he said. "No word from him. He and Virginia were having some trouble I think, but nothing serious. And then." He lifted his hands as though describing an explosion. "Nothing."

"He took off?"

"No phone call, nothing. Not answering his phone or e-mail, Facebook, whatever. No offense, I know the two of you had your falling out. I just thought you might have heard something. If you're still, ah, in touch with that old crowd.

Virginia's just, she's been wrecked by it." I thought of the cool way she had adjusted her glasses, the way she drank her wine. She didn't seem wrecked. But she was good at hiding things.

"Was he still working for you?" I asked.

"Yes. Left me in the lurch a bit with a couple of things." He waved as though brushing away a mosquito. "But that's neither here nor there."

"I'm not in touch with that old crowd, not that much," I said, using his words. The crowd of dealers and users that had been a big reason to leave Sydney before I found myself arrested or worse. Julian had been part of it, but it always seemed like a part-time interest for him, a hobby. His uncle was a judge. His father was a solicitor, with a house in Cremorne that made Fred's look like a boat shed. Julian was just passing time before entering that kind of life; they would have bailed him out if any kind of serious trouble had loomed, or spirited him away to dry out if his habit got out of control. Which it never seemed to do. When he started working for Fred, I thought he had taken that step into the world of money and privilege. That happened just after he started seeing Virginia. Or just after he started seeing her publicly. I found out later that before she broke up with me, she had been sleeping with him for months. It was hard to muster any concern for Julian.

It had been me who had introduced him to Virginia, when I brought him along to a party at the Dawsons' one weekend. He was the new kid at school in our final year, arriving with rumors that he had been expelled from two others. Parents loved him, with his easy, disarming smile, his apparent lack of teenage angst, his guileless charm, his storybook name. I fell for it myself, but I was disappointed in Virginia when she fell for it too.

"Was he in any trouble?" I asked. Maybe he hadn't left the old crowd after all.

I expected Fred to say no and I think he was about to. But he said, "I've started to wonder."

I hadn't tasted my beer and it was impossible to eat the pavlova while holding it. I looked for a place to put both of them down before I left.

"His parents have been to the police." Fred shook his head. "It's not like him to disappear like that." He seemed to be wounded on his own behalf as much as Virginia's. Julian was easy to love, and Fred was someone who loved people easily. "I'm used to seeing you with your camera in hand," he said, changing the subject. "You know Derek, don't you? Derek March? He's here somewhere."

"I think I met him once or twice." Derek March had been a frequent visitor to the house when I was there, often around for drinks or dinner. Decades ago he had made a name overseas with his photographs of musicians and their groupies. Now he attracted controversy with portraits of young girls and boys, posed in situations from basements to darkened playgrounds. Virginia and Skye had appeared in some of his photographs.

"What's your situation, work wise?" Fred asked me. "I know Derek's looking for a studio assistant." He led me through to the big living room, where Derek March was seated in a corner talking to a young woman in black, a glass of red wine in his hand and a bottle on the coffee table in front of him. He still had that slightly emaciated Keith Richards look, his face more lined than I remembered, his deep-set eyes an unsettling pale slatey blue.

"The man of the hour!" he said when he saw Fred, raising his glass.

Fred introduced me as an old friend of the family, a great

talent, just returned from overseas. March was used to young artists seeking favor. The woman sitting with him was probably one of them. His gaze grew more sober as he examined me.

"Fred said you might need an assistant," I said. I did need work. I liked the idea of being back in a darkroom, the closeness of the space, the fumes of the magical chemicals, the concentration.

"Let's talk," he said. The young woman reached for the bottle. He tilted his glass toward her and she refilled it. "Come and see me at the studio. Two-forty Denis Street. Not far. Other side of Balmain."

"Thanks," I said. "When?"

He waved his glass around a bit so that the wine came close to sloshing over the edge. "Next week will do. You can usually find me there. Don't make it too early."

One of his pieces hung on the wall across from us, a photograph of Virginia. She looked as I remembered her when we met in high school, her dark hair long and wavy, her lipsticked mouth somewhere between sullen and humorous. Her face was the only spot of light in the image, shadowy trees in the background, her arm on a fence collapsing under the weight of ivy.

Fred put one hand on my shoulder. "Now excuse me while I mingle," he said, smiling, his work done, the introduction made, the favor conferred.

I was making my way along the stone path that led to the front gate, when Skye appeared, stepping on tiptoe over pebbles and the hard little seeds from overhanging bottlebrush trees. "Where are you going?" she asked, falling into step beside me.

"Home." Back to Surry Hills where I was staying in a musician friend's flat, empty while he was on tour. *Home* didn't sound right.

"Do you still sell drugs?" she asked.

I stopped and faced her. "What? How old are you, fourteen?"

"You were fourteen," she said. "You and Virginia." She was wrong, but not by much. By fifteen we were trying something new every weekend.

"Forget it," I said. "And no, I don't."

She came closer and put her fingers around my wrist and bit her lip. Her eyes were bloodshot and I wondered whether she was stoned. I pulled my wrist away, hard.

"Ow," she said in a hurt little voice.

Fred called her name from the deck. I headed toward the gate.

"Fuck you, Rob," she called after me.

Most of the time in high school I had envied Virginia her family, but there were times like now when I closed the gate behind me with a sense of escape that took me by surprise with its force.

A few days later I found myself at the Clock Hotel in Surry Hills, drinking alone. Years ago this had been a frequent haunt of the old crowd, as Fred had affectionately called them. Since then it had received a makeover and now sold boutique beer. I didn't expect to see any old faces, but then I caught sight of one at the other end of the bar. Finn. He had grown a long, solid-looking beard, and it took me a moment to recognize him. He glanced over and saw me and frowned and smiled at the same time. His hair had grown longer, and it suited him, like the beard. He walked over with his glass in hand.

We talked about what he was doing and what he was planning to do, a familiar conversation. He was working on some amazing home brew, organic and heirloom, he said, better than this overpriced shit at the Clock. Planning to develop it, expand. He always had ambitions that he made sound convincing. I wondered if he was still selling from here. I remembered Fred's anxiety, and asked Finn if he was in touch with Julian. He shook his head. "Weird," he said. "No one's seen him." Julian had put in an order with him, he told me, a month or two earlier, not a big one, just a small one, but he never showed up to collect. "I thought maybe he'd taken off overseas, like you." He smiled. "Or somewhere. Maybe there was some kind of trouble, I don't know. He always said he wanted to go to Tasmania." He shrugged. "Maybe he just moved back to Cremorne. What does Virginia have to say?" He tried to sound casual.

"He's away for work."

"What about her sister?" he asked.

"What? Skye?"

Finn put his glass down on the bar and studied it. "Too bitter for an IPA."

"What about her?"

"Just wondering," he said. "She's a bit of a wild child. And now I'm off. Internet dating." He smoothed his beard. We said goodbye.

I lost my way a couple of times getting to March's studio, turning through old streets no wider than a lane, sandstone curbstones and asphalt footpaths broken up by eucalyptus roots. Glimpses of water, eerily flat in the late-afternoon light, showed through gaps between houses, and glinted through windows in Victorian terraces with all the inner walls knocked out, everything given over to the view beyond. Expensive cars were parked on March's block with half their wheels up on the curb to make space for other vehicles to pass through the narrow street. I recognized Virginia's old car, a blue 1980s Mercedes sedan, parked at a haphazard angle. She worked for the gallery that represented March; she was visiting for something to do with that, probably, and I was surprised to find that I didn't particularly want her to be here. A high wooden gate in a brick fence led to the studio, a tall boxy structure clad in corrugated iron and half covered in creeping ivy, set back from a brick courtyard. The front door was ajar, but there was no answer when I knocked. The place was heavy with quiet, cut with the sounds of insects intermittently buzzing.

"Hello?" I called as I pushed the door. Inside was an open space like a warehouse with a room toward the back that looked like a darkroom. A half-assembled motorcycle sat in one corner surrounded by parts and tools. Stairs led to a loft, a bed strewn with clothes. Blinds let through slivers of light.

March lay on a low sofa, his eyes closed. Skye sat in a high-backed leather armchair across from him in front of a white fabric screen, hands resting neatly on the arms of the chair, her head tipped back, eyes open and unfocused. Her tawny hair was down and she was naked. Between her and March was a camera on a tall tripod. I waited for one of them to stir, but neither of them did.

"Skye?" I said. She was wearing long dangling earrings of silver and jade and they swung as she turned her head toward me. She smiled dreamily.

Stuff covered every surface apart from a clear space around Skye's chair: ashtrays, books, glasses, bowls, vases full of dead flowers. March hadn't moved; I looked closer and saw the belt around his arm, the syringe on the coffee table. His lips were tinged with blue.

"Fuck," I said. I knelt by him and put my fingers to his wrist, his throat. Nothing. His skin felt warm.

"Fuck," Skye said, in a mumbled echo.

His head lolled when I pressed his throat again, and this time I felt it, a feeble beat. I pulled out my phone. No signal. "Is there a landline?" I asked her.

She sighed. "Somewhere."

I saw a telephone on a table, a plastic handset with a tangled curly cord, and dialed, and gave the information. An ambulance would be with us shortly, I was told. I looked through the cabinets in the bathroom, the stinking darkroom and the untidy bookshelves, to see if there was any Naloxone. There wasn't. Skye hadn't moved from her chair. I found her clothes behind a sofa and brought them to her. She held them limply.

I checked March again, tried to pull him upright, and managed to get his head elevated on a couple of cushions. His chest rose and fell with shallow breaths, ribs visible through his thin shirt. I didn't want to look at him.

He wasn't dead. I repeated that to myself, fought to stave off the panic. Part of me was back in a Hoxton bedroom, frantic, hopeless; time was a plastic spool of film and sound that stuttered and spun like a trap. I tried to close it off, focused on examining the camera while Skye started to dress. It was a beautiful machine, a Canon with a lens that would have cost as much as a first-class ticket to London. It held old-fashioned film, no digital screen to scroll back through. I opened the camera and pulled out the film. There were a few other rolls on the table and I pocketed them. Skye was still struggling to get her T-shirt over her head. I went over to a bookcase with a shelf of photo albums and pulled them out, looked through until I came to one filled with pictures of her and other girls. Not Virginia. I saw enough before I closed it to see that they were not all recent; some of Skye were a couple of years old at least. Beautifully composed, printed on quality paper, artful and obscene and poisonous. I pulled out another album. More girls, older-looking prints. I fought the urge to tear them all to shreds. I left the album open on the coffee table for the medics, and held on to the one with pictures of Skye. It felt like a futile gesture. There was probably a computer somewhere with a whole vault of digital versions of the images.

I found the keys to the Mercedes in Skye's miniature leather backpack, in among cigarettes, sticky pots of lip gloss, gum, and coins. A siren sounded in the distance. There seemed to be little point waiting and I badly wanted to be somewhere else.

"Let's go," I said. She stood up and pulled her shirt down to her waist. Her hips were narrow as a boy's. "Put on your skirt." I looked away. She glanced at March for the first time and blinked. He was still breathing. "The ambulance is on the way," I said.

"Why?" she asked. She reached for a clear flat plastic bag of tablets, little white oblongs, on the coffee table near an ashtray.

"Leave it," I told her, but she held on to it and I didn't feel like arguing.

The sirens were properly loud, just blocks away, by the time we reached the Mercedes. I opened the passenger door for Skye but she ignored me and slumped into the back. I sat behind the wheel and turned the key. The engine kicked into life with a deep grumble. I remembered the feel of the hand brake, and had a sudden memory of Virginia in the driver's seat, her hands on the wheel, the loose elegance of her slim wrists. The gears creaked.

The weather had changed; storm clouds turned the light dim and green, and rain spattered the car roof. A pair of white cockatoos swooped onto the telegraph pole at the end of the block, screaming in outrage.

"Home, James," Skye said, and laid herself down on the backseat. I couldn't tell whether she understood what she had witnessed, or if she didn't care.

"Put your seat belt on," I said.

"Fuck you, Rob," she mumbled. The earrings made a little thump as she dropped them onto the floor.

Maureen opened the door when I rang the bell. I had the album under one arm, Skye's backpack over my shoulder, Skye leaning on my other arm. "I found her at Derek March's studio," I told Maureen.

"Okay, come in," she said after a long pause. "Virginia isn't home."

Skye let go of me and headed toward the bathroom.

Maureen poured herself a glass of wine in the kitchen, but didn't offer me anything. "Thank you, Rob. It's such a problem, with Skye. Chemicals," she said disapprovingly, as though Skye had been shooting up bleach. "It's out of control," she complained, but she didn't sound convincing. "I've tried to tell Fred." I wondered if she hadn't heard what I'd said. She turned away, putting the bottle back in the fridge.

"She was at March's studio," I repeated, and put the album on the kitchen counter. I thought about how to tell her about what I had seen. And then I saw the way she was looking at the album, and the way she looked back at me. There was anxiety in her face, but it wasn't for Skye. I had the feeling that the contents of the album would not be a surprise to her. I remembered Virginia's stories, of being taken to the studio by Maureen with Skye, being left to play with the pottery wheel in the courtyard while the adults stayed inside.

"He overdosed," I said. "We left before the ambulance got there."

"The ambulance?" she asked, frowning. She felt for her necklace, a string of chunky, colorful beads.

"He'll be okay."

"But you said an ambulance? What happened?"

I tried to sound confused and stupid to deflect her questions, my patience suddenly gone. "I don't know where they would have taken him," I told her. "The Balmain Hospital? I don't know. Sorry."

She looked weary and disappointed in me. I imagined that Skye was familiar with this look; Virginia and Fred too. I didn't believe that she was ignorant of any of it: the drugs, the photographs. She took a packet of cigarettes from a high corner shelf—a halfhearted hiding place—and lit one. Skye shuffled out of the bathroom toward the lounge and the bleep of the television being turned on reached us a few seconds later.

The pathway was slippery with rain as I made my way to the street, but the storm had passed; already there was a patch of hollow blue sky over the bridge. I walked the meandering blocks to Darling Street and down to the water to wait for a ferry.

Virginia called me later that night. I had drunk with dedicated speed at the first place I found at the quay, a cramped pub in the Rocks full of American tourists, but it didn't blunt anything as much as I wanted it to and I left when the karaoke started. Virginia thanked me, demure and sincere sounding. Maureen hadn't told her about the photos, it turned out, and she was quietly furious when I explained. She remembered a session Skye had done for March the previous year, but thought that had been the last time, and it had seemed to be above board, something for his new series.

"I took the film," I said.

"It will be on his computer, though, or someone's computer," she said.

"I know." It was probably just a matter of time before the photographs showed up online, if they weren't there already. I was in no hurry to find out. "I have your car keys," I told her. I had found them in my pocket when I reached for my own door key.

Virginia made an impatient noise. "I can't believe she took the car again." There was a big age gap between them, ten years, enough to make the sibling relationship tenuous, but Virginia's exasperation somehow seemed entirely belonging to a sister. She downplayed her protective instincts, as though they were an embarrassment, and irritation was one of her covers.

I couldn't tell if our stalled exchange was one of intimacy or estrangement. I set the canisters on the kitchen counter and pulled out the rolls of film, flimsy ribbons that turned dead brown in the light.

Skye answered the door when I went over the next day to return the keys. Despite the heat, she was wearing tracksuit pants with a hooded jacket zipped all the way up, her whole body covered apart from her bare feet. I pushed away a memory of her golden skin against the leather chair in the studio. Her cheekbones glittered with powder.

"Come on in," she said, and I followed her. Burning December sun poured in through all the glass. The bridge was a crisp piece of geometry across the water, the view fringed with drooping gums, a postcard. "Virginia's at the gallery. Some kind of photocopier emergency? You can wait for her if you want." I held on to the keys in my pocket, unreasonably disappointed. Skye folded her arms with her back to the light. "I was just about to take the boat out. Do you want to come?"

"Sailing?"

"Yes, stupid." She went to the door and slipped her feet into canvas sandshoes. I had never learned to like sailing, the few times Virginia had taken me. But my hangover made me slow and pliant; I went along with it.

The sailboat slid through the water, out from the shade of the dock and into the bright afternoon. The deck was scrubbed clean and white, and I sat on a bench near the stern and closed my eyes for a moment. The harsh sun and salt spray felt kind for those long seconds, convinced me that they could scrub me clean too. Skye moved with compact assurance as she adjusted the sail, coiled ropes, tied complicated knots. I didn't embarrass myself by trying to help. She stepped down into the small cabin and came back with a bottle of water.

"Thanks for yesterday," she said, handing me the bottle. She said it as though it was any old thing, no big deal. "He's fine, by the way. Apparently."

Half my night had been spent fighting memories of March's prone body, the terrible bluish slackness of his skin, and the other half dreaming of London. All night with the comatose and the dead.

"No worries," I said.

The water around us sparkled and shined, giving away nothing of its true depth, and the boat rocked gently. Skye unzipped her jacket and sat across from me with her elbows on her knees and talked. She had been photographed by March for his "private collection" a few times, she said. He didn't pay her in money, only in drugs. She made it sound like a fair swap, or rather she was convincing herself that it was.

"Isn't he friends with Maureen?" I asked.

She snorted. "Friends. Yeah."

I asked about Fred.

"He loves Derek. He loves all that free-spirit, hippie artistic bullshit," she said. "He just sees what he wants to see. Like everyone." Skye checked the sail, lifted a snaking end of coiled rope, dropped it again. "So, do you have anything on you?" she asked, standing with one hand on her hip.

"You keep asking me that," I said.

"Yeah, I do." She shrugged her hoodie off, leaving her shoulders bare in a thin camisole, flirting. She stepped closer so that we were almost touching.

"Skye, come on," I said, shifting. "Don't."

Her expression clouded. "I hope you got a good look yesterday. Enjoy yourself?"

I drank my water, shook my painful head. This whole sailing thing was a mistake.

She collected her hoodie from the floor. "Julian wasn't as pure and good as you," she said. "He loved to come out for a sail." She played with the zipper, which seemed to have stuck, and tossed the thing onto the bench across from me. "He used to make me a drink, a 'Julian Special.'" She bit her thumb, chewing the worn-down nail, worrying the skin with her teeth.

The bottled water started to taste stale and metallic. It took a moment to understand what she was telling me, and then another moment for the instinctive disbelief to fall sickeningly away.

"Dad thinks he was such a saint," she went on. "I said I'd tell him. I'd tell Virginia. He said I wouldn't, and that even if I did, he'd just say it was bullshit and I was a jealous little bitch, jealous little sister. And he said everyone knew about March's photos, everyone knew I was a slut."

The boat floated in the water, going nowhere, stilled against the breeze. She talked quickly, with anxious animation. "I switched the drinks. He didn't notice, he was stoned anyway. He was right there, where you're sitting. Passed out." She paused, staring at the bench, and shook her head. "I was so sick of it, you know? And I just thought, *I know what it will be like, he just won't tell me next time he mixes the drinks, and that would be worse.*"

"You didn't think they'd believe you? If you told them?"

Her face lost its hardness, threatened to crumple. "Maybe, yeah. But I didn't want them to know." She was ashamed, she was trying to paper it over, and I felt the bitter tide of my anger rising again, that impulse to shred the photos, to wreck the studio. To leave the man dead and alone. "I think Virginia kind of knew, for a while," she said. "I don't know." The idea was unthinkable: I pushed it away, but it pulsed with cruel possibility.

"So where is he?"

She looked back toward the house. The boat seemed to be traveling so slowly, but we were farther out into the harbor than I had realized. The bridge cast a perfect shadow of itself onto the water. In the distance Luna Park showed its ghastly open mouth, its Ferris wheel an oversized toy. "We should head back," she said. "Virginia's probably home."

I wanted to know, although part of me wanted not to. "Skye, where is he?"

She gazed at the little waves slapping the hull. "Stop looking for him," she said, her voice tired and flat. "He's not coming back." The boat felt suddenly like a flimsy thing, suspended over cold depth. She adjusted the tiller, her body again filled with focus, tuned to the machine, the water, the weather. We picked up speed. "I could have said it was an accident and he fell, he was drunk, whatever." The breeze carried her words away as she spoke. "But maybe it wouldn't have looked exactly like that, his body. I don't know."

He was in the water then: this was what she had been telling me. Not telling me. I didn't know how long bodies stayed underwater. A long time, probably, if weighted correctly. Every object around me now seemed full of sinister possibility: the new-looking anchor, the coiling rope, the heavy wooden boom of the sail.

"What about Virginia? Does she know?"

Skye shrugged. "Maybe she guessed." Her confession was over, such as it was; she would not look at me, or the water, only toward the house. The breeze lifted her hair, blowing it across her mouth and her eyes. She was a girl again for a second, lanky and unself-conscious, inhabiting the child I remembered, and then the impression slipped. "You don't have to tell her," she said.

If not me, then who would? I tried to remember if we had been like this at fourteen, with this kind of remove from moral structures. I could imagine it in Virginia, but I didn't trust anything I remembered of my own past self.

I tried to see something of Virginia in her, as though finding likeness between them would somehow provide a clue to the whole tragedy. I found only superficial resemblances. The tilt of her jaw in profile, the shape of her brow. Skye's tawny blond hair was nothing like Virginia's sleek dark mane. Maybe Virginia had once been this brittle, but surely never this damaged. To me she had always been imbued with a terrible power, all due to my adolescent desire.

Had Virginia returned to the house, shadowing her sister, to learn the truth? Or to protect her in case the truth leaked out? I reached inside for the familiar longing for her, and was surprised to find it flattened, somehow two-dimensional, a dead echo of itself. The glare was just starting to leach out of the sunshine as the afternoon turned toward evening. The shadow of a tall gum tree fell across the dock as we approached, and for a moment I saw March's photograph there, Virginia framed by darkened greenery, waiting.

THE BIRTHDAY PRESENT

BY MANDY SAYER

Kings Cross

Frank lived in a dive in Kings Cross filled with junkies and prostitutes. Three stories high and about a hundred years old, this hotel was either rented by the week, or by the half hour, depending on your requirements. Frank had rented room 11 for as long as he could remember, because he worked as a courier for the neighboring strip joints and clubs. Now in his midsixties, he'd done the same job for almost half a century, and was ready to pass the business on.

Frank rose at about five p.m., as he did most afternoons, and showered and shaved in the shared bathroom—a mold-furred cubicle with leaking taps and a dedicated sharps bin. Back in his own room, he dressed in his best suit—the one he reserved for funerals and court appearances. His only son, Jimmy, was turning eighteen today.

He checked the duffel bag in the wardrobe, which contained thirty-four grand in cash. Frank locked the wardrobe and shoved his revolver into his inside coat pocket. As he opened the door, he glanced again at the eviction notice lying on the floor: the Astoria had been sold to a foreign company and all tenants had to vacate the premises by the end of the week. The word on the street was that it was going to be renovated into multimillion-dollar apartments.

He stepped out onto the footpath. The neon sign from a bar across the road blinked erratically. A siren wailed in the distance. In the old days, the locals had called them "Kings Cross lullabies." And back then he used to deliver chicken dinners and hamburgers to all the hungry strippers on eight-hour shifts stuck in joints along the Golden Mile. Now, most of the clubs had shut down due to 1:30 a.m. lockout laws. These days the only orders he received from working girls were for ice and Ecstasy.

He was to meet his son at an old haunt farther along the Golden Mile, at a restaurant that had once belonged to his first boss, Lionel Silke, the former King of the Cross. Everyone around town knew that Silke had earned his title by bribing cops, blackmailing politicians, and dealing smack. His nickname had been Sir Untouchable. Frank remembered that at the height of his fame, Silke had owned five strip clubs, as well as twelve nightclubs, six restaurants, and three illegal gambling dens. He'd also bought up a high-class brothel.

Frank strolled south down Darlinghurst Road, weaving between the scores of suited professionals pouring out of the train station on their way home from work. Most of them were carrying briefcases and muttering into headsets, not watching where they were walking, and bumping into each other. These were the kind of people who would move into his hotel, once it had been turned into slick apartments. Farther down, outside McDonald's, Frank saw a big-breasted blonde in her late sixties wearing thigh-high boots. Doris had kept an eye on him when he'd first come to the Cross, and had once given him a spirited blow job in a darkened doorway of Kellett Lane. Doris didn't drink or take drugs; the only times she was forced to work the streets were when she ran up too many gambling debts. Frank picked up his pace and rushed toward her—a friendly face from an easier time. But when he got closer he realized the woman wasn't Doris at all—just a grandmother with a beehive hairdo, holding a baby in her arms.

Frank crossed the road. All his mates were now dead or in jail. There were only two or three hookers left on the street, and they were just weepy teenage girls who lived under the railway bridge down the hill in Woolloomooloo. The joint that used to be the Pink Pussycat had been renovated into a home-wares store, the former sex toy shop next to it was now selling scented candles and lead light lanterns.

Through the restaurant window, he could see Jimmy sitting at the front table, clutching a can of VB, gazing out at the passing parade. Father and son locked eyes and briefly waved to each other. Jimmy had been the unintended consequence of a conjugal visit at Silverwater when Frank had been doing time. The kid had grown up with his mother, in a government flat in the coastal town of Wollongong. She was a woman who preferred rough trade in the form of men who were doing time. Jimmy was a tall, pale-skinned boy with rounded shoulders, who always looked as if he'd just been punched in the gut and was still striving to catch his breath.

Frank opened the door and they shook hands. "Happy birthday, son," he said, motioning to the waiter. Every year they did this—celebrated Jimmy's birth—while the mother had the son at Christmas and Easter. Frank whispered an order over the bar and sat down at the booth. In the sixties, the restaurant had been filled with dark wood furniture and had served heavy Italian food; today it was a minimalist white box with a blackboard menu featuring something called "Truffle Foam."

He took his phone from of his pocket, turned it off, and rested it on the table. "So, how's your mother?" he asked. He automatically took out a cigarette, remembered the new antismoking laws had just come into effect, and, sighing heavily, slid it back into its pack.

Jimmy shrugged and replied, "Or'right."

Frank saw the kid was wearing tracky-daks. Well, that was the first thing that would have to change. And he'd have to learn to speak properly. No one in this town respected a mumbler. Or a man who couldn't look another man straight in the eye. If nothing else, Lionel Silke had taught him that.

The champagne arrived in a silver bucket and the waiter poured them two fizzing glasses. From the blackboard menus they ordered organic pizzas topped with homemade goat cheese. Frank toasted the kid's birthday and they both began to drink. They made small talk until the food arrived and then ate in silence.

Frank wiped his mouth with a serviette and drained his glass. "Son," he said, "now that you're all grown up, there's something I need to tell you . . ."

Jimmy stopped chewing and met his father's eye. "Is it about Mum?"

Frank shook his head. "No, it's about family. My side of the family."

Jimmy sat back and fingered the stem of his glass, waiting for him to continue.

Frank gazed through the window, watching a small package exchange hands outside the railway station. "You know it was my older sister Nell who got me my first job up here in the Cross?"

Jimmy looked at him blankly and shook his head.

"She was an exotic dancer in a few of the clubs. She worked with snakes."

Jimmy's eyes widened.

"And it was her idea to have someone deliver takeaway

food to strippers in the clubs. I worked for tips. And boy—were they generous."

From a passing waiter Frank ordered two shots of whiskey and asked for the bill. He explained to Jimmy that when he'd first started the business, he'd been only fifteen. Within a month or so, working every night of the week, he'd made enough money to move out of his mum's home.

His single mother had three other kids to raise and was happy to have one less mouth to feed. Soon young Frank had set himself up in an attic room on Victoria Street, two blocks from the Golden Mile, while Nell lived on her own in a posh apartment on Macleay Street. It was the late sixties and the Cross was crawling with American servicemen on R&R from Vietnam.

The bill and the whiskeys arrived and again Frank reached for his cigarettes. "It was all going along hunky dory. Business was good." He downed his shot and Jimmy followed. "Even Lionel Silke got me working for him. Running errands and shit like that."

Frank picked up the bill, ran his eyes over the figures, and dumped a few notes on the table. "I got you a present, son," he said, standing up. "But I left it back at the hotel." He pulled a packet of Camels from his inside pocket. "C'mon, Jim, let's walk and talk." He patted his coat pocket and was reassured to feel the lump that was his gun.

Out on the street, Frank lit his smoke and they strolled beneath the blinking neon lights. He had no other children and was greatly relieved to have this father-son discussion. He had to tell somebody—preferably his own son—before he kicked the bucket.

"There was a time when Silke owned every joint in this town," Frank recalled, gesturing down the street. "And even though he was a gangster, he always paid on time. And he always paid in cash."

Jimmy nodded obediently and shoved his hands in his pockets.

"You're probably wondering why I'm telling you all this," said Frank. "Don't worry. You'll see."

They crossed the road, dodging traffic. Frank ducked into a bottle shop and bought a liter of bourbon. Back on the footpath, he cracked the top, took a gulp, and passed it to Jimmy. They kept walking north, toward the fountain.

"Then one day," Frank continued, lighting another Camel, "all of a sudden, it's my eighteenth birthday. And all the girls in the clubs are making a fuss of me. And then I get this message. From Lionel Silke. To meet him in his office."

"What'd he want?" asked Jimmy, suddenly interested.

They passed a man begging for change and Frank slipped him a note.

"What'd he want?" echoed Frank, snatching back the bottle. "Well, he wanted to show me how much I meant to him." He pointed to a corner building across the road. "See that second floor? That was his office—" He sat down on a bench and took slow swigs of the bourbon.

Jimmy remained standing, impatiently shifting his weight from one leg to another.

"So I go up the stairs and see him standing at his filing cabinet. Suddenly he pulls out a gun and points it at me. Right at my fucking head."

Jimmy paled and glanced around the street.

"Don't worry, kid," said Frank, stifling a laugh. "The next thing I know, Silke is handing me the gun and wishing me a happy birthday."

Jimmy looked puzzled and so Frank stood up to explain.

"Y'see, the Yankee sailors were bringing heroin off the ships and Silke needed a go-between to get the gear around. The gun was for my protection, see?"

The kid's eyes widened and he nodded several times.

"And after Silke gave me the gun, he told me there was only one rule . . ." Frank paused for theatrical effect.

"And what was that?"

Frank pursed his lips. "Only pull the trigger in self-defense."

He passed the bottle back to Jimmy and they continued strolling north. The sickly sweet smell of the nearby ice cream shop wafted down the footpath. Frank went on with the story, saying that his job had been pretty easy at the time: getting down to the Garden Island docks before dawn, exchanging cash for small brown parcels, and transporting them back to Silke's office, where they'd be cut, repackaged, and sold to the dancers and customers. Silke would put up the capital and split the profits with his teenage protégée.

"For a while we were pretty tight," said Frank. "He hired me as his driver, his bodyguard, and his ear on the street. Any bullshit going down and I'd report straight back to him. He gave me heaps of bonuses . . ." They came to the Astoria Hotel and Frank flicked his butt into the gutter. "Life was pretty shit-hot, you know?"

Jimmy smiled crookedly and let out a burp. Frank could tell the kid was already half-maggoted—the flushed faced, the swaying head. "C'mon, son," he said, cocking his head at the double doors.

He led the way past the dozing clerk and up a flight of stairs pocked with cigarette burns. Everything smelled of stale spew and cheap disinfectant. Frank unlocked his door, kicked the eviction notice out of the way, and ushered the kid inside. He flicked on the light and opened the bay windows overlooking Darlinghurst Road. Setting two chairs before them, he told the kid to make himself at home. For a few minutes they sat side by side in silence, passing the bottle back and forth, gazing out over the kingdom that had once been the Cross. Car horns bleated and two hookers were yelling at each other in front of the El Alamein Fountain. Still, it would never be like the old days again.

Frank rested his feet on the sill and Jimmy asked what happened next, about the business with Silke.

"A few months passed," Frank said. He shrugged. "Life was good. Silke gave me a secondhand car. Treated me like family. Quite a few times he took my sister out and sometimes we'd all eat dinner together." From where he was sitting, Frank could still see the window of Silke's former office on the corner of Rosyln Street.

Jimmy shifted and crossed his feet on the windowsill too. Frank glanced at him and thought they looked like the sheriff and the deputy in some Western movie, just waiting for some trouble to gallop past their porch.

"Then one night I'm walking through one of the joints backstage when I hear this terrible ruckus. Chairs falling over. A woman screaming." Frank took a long swig of the bottle and wiped his mouth. "So I bolt up the stairs and there is Silke, beating the shit out of Nellie. Whacking her across the face. Slamming her against walls. Dragging her across the room by her hair. Before I knew what I was doing, I had the gun in my hand. I don't think I even aimed—I just fired the fucking thing—and the next thing I know, Silke is dropping to the ground and this gutful of blood is flying all over me."

Jimmy pulled his legs from the sill and sat up straight.

"Then Nellie went berserk. Started yelling and whacking and punching me around. *How could you do that?* she screamed. *After everything he's done for you?* She cuffed me in the mouth. *You meant more to him than any . . . He treated you like a . . .*" Frank's voice trailed off and he shook his head. "And then it all made sense, Jimmy."

"You killed your own boss?" asked Jimmy.

"No, fuckwit. I killed my own father. I just didn't know it until then."

Jimmy's expression blanched into one of shock. He was gripping the arms of his chair as if he were trapped in a plane taking a nosedive.

"You see, Nellie was fifteen when she first came to the Cross and started working for Silke. And he was already married."

The kid frowned and wagged his head back and forth in disbelief.

"She refused an abortion." Frank stood up, walked to the wardrobe, and pulled out the duffel bag. "And Mum—well, my grandma, really—she raised me as her own." He dumped the bag on the bed and gestured to Jimmy.

The kid rose and lifting the bag, yanked back the zipper. A few wads of cash dropped onto the mattress. Jimmy's eyes widened again.

Frank drew his phone from his inside pocket and clicked on his contacts list. "Two suppliers. Seventy-eight clients. All yours." He placed the phone beside the duffel bag. "But on one condition," added Frank, drawing the revolver from his inside pocket.

Jimmy flinched. He went to say something but stopped himself.

"Look, I never did time for the murder." Frank stepped closer. "Nell took the rap."

Frank leaned forward and held the gun out handle first,

but Jimmy backed away. "Can you imagine the cocksucking guilt I've had all my life? It's a fucking Greek tragedy!"

Jimmy glanced frantically around the room, then fixed his eyes on the mobile phone and the bag of money.

"You haven't got the guts, have you?"

The kid ran a hand through his hair. He sat on the windowsill and then stood up again.

"Please, son," said Frank. "It won't be the same if I do it myself."

The kid cleared his throat and spat out the window. For what seemed a long time he just leaned against the sill and gazed out over the street.

"You know the saying, son: *An eye for an eye.*"

Jimmy turned and the two men stood staring at one another.

Finally, Jimmy extended a trembling hand to Frank. He slowly took the gun and held it in both palms.

Frank raised his arms, as if in surrender.

Jimmy lifted the revolver and aimed it straight at Frank's head. "What the fuck?" he said. He let out a crazed laugh. "You're not my real father anyway."

GOOD BOY, BAD GIRL

BY JOHN DALE

Newtown

Jazz came out onto the porch in bare feet to watch the dogfight. Day or night, there was always something going on in this park. That's why her nan kept a special chair outside with a leather cushion; most mornings she sat out here pulling faces at people who passed. Jazz leaned on the spear-tipped fence and watched a man and a woman struggling to separate their dogs. Finally the man pulled his boxer off by the collar, yelling, "Good boy, bad girl!" The tiny white shih tzu stood her ground, baring her teeth, and her owner, an old woman with see-through hair, patted her dog's flank and said in a voice loud enough for Jazz to hear, "Clever girl."

Backpackers were lying around on the grass smoking dope and drinking goon. In an hour or two they'd make their way down to the clubs, pubs, and cheap eateries on King Street. Jazz had lived in her nan's house all her life and she couldn't imagine living anywhere else. Memorial Park and St. Stephen's Church with its graffitied sandstone walls was her front yard, though recently at night the park attracted ice addicts and undercover cops.

Newtown was the place to be, but it wasn't always so. When Jazz was a kid, it was a different world. Her nan would call from the kitchen, "Jazz, go get your father for dinner," and she'd run barefoot up Church Street to the Shakespeare, push on the heavy wooden door with both hands, and through the fug of cigarette smoke find her way to the back bar where the TAB was; she'd weave a path between the big bellies and tug her dad's sleeve, looking around at the faces of the council workers and the coppers from the Police Youth Club. When he was done drinking, her dad would squeeze her hand and she would lead him home down Crooks Lane. Most nights ended peacefully with her dad snoring in his armchair, but there were other nights when he broke a glass or chipped a tooth and his mood would turn on a sixpence, and she and Nan would retreat to their bedroom and watch TV together on the portable set, fiddling with the rabbit ears, while her father vented his rage on doors and crockery, cursing her mother for dying on them.

It still surprised Jazz how many people knew her dad, for he never became a household name, but he always gave it a go, and at his memorial service in St. Stephen's there were over three hundred people in attendance: stand-over men, boxing trainers, Bluebags supporters, battlers from the housing commission flats, and that little rooster fella from 2GB who told everyone that "Spearsy had the heart of a champion, was a champion bloke."

Afterward there were egg sandwiches that Jazz had cut the crusts off herself, and she heard one wag say that, "Spearsy wouldna come to his own funeral if he'd a-known there was no grog." She'd wheeled her nan home and at five o'clock she began her shift at Liquorland.

The steam had cleared in the bathroom and Jazz dried her hair and applied mascara and her favorite dark lipstick. Her childhood was rough and ready but it wasn't as disadvantaged as her welfare officer said. She had free range of the park and the churchyard and when she was little she'd played hide-and-seek behind the headstones. Everyone's got misfortune in their family is what Jazz figured, and if people thought they could avoid tragedy by having truckloads of money and a four-bedroom mansion right on the harbor, they were mistaken. Her mum and dad were party people and they took her everywhere. Once they left her at the Courthouse Hotel and came back after closing time to find her eating sausage rolls and drinking lemonade with the publican's Down syndrome grandson. You learned more about life sitting in a Newtown beer garden than you did watching *Sesame Street*, that's for sure.

Those old Newtowners were a different species, the way they spoke out the sides of their mouths, the way they expressed emotion with both hands.

Jazz wasn't abused or nothing like some of them Catholic kids and she had her nan. When he passed out dead drunk on Gardeners Road, Jazz's grandfather was run over by a steamroller. Her dad loved telling that story, how he had to identify his father's disfigured remains in the Glebe morgue.

Jazz zipped up her giraffe-print dress, the one Lockie liked, and slipped her feet into flats. She went down the hall to find her nan sunk in her wheelchair watching *Animal Kingdom*, a glass of water and a box of Arnott's crackers on her tray. Nan liked to suck on the barbecue shapes without her teeth in. Jazz changed her nan's bag and cleaned her face with a washer. Her phone buzzed and she read the single-word message: *Parking.*

"You remember Lockie, don't you, Nan?" Her nan stared blankly at the TV. Some days she appeared to understand what was going on, but mostly she occupied a different time zone. Jazz wasn't one of those ungrateful young women who dumped her last remaining relative in an aged-care unit; she knew how to care for old people. Before her mum died, she'd promised to buy Jazz a dog but she never did. Anyway, where would she fit a dog in a single-story, two-bedroom terrace? That's why the park was so important. She strapped her nan's legs securely in the wheelchair so she couldn't fall out and squashed two ants climbing up the edge of her tray.

"Won't be long, Nan," she said. Lockie had something important to tell her tonight and she suspected he wanted to ask her to marry him or else move in together now that he'd finished his law degree. She'd thought it over long and hard. Her nan would have to come with them or else Lockie could move in here, help out with the showering and toileting; it hurt her back lifting Nan in and out of the tub.

Her girlfriends said she had snared the man of her dreams, tall, athletic, handsome, with rich parents. Mr. Perfect. Of course Lockie had his little kinks, but he certainly wasn't her worst BF; she'd had her fair share of disasters in the past, and it was a pleasant change to go out with someone from the North Shore. Hunters Hill was as far removed from Newtown as you could get.

The doorbell rang while Jazz was fixing her hair. She walked down the hall and opened the door.

"You look nice," Lockie said. He was wearing a bright pink Tommy Hilfiger polo with bone-colored chinos as if he'd dropped by for a round of golf. He leaned in close: "You smell good, what is that?"

"It's me."

"Nice," he said. She stepped outside and pulled the door shut and he put an arm around her waist as they walked. Up close he smelled of cologne—too much cologne.

The iron gates to the churchyard were open and the rector was chaperoning a party of Japanese guests through the grounds. The private cemetery was popular for weddings although it struck Jazz as a strange place to get married.

Lockie had everything planned for the night. A few drinks and a seafood meal followed by sex in the backseat of his father's car.

"We need to talk," she said.

"Later," he said. "Let's enjoy ourselves first."

She took that to mean, *Don't spoil my night*, but Lockie was the one who did most of the talking. She mainly listened and tuned in and out when necessary. She was happy for him to pick the pub, book the table, and order the wine. He liked to be in control, play the grown-up. From experience, she figured it was best if she just went along with things. They walked up King Street past the *Tear Down Capitalism* posters, the pie and burger joints starting to fill with customers, cars and buses running bumper to bumper. When did it become fashionable to eat your dinner with a lungful of diesel fumes?

Lockie was talking but she found it hard to hear over the traffic noise. "Sorry?"

"So many weirdos out," he said. "It's great."

She took that as a compliment from a Hunters Hill boy who went to St. Joseph's College and then Sydney Uni. She didn't hold it against him, having a privileged childhood; she was never envious of others because she had a theory that it all evened out in the end.

Lockie whispered in her ear how much he was looking forward to doing it in the X5. "Hope to Christ it's safe parked there," he said.

A group of shaved-eyebrow guys were staring from the Italian Bowl, checking out his rig. Unlike her previous BFs, Lockie never ogled other girls, never even glanced out the corner of his eye at a pretty girl, or commented on their attributes; it was almost as if he wasn't interested in other women. Sometimes she asked herself if Lockie was gay, but no, he couldn't be. He was like a horny puppy dog, always rubbing up against her, always touching her butt.

He stopped at the entrance to the hotel, checked his app to make sure this was the correct address, confirmed it was. "The crispy soft-shell crab is the go apparently," he said. If only he'd asked her instead of Google, she could have told him this was her father's former local, transformed into an upmarket eatery. Downstairs still retained its sour, beery, wet-carpet odor, a few gray-faced men drinking alone at dark tables, a bluish flicker from Sky Sports, a buxom barmaid playing with her split ends. No different from twenty years ago, but upstairs—Jazz couldn't recall there ever being an upstairs—upstairs there was light and a beer garden with potted plants and climbing vines and tables that faced an open-plan kitchen where short-order cooks flipped meat and fish and red capsicum over a stone grill; there was a wine list and specials on a chalkboard and photos plastered on the walls of what Newtown must have looked like in her grandfather's day before he was run over by the steamroller. The twin barmaids were younger than she was and fashionably pierced.

"What do you think, Jazz?" Lockie asked proudly, as if he'd built this rooftop courtyard himself. Like most men, Lockie liked to be praised for little things.

"You did well," she said.

He went to the bar and ordered drinks: a full-strength pale ale for her and a light lager for himself.

Never trust a man who drinks light beer, her dad used to say. Or was that her mum? Neither of them had worried about drunk driving.

Jazz watched Lockie return—confident, broad-shouldered, attracting male glances.

"The marinara looks awesome!" he said.

"This used to be my dad's old pub," she told him. "They didn't serve food back then, only crisps and beer nuts."

"So much character," he said. "My parents would love it."

"I must meet them one day."

"Oh, you wouldn't like them, Jazz. They're very left wing."

What did he mean by that? Was he ashamed of her? Did his parents even know he had a girlfriend? Wasn't it peculiar how you could sleep with someone, go out to dinner with them, see two Ryan Gosling movies in a row, and still never really know them? Even after eleven months she didn't know Lockie and he sure as hell didn't know her.

"I haven't told you my news," he said. "I won the Sociological Jurisprudence Prize."

"Wow," she said.

"One hundred forty dollars, awarded to a final-year law student."

They toasted his success. When the plates came, he talked about how this award would improve his chances of working for an international NGO. His life stretched out in front of him like a brand-new superhighway, while hers was a bumpy, winding back road filled with potholes.

"You should do a course," he said, sifting through his marinara for shellfish.

"Like what?"

"Bookkeeping. You can't go on caring for that old woman forever." Soon as he said it he tried to backtrack, mumbling through a mouthful of spaghetti how it was better for senior citizens to be with people their own age, that modern nursing facilities had improved their level of aged care exponentially.

"So what are you suggesting?"

"Let's not discuss it now," he said.

"You brought it up!"

He gave her a look to indicate her voice was loud. A couple at the next table glanced over so she breathed in deeply and said, "I know what I'd want if I was her age."

"And what's that?"

"To die in my own home."

He didn't argue, wasn't going to spoil the evening. His crab, he told her, was superb. She didn't tell him her dish, the one he insisted she order, was bland, the seafood overcooked and drowning in a watery sauce.

"Don't look now," he whispered, "but there's a guy who keeps staring at you."

The man was seated alone in the corner: coarse red hair, ruddy complexion with pitted skin. She had a feeling she had seen him somewhere but couldn't place where.

"You know him?" Lockie asked.

"Not sure." The guy was wearing a tight-fitting white shirt, unbuttoned to reveal the links of a gold chain. He was chewing, deep in thought, but at that moment he glanced up from his T-bone and gave her a curt nod of recognition. She leaned back in her chair.

"Looks like a cop to me," Lockie said.

Now that Lockie mentioned it, he did look like a cop. She'd met her fair share of detectives when her father was alive. His suit jacket was slung over the back of his chair and although overweight, he had the physique of a man who used to work out. He stood up, a red napkin tucked into the belt of his trousers.

"Oh shit," Lockie said, "he's coming this way."

Jazz put on the smile she used at the bottle shop. The man stopped at their table and said, "You're Spearsy's kid. Jasmine, right?"

"Yes," she said.

"Just wanted to say, your old man was one of a kind. They broke the mold when they made him." He took the red paper napkin out of his belt, wiped his mouth, then balled it on the floor near her feet. "Sorry to hear about your mother too," he said. "Real shame what happened there. Real shame."

She nodded.

"Just thought I'd say hi." He made no attempt to move on toward the bar, seemed to be waiting for an invitation to join them, but Lockie didn't offer any encouragement. Jazz sensed hostility between the two men. "Decent send-off, all them speeches, Johnny woulda been proud . . ."

"Sorry, I've forgotten your name," she said.

"Kenny. Call me Kenny."

"Like the movie?" Lockie put in.

"What movie?" The man gave Lockie a stare, then lowered his voice: "You wouldn't know where I can buy some marijuana, would you, son?"

"What?"

"My niece has cancer, and smoking weed relieves the pain."

Jazz said, "There's a guy down at Redfern Station—"

Lockie kicked her under the table. "Sorry, can't help you."

The man nodded as if he was weighing up his response. "Nice shirt, son. Is that peach?" And turning on his heels, he walked over to the bar, bouncing his keys in his hand.

"Told you he was a cop," Lockie whispered.

"He didn't like you very much," Jazz said.

"Guy's a creep. I thought he was going to pop the buttons on his shirt. And see that hair, some kind of wig—"

"Now I know where I saw him!" Jazz cut in. "At the park." She told Lockie about the dogfight between the shih tzu and the boxer. "The guy was the boxer's owner but he wasn't wearing any suit."

"So he *is* a cop!" Lockie said.

"How do you figure that?"

"You told me undercover cops patrol that park looking for ice dealers."

"Did I?"

Some men were like dogs the way they took an instinctive dislike to each other and started barking. Lockie was still yapping, worked up about this stranger standing over at the bar chatting to one of the identical barmaids.

"There's a difference," he said, "between entrapment and a sting operation designed to catch a person committing a crime. What he was trying to do was entrapment."

"But you don't sell dope," she said.

"I would never ask a complete stranger in a restaurant where to buy marijuana, would you?"

"It's Newtown, Lockie. Forget about it."

"I find people like that so obnoxious."

"Let's get out of here."

She led him down the stairs, through the public bar, and out onto King Street. Crowds of people swept past, car horns blaring, colored lights flashing. She felt the heat of the pavement through her shoes. They looked in shop windows and walked off their dinner in silence. When they turned onto the quiet of Church Street, Lockie was still brooding. Jazz stopped outside St. Stephen's Church. The gate was unlocked.

"That's odd," she said, "the rector always padlocks it at dusk." She pushed on the heavy iron gate which gave a rough grinding sound as it swung open.

"What are you doing?" Lockie grabbed at her arm.

"I want to show you the churchyard at night."

"It's trespassing."

She steered him past her favorite old fig tree, black shapes flitting between its branches. Clouds obscured the stars and the gravestones shone in the moonlight. She showed him the monuments she liked the best: the figure of a grieving woman, a ship ploughing through the waves.

Lockie displayed no interest in these stone carvings; all he wanted to do was get back to his father's car. "This place gives me the creeps," he said.

"Why don't we do it here?" she suggested.

Lockie looked around at the swaying oak trees. She could sense the idea appealed to him.

"What if we get caught?"

"Who's going to find us?" She didn't mention the graffiti gang who scaled the walls to spray their tags or the bicycle cops who sometimes pursued them. She didn't mention how she used to come here with her previous boyfriend. She read the names of someone's beloved on a cracked headstone nailed to the bottom of the wall and then she knelt and unzipped his chinos and took him in her mouth. Kangaroo grass brushed against her legs. Once, she'd asked how old he was when he'd first had his cock sucked, and he'd answered, "Fifteen. At Joey's."

"By a woman?"

"You're the first," he said. Of course she'd suspected he was a virgin, all that studying law and going to the gym left no time for girls.

He lifted up her dress and rolled down her underpants. When he laid her gently on a horizontal slab, the sandstone felt cool against her bare skin but not unpleasant. Jazz closed her eyes and let the moment carry her. His breathing grew rapid and a cricket chirped and then a jet roared low over Newtown, muffling his cries. Afterward she held onto him, not wanting him to rush off.

"We need to talk," he said. Glistening with sweat, he rolled off her onto the worn slab. Low spiky bushes surrounded them. "Don't get me wrong, Jazz," he began. His voice sounded nervous. "I like being with you, I really do, but I don't know if we're suited. I mean, we can still be friends, see each other now and then . . ."

She sat up and searched for her underpants, then smoothed down the giraffe-print dress she had worn especially for him.

"There's no other woman, if that's what you're thinking. I just need to focus on my career. The next few years will be critical."

Jazz let him talk. *Men always let you down*, her mum used to say, *you can't rely on them for anything*. What would Lockie think of her in the years to come? Would he look back on their hasty sexual encounters with fondness or would she be quickly forgotten in his scramble for success? He never said it, but this is what he thought: she was not good enough for him.

He tried a change of tone, almost jocular: "You'll probably thank me one day, Jazz."

Something heavy moved near the wall and Lockie jumped to his feet. He buttoned his pants and grabbed a thick branch from the ground and raced over, thrusting the bushes aside. Jazz assumed it was a dog trapped in there or one of the local taggers.

A man ran out from the bushes straight at Lockie, who yelled and brought the heavy end of the branch down hard on the guy's head. The sound it made was like a timber crate being split with an axe. Stunned, the man swayed, mouth agape, then fell forward. His forehead struck the edge of a stone urn with a loud crack and he landed sideways on an unmarked grave, arms and legs sprawled, not moving.

Jazz ran over and knelt beside him. It was the man who'd

approached them in the restaurant. She saw the depression in his skull and placed two fingers against his carotid artery. Nothing. By the light of the moon she could tell he was gone. She'd seen two dead parents up close and knew that look. Wedged between the fingers of his right hand was the smoldering remains of a joint. So he had scored, after all.

Lockie tossed the branch into the bushes and covered his face with his hands. "Oh God," he said, "I've killed a cop!"

"Why'd you do that?"

"He freaked me out, he came out of nowhere, I thought he was going to rape us . . ."

Jazz slipped a hand inside the man's suit jacket and found his wallet. She flipped through a bunch of store cards looking for ID and there it was, a business card: *Kenny Gelder. MEMBER. REIA.*

"He's no cop," Jazz said. "He's a real estate agent."

"This isn't happening!" Lockie was taking rapid breaths and looking up at the church steeple as if praying for a miracle.

Jazz touched the man's coarse hair. Lockie had got that wrong too; it was no wig. Poor old Kenny with his bad skin and ruddy complexion.

"I'm fucked," Lockie said.

"Tell the police it was self-defense."

"I can't go to the police. My whole life would be ruined. My father is a lawyer. My grandfather was attorney general."

"Maybe they'll get you off then," she said.

"What was I doing in this churchyard? Having sex on a gravestone. Oh yes, that would look brilliant for my future employment. Why'd you bring me here?" His voice rose in anger. "Why didn't we go back to the car?"

Surely he was not trying to blame her? She had a good mind to walk away and leave him to deal with it. But Lockie started to quickly backtrack. He was not the violent type, he'd never been in a fight before, not since high school. "What am I going to do, Jazz?" His eyes begged her. She stood up and held him in the dark. The moon had slipped behind the clouds and a few faint stars were the only light source.

"I'll help you," she said, "but this has got to be *your* decision."

He wiped his nose and nodded.

"First thing, we need to get rid of his phone; second, the cops will interview everyone at the restaurant. We tell them we last saw him talking to the barmaid."

"What about the body?" Lockie asked, staring down with distaste.

"We dispose of it."

"I'm not chopping it up!"

"If they find his body it's murder, at best manslaughter. If they don't find a body it's a missing person. Big difference in priority." She bent over Kenny and patted his trouser pockets, retrieved his iPhone, checked a message on the display, then snapped his SIM card in half. Poor Kenny, he was out celebrating a house sale. Who would feed his dog?

"Wait here," she said.

"Where you going?" Lockie called after her. "Jazz . . ."

One thing her father had taught her was to never panic when you are in a fight; keep calm and wait for your moment. When she was twelve years of age, he took her to the gym in Erskineville, put her in with a fierce girl with cornrows who tried to knock her head off, but she did exactly what her dad had taught her, slipping and countering, sliding her feet in and out of trouble, moving her head and rolling her shoulders until that big islander girl had punched herself out. Her dad and his boxing mates cheered her on from the ropes. He never encouraged her education, never took her anywhere that didn't involve his drinking, but she'd learned how to weather life's blows from him.

She pulled the cemetery gate shut and walked down Church Street, flying foxes squabbling overhead, then turned onto King, pushing between crowds of diners and drinkers. She dumped the phone and the SIM card into an overflowing bin, making sure the bouncer obscured her from the hotel's CCTV cameras. Cockroaches scuttled past her feet on the greasy pavement. After the council trucks rolled through in the early hours of the morning, there would be no sign of Kenny or his phone. She went home and found Nan asleep in front of the TV. She grabbed a short-handled spade from the old brick shed under the mango tree and rolled it up in her yoga mat. At the churchyard she pushed softly on the iron gate and crept up on Lockie, who was sitting on the edge of a tombstone, hands covering his face. The enormity of what he had done had paralyzed him into inaction.

Jazz unrolled her yoga mat. He blinked at her with self-pity then followed her cautiously along the west wall until she stopped between two gravesites overgrown with weeds and tall grass. A horizontal slab covered one of the graves, the engraved names erased by the elements. Jazz worked her spade in under one corner of the slab but couldn't shift it. She heard the *woo-hoo* of a powerful owl. She looked around and tried again. What panicked her most was that underage drinkers would discover them.

Lockie removed his polo and, grunting, lifted the slab off with a *pop* like a tight lid coming off a jar. Underneath was a deep sunken hole where the rain had got in, giving off an earthy smell of rot. How many bodies were interred below, Jazz didn't know; she hoped poor Kenny wouldn't mind spending eternity on top of strangers. Together, they dragged his body over by his legs and rolled him into the hole and covered him with a layer of dirt and then maneuvered the stone slab carefully back over the top. Volunteers from the church often tidied up these neglected gravesites, but you couldn't tell the slab had been disturbed. It was airtight and partly hidden under the Chinese elms. No one was going to bother around in there.

She dropped a branch and sprinkled leaves over the adjoining grave and rolled the spade up in her yoga mat and gave it to Lockie, who looked at her strangely, as if she had done this type of thing before.

On the way out she showed him where she had scattered her mum's and dad's ashes at opposite ends of the churchyard so they wouldn't argue with each other. St. Stephen's was her favorite parish church in the world and the only one she'd ever been inside of. Years ago, her nan knew everyone on this street, families who had lived in the same houses for generations, but that sense of community was gone. People had to look after themselves these days. She secured the heavy padlock on the iron gates and slipped her arm around Lockie's waist. She had never known him to be so quiet. Maybe this could work out between them. She could use those gym muscles. She asked him if he would do her a big favor: "Help me carry Nan to bed?"

Without hesitation he said yes.

"I couldn't stick Nan in a nursing home," she told him. "We need to look after her properly . . ."

The word *we* didn't seem to faze him. Since her father had died, she had wanted a man she could rely on, someone she could trust. That's what a real relationship was. Of course, he would need to make adjustments. She thought of his smooth, hairless chest shining under the moonlight. Her girlfriends were right. She had snared the man of her dreams: tall, strong, handsome, with rich parents. Mr. Perfect.

IN THE DUNES

BY ELEANOR LIMPRECHT

Maroubra

The week before council collection the footpaths are stacked with people's unwanted stuff. Snapped surfboards, plastic baby walkers, stained office chairs, and dinette sets from the eighties. Rusted-out bicycles, suitcases with broken zippers, cracked terra-cotta pots, box set televisions, and weight benches spilling foam. Alf does the drive round in his dual-fuel Falcon Ute with Marnie sitting shotgun. He keeps the engine running since the Falcon can be finicky about starting.

Marnie slides out and checks the gear over while he idles beside the curb. She knows the drill by now. Does the chair have a broken leg? Has the cord been chewed by a rat while it moldered in the garage for twenty years? Seriously, though, you wouldn't believe what people give away. Just because two-thirds of it is crap doesn't mean that there aren't some genuine treasures in the remaining third.

Marnie doesn't jump at the chance to come along these days but she still does if he insists. She sits sullen and silent beside him. Used to be it was like an adventure together, a treasure hunt, some of their best times. It's harder and harder to know what's going on in that head of hers now. She fixes dinner like her mum used to, puts the laundry on, and sometimes even watches the telly with him, but most of the time she's either in her room with the door shut or present but not, looking at her phone, sending messages to the friends he's never met since she doesn't bring them home.

Tonight they find a bedside table with all the drawers working, a set of barbecue tongs which look like they've never been used, an old dog house which he'll fix up and sell on Gumtree, and half a dozen romance novels which Marnie shoves beneath her seat. He'd have thought at fourteen she's too young to be reading that rubbish, but he keeps his mouth shut. Since her mum died two years ago—just after Marnie got her period—he's realized that trying to talk about those things, female things, just makes it worse. Makes her face get all splotchy, her eyes squeeze shut, and the rolls of fat around her middle shake as she cries without making a sound. She needs a mum for these things, but what's Alf to do? Not as though he can just put an ad on Gumtree for one. And the rest of the family—his and Em's—are back in the UK. No aunties to take the girl aside and show her how to shave her legs, how to cross them when she's wearing a skirt or dress.

It doesn't help, Alf thinks, driving down to Marine Parade from Lurline Bay, past the huge boxy houses with tinted windows, landscaped gardens, and backyard pools, it doesn't help that Em and he always kept to themselves. Ever since they'd moved into their flat overlooking the rifle range and the headland at South Maroubra, they'd agreed: there's no problem worth burdening strangers with. They kept Em's illness quiet, the years of dialysis treatments, the long absences from work which caused him to eventually lose the council job. Ten years he drove the street sweeper. Well too. Never a gutter left clogged with wet leaves. He still finds himself angling his Ute toward curbs, hugging the very edge of the road.

He drives toward the long flat stretch of beach, rolling down his window to feel the kick of the southerly wind, and pulls over to watch the surf. It's slate blue and churny, there's some swell at the north end and a few board riders braving the dusk for it. There's the salty seaweed smell he'll never grow tired of and the stretch of promenade speckled with dogwalkers and teenagers reluctant to go home. The boxy pink North Maroubra surf club building beside the showers and picnic tables, some seagulls still scavenging in ghostly flocks. Beside the curb where they've pulled up, someone's left their Macca's rubbish, crushed cups and grease-spotted bags. Lined up on the footpath are empty bottles of VB, Tooheys New, silver blue cans of UDL. Marnie ducks her head like she always does these days, he can feel her fear like you feel a dog's. She takes after her mum, who was never keen on the beach.

"It's hard for a big lady," Em used to say, "to feel comfortable parading around in next to nothing in broad daylight."

Marnie's built like Em, solid and only more so in the past two years. Her school uniforms they buy at Kmart because the sizes run too small at the school uniform shop. Her other clothes they buy at the Vinnie's on Anzac Parade, and Marnie won't even try them on, just finds the biggest-size jeans or jacket, shapeless dress, and passes them to him to take to the white-haired lady with shaky hands at the register.

"Can we have KFC for dinner?" she mumbles now, looking at the phone in her lap. It's the first sentence she's spoken all afternoon.

"Alright," he agrees, on a whim. "Just this once." It's worth it for the quick moment she glances at him, the almost smile, before turning back to the shiny surface of her phone.

As he drives away from the beach and the breeze, up Maroubra Road into the tangle of ugly shops around the Junction, he promises himself that tomorrow he'll start talking to her about eating healthy, about losing some weight. He'll buy the fruit and veg he keeps meaning to buy from that nice Indian couple at the South Maroubra shops instead of the frozen dinners from Woollies they started buying when Em got sick.

They finish the bucket of lukewarm chicken in front of the six o'clock news. There is a woman in Quaker's Hill who abandoned her baby the night before in a storm-water drain. The bub was found by a cyclist who heard the cries riding past, and went to investigate. The anchor—serious-faced—says the mother turned herself in and was charged with attempted murder. Marnie's been looking at the screen in her lap instead of the telly but the taps on her phone slow like the drops at the tail end of a rainstorm.

"What a tragedy," Alf says, shaking his head. "A horrible thing to do."

Marnie gets up and leaves, not saying anything, shutting the door to her room. *What's gotten into her?* he wonders. Em would have agreed, might even have cried the way she did when they had stuff on the news about abandoned children or babies who'd been hurt. There's still a row of photographs of the charity kids Em sponsored on the windowsill, dark-skinned children with tangled hair and faded T-shirts, even though they stopped paying the monthly charity bills when he lost his job.

Tomorrow, when Marnie's at school, he'll tidy up, throw some of those old faded photos away. Then he'll scrape back the peeling paint on the doghouse, sand it, and give it a fresh coat. White, maybe. With blue trim. He still has a tin of blue paint which Marnie chose for her room—she must have been nine or ten. It had been pink before that and Marnie decided one day she hated pink. "It's what they do," Em had said, smiling as she shook her head. "Turn against their parents." But it was different, then. Alf knew Em was proud that Marnie was making up her own mind about things. Figuring out what she liked, rather than what was expected of her.

That night he goes to sleep thinking about Marnie when she was born, her new-baby smell, the creases in her legs which Em would powder so they didn't get red in the heat. Em did everything, nearly everything—that was part of the problem. Maybe if she'd let him help out a little he wouldn't be so lost now that she's gone.

It's odd because he hears the sirens that morning—a week later—but doesn't think twice about it. He's been outside working on the starter motor; it's a still day, hot, and he's planning a swim in the afternoon, thinking of the surf crashing over him and cooling his skin. The locusts are screeching beyond the fence in the rifle range and the crows are perched on the power lines, their caws punctuating songs from the oldies station on the radio, the distant thrum of the surf. But he ends up getting lost in the work, that feeling when you're so caught up in what you're doing that suddenly it's dark and you don't know where the day has gone. He's swum after dark once or twice, but to tell the truth, it scares him. The thought of sharks lurking in the murky dark water, of getting caught in a rip with no one to see you go. Alf loves the beach but he doesn't know it, he's come to it late in life and it's like a language he'll never be fluent in, no matter how hard he tries. He imagined once that Marnie would know, growing up on the doorstep and all, but he was wrong. Turns out she's inherited her parents' fear.

It isn't until the news that night that he hears what the sirens were all about. They found a newborn buried in the South Maroubra dunes, just fifty meters from the South Maroubra surf club, scrub on both sides. A little corpse in a shallow grave. It's awful, it is. Some nippers found it during races on the beach. They'd not made the final round and were digging while they waited for the faster kids to finish running. Little fellas, not older than six or seven. Their parents thought it must be something else—a big fish, maybe, an old doll—but the kids were sure of it. Then it was police up and down the beach, the south end taped off, autopsy kits beneath a police tent underneath the beating sun. There's a press conference with the police superintendent, who tells a pack of journos that homicide detectives are helping local police with their investigations.

Marnie is in her room and he knocks on the door, "C'mere, love, have a look at this," but he just hears some muffled words and then a sharp—"I'm on the phone!"

She's been off sick all week, gastro, running back and forth to the loo. The only time she's been out was to go to the chemist and Alf didn't realize she was gone until she came home, wearing a big puffer jacket in spite of the heat, a white paper bag clutched under her arm. He got upset, saying she ought to have let him go for her, but she just said, "It's embarrassing, Dad," and slammed the door to her room. She hasn't been eating, so he's scavenged around: biscuits and cheese, frozen pizza. They're interviewing the nippers' parents now on the telly. Parents who during normal Sunday mornings have no greater dilemma than what coffee to order and whether or not they'll jump in the surf themselves.

"Who could do this?" the mum on telly says, her eyes hidden behind those big round sunglasses all the young women now wear. "What kind of woman would do this to her baby?"

Her voice breaks in the way that reporters love, and they flick back to the studio, where the regular anchor is sitting at the desk with his most serious expression, shaking his head. "And now over to Dan for the weather."

"Awful," Alf mutters, "just down the road." He gets up to grab a beer from the fridge. The fruit and veg he bought at the beginning of the week are wilting in the crisper. There is a dark shape in the doorway at the edge of his vision, gone before he can turn toward it.

"Marnie?" he calls. Now the soft click of her shutting the door to her room. It's no good. She didn't used to hide in her room all the time. Even if she is sick, she must need something. He knocks at the door.

"Can I get you a lemonade?"

"I'm fine, Dad. Go away."

He knocks again.

The door opens a crack, her face swollen and red with fury. The rest of her, though—there's not as much of it.

"What?"

"I'll take you to the doctor, love. Look at you—you've lost weight."

"No, Dad!"

He's surprised how she reacts. Marnie loved the doctor as a girl. When Em got sick she went along to every appointment, stroking the glossy magazine covers in the waiting rooms, keeping copies of the scripts and receipts in a neat folder. Sometimes she went in his place, missing school to accompany her mum. Em seemed to sense how Alf hated the hospital. He felt like the walls were closing in on him, bright white above hard clicky floors. Like the words the doctors used were sharp little barbs placed to puncture his veneer as a husband, as a father. To peel it back, exposing the failure he really was beneath.

"I'm feeling better."

"At least let me in."

She looks behind her, then steps aside, gripping her phone in her hand. There are piles of clothes everywhere, small mountains of fabric piled against the blue walls. There's a poster of an airbrushed boy band above a corkboard of photos, mostly of her and Em. Crumpled tissues like small squashed flowers. The room smells sour, like unwashed flesh.

"At least open a window. C'mon, love."

She does. She has lost weight; he can't help but be relieved to see it. But she looks pale. He sits at the edge of her bed.

"What can I do, Marnie?"

"What do you mean?"

"I'm yer dad. What can I fix for you?"

"I'm fine," she says, but she clearly isn't, because her chin quivers. Tears have already started streaming down her face, and she wipes at them with a dirty fist. "I'm fine."

And then she tells him.

Everywhere they keep asking for the mum to turn herself in. "We're here to help. You need our help." But it's too late for their help now.

The help would have been good before, she says, when it started. When she bled through her sports uniform at age twelve, and the whole class laughed, and the gym teacher just told her she should look after herself better. Who was there to show her how? When the boys said she was too fat to fuck, and she proved them wrong the only way she knew.

Brayden didn't talk to her at school, but he texted. He liked green jelly frogs, he was always eating them at the bus stop. When they snuck into the rifle range after dark, he held back the wire-cut fence so it didn't scrape her bare legs. When they spread out her jumper to lie on, he said the rustling sounds were rabbits. Not snakes.

The birth is still a blur. The pain that started mild kept on building through the night until it was so bad she was sure she'd die, she'd be torn in two. Then it finally came, the gory mess of it, like someone bled to death in her sheets. The second lot of cramps and the sloppy hunk of meat which came at the end of the cord. The fucking bread knife, would you believe, to cut the blue of the cord, stumbling to the kitchen all torn and bloody holding the hot little slippery thing in her arms. The crying that wouldn't quit. She had to fix it. No one could know. Wrapped it tight, stopped the noise, covered it until it stopped. No one could see. She'd take it away. Cover it up. Hide it somewhere. No one would know. The beach just there. Afterward she found herself stuffing her bedsheets into a bin liner. Was it even her? Shoving the bag into the red-lidded rubbish bin. She put fresh linen on the bed, scrubbed the lino where she'd dripped on the kitchen floor.

Did she feel anything?

Dizzy. Sand in her nails, all week finding grains of it in her hair. Cramps which left blood in her underpants, so much blood. She was scared to buy the maternity pads so she bought regular and wore them two at a time. Tits hard and hot and sore.

Alf says, "I wish you'd told me."

"Will the police come get me?"

"If they do, we'll deal with it. I'll be right here." He puts his hand awkwardly on her shoulder, which is still shaking. She half leans into him. She will live with this—the knowledge of it—always.

That night he dreams of his wife, her body washed up on the sand. Marnie clawing the bloated corpse. He wakes up, shorts wet from sweat. He thinks about the call he would need to make. The words he would have to say. He holds his hands over his face and weeps like he didn't when Em died.

Alf sees on the news that a local woman, a mother of three, has unofficially adopted the dead baby, named her Lily Grace and given her a burial in a local cemetery. The real mother has failed to come forward, despite repeated requests and investigations. There have been many leads but all have come up empty. This other woman organized a memorial service where they released butterflies from a cage, carried pink balloons, and suspended the tiny white coffin into the grave on pink satin ribbons. Inside the coffin, the reporter says, the infant's body is flanked by a teddy bear, dressed in a gown made from a gently used wedding dress. This other woman is interviewed, wearing black, saying, "I wanted to do something for the girl." For a minute Alf wonders which girl she means. He turns the telly off. It's time he stopped watching the news.

There are nights where the surf is louder than others, crashing so close it sounds like it's hitting the building they live in, as if it might pound down their door, pool beneath their beds, carry them away.

There are nights when cats yowl in the streets, fighting, mating, their cries like those of human babies.

Those are the nights he wakes in terror. Opens the door to her room. Marnie sleeps—almost peacefully—in the glow of the streetlamp. He pulls the curtain shut.

There is no baby. Never was.

IN THE COURT OF THE LION KING

BY MARK DAPIN

La Perouse

I was two-out in a one-man cell in the hospital wing at Long Bay, sharing a shitter with Roman Vasari, the only other innocent bloke in the place. It was a greasy Monday in December and I was awaiting trial for the murder of my best mate Jamie—who, as far as I knew, wasn't even dead. An angry screw escorted me to the door of the cell where the Lion King lay in his underpants, too fat to stand. The Lion King pretended he hadn't seen me and he pulled at his cock, then he looked up and asked, "Do you know who I am?"

"You're the Lion King of La Perouse," I said.

His cellie handed him a chicken leg. The Lion King accepted it with his cock hand.

"Where are you from, eh?" he asked me.

"I grew up in WA," I said.

He nodded, as if he had known. Or as if he had known I'd say that. He wiped his lips with the back of his hand. "I sent for you," he said to me, "because I heard there was a white man called Chevy in a cell with Vasari. You're as white as fucking pavlova, but your cell plate says, *Chevapravatdum-rong*. How does a pavlova get a name like that?"

"My dad's Laotian," I told him.

He laughed, as if I'd said he was a Martian. "And what the fuck is a Laotian?"

"Laos is a country next to Vietnam," I said.

"I know where Laos is, you stupid cunt." The Lion King picked shreds of chicken from between his teeth. He scratched around in his pants. "So you're not white?" he said, eventually.

I shook my head.

"And you're not yellow?"

I dropped my eyes.

"And Blind Freddy can see you're not fucking black," he said.

I nodded.

"Do you know what that makes you?"

I shrugged.

"Dead," he said.

Jessica Solomon wore a snug skirt and a weightless blouse. We sat across an empty table, players without a game. She told me it wasn't looking good for me but everything was going to be alright. I was in no mood to embrace the contradiction.

She asked about the Vientiane project. I said it had been going well until I had found myself in my present difficulties. I actually used those words—"present difficulties."

I should have been in Laos that morning, drinking strong, syrupy coffee, inspecting the site. "Zero environmental impact," I told my lawyer, as if that might impress her.

The government had approved the plans, and I had a business-class ticket to Vientiane via Ho Chi Minh City, but my reservation was on hold until the police realized I hadn't killed my best friend. I had been refused bail since the cops knew about Vientiane and suspected I might have a second passport. They were holding me because they were certain that Jamie was dead, though they couldn't locate the body.

"They think it was gay panic," she said.

I laughed. Jamie was the best man I knew. I would have been proud to believe he wanted me.

"The Lion King wants two hundred bucks a week," I said. "It has to be paid to an electrician in Tempe—he said you'd know him."

Jesse nodded. "I can do that for you," she said. "But don't trust the Lion King. He'll only protect you from himself, and he'll probably have you bashed anyway."

"What for?" I asked.

"Control."

I knew I was never going to last in jail.

I watched Vasari draw a comic strip in his spiral-bound sketchbook. He said he was making a graphic novel about prison life. He pronounced the *p* in graphic, as if he had read the word but never heard it spoken.

He showed me the opening pages of his story: a young Vasari, with a flick of black hair and a square jaw, was loaded up with home bake by cops who couldn't get him on a breaking-and-entering blue.

He asked to see one of my drawings. I told him to look out from the hill around Area One to Military Road, where Port Botany Towers rose from the docks like twin Ts joined at the ascenders. The bridge between the towers was a terraced garden. We won every award in the industry for Port Botany Towers.

"The Lion King doesn't like that building," said Vasari.

He rubbed the ledge of his nose.

"Everyone's a classicist," I said, "when it comes to architecture."

Vasari farted like a foghorn, to show what he thought of the Western aesthetic tradition.

* * *

As a remand prisoner I didn't have to work, but I volunteered as a porter in the hospital. The ward was choked with bed blockers stealing nurses' time from dying men. I sat with the vanishing and held their hands, then carted bags of wet test tubes, jars, and needles to the incinerator, wearing gloves that gave me bear's paws.

One of my patients was Vietnamese. He said he'd never met a man with a face like mine and a name like Chevapravatdumrong, but that when he looked closely, he could see parched rice fields in my eyes. He warned me the other Viets were coming for me. They thought I was trying to pass as a skip. They would take those eyes from me. He said I would have to pay two hundred dollars a week to the 5T. I said I needed the money for my defense. He laughed and said, "You've got that right."

A nurse perfumed with iodine advised me to go into protection.

"But I'm not a rock spider," I said. "I'm not even guilty."

The men with HIV divided themselves into needlesharers and cock-sharers. They said their disease was no longer a death sentence; it had been commuted to life. I wheeled their waste to the basement. I practiced deep breathing to try to keep calm, but panic chased the breath out of my lungs. I vomited in my cell, and my fingers shook as I tried to clean myself up.

The Lion King's cellie sat beside the Lion King's bunk, rolling White Ox tobacco. When he finished making a cigarette he placed it between the Lion King's lips and lit it for him. Smoking was banned in jail, but the Lion King had earned unofficial privileges in unofficial ways.

"I hear you're an architect," he said. "What does an architect do? Take it up the arc?"

I blinked smoke from my eye.

"A bent fucking bird tells me you designed Port Botany Towers. I hate that cock-sore. What's it supposed to be, anyway?"

"It's a landmark symbol of the regeneration of a dockside suburb," I told him, reading the brief from memory.

"It's my fucking suburb," said the Lion King. "I grew up five minutes from this fucking jail. And do you know what your building looks like to me?"

"Most people say it reminds them of a Japanese gate."

"I couldn't give a fat-arsed fuck," he said. "To me, it's two Ts, and those two Ts stand for Trent Taylor and the Tasman Tigers."

I didn't know what he expected me to say.

"Every fucking morning," he continued, "when I went out on a work party, I used to see your fucking Trent Taylor Tasman Tigers Tower and think to myself, *I'd like to get my hands on the cunt that built that, because I've got a strong fucking feeling that he put it there just to piss me off.* In the end, I stopped going out on work parties, because I couldn't bear to look at the fucking thing." He patted his hairy stomach. "That's when I started putting on weight. No fucking exercise except this—" He pulled vigorously on his cock. "I knocked Trent Taylor. Did you know that?"

I told him I didn't.

"So why do you think I'm in here? Because I like the smell?"

"You were president of the La Perouse Lions," I said, "at the Moorebank massacre."

"Fucking oath I was," said the Lion King. "And I knocked

President Trent fucking Taylor, because the dog deserved to die." He turned to his cellie. "That's right, isn't it?"

"Fucking oath it is," said his cellie.

"What're you in here for?" the Lion King suddenly asked me.

"Murder."

"No, what're you in *here* for?"

"I got arrested," I said, "and refused bail."

The Lion King looked at me, disgusted. "Do you know how many blokes I've knocked?"

I couldn't tell whether he wanted me to guess low or high.

"Five," I said. "Something like that."

"Six. Three at Moorebank, outside the pub, and three Tigers who came in here after me, looking to get square for their brothers."

Again, I didn't know how he expected me to react.

"And now the Tasman Tigers are extinct," he said, and smiled nicotine-piss, spider-cracked teeth. "What're you in here for?" he asked me again.

A new Viet arrived on remand. He followed me around for days but seemed reluctant to approach. I guess he was scared, because it was a frightening thing to have to do. When he finally cornered me, he was apologetic, although he needed me to know that this was all my own fault. If I had cooperated, I would have been fine.

He was searching for the strength to stab me.

"Why don't you just tell them you couldn't find me?" I said.

"Because you're a fucking traitor." His voice was high and glassy.

"And who have I betrayed?" I asked.

"Listen to you," he said. "Talking like a fucking . . . architect."

I had never been to another place where it was a joke to be an architect.

He was bigger than me, but not by much. He wanted me to say something else so that he could get angry.

"Go back to your cell," I said.

"Don't tell me what to do, you Laos cunt." He stamped his feet to send his heart charging.

This is it, I thought.

Prisoners were allowed to make calls from the wall phone by the guardhouse at the entrance to the wing. I knew the screws were listening in, but I wasn't breaking any law. My call diverted from a fixed line on my desk in the office to an Android in my safe to a satellite phone in a Toyota Land Cruiser.

"It's me," I said.

"And me," he said.

I could hear warmth and waves.

"What's it like in there?" he asked.

"Like school," I said. "Except worse. What're you doing?"

"Fishing."

"Caught anything?"

"Sweetlip, cod, and mullet," he said.

"Sounds like a law firm."

"You should hire them."

"I already did," I told him.

He laughed. "Give my regards to Sweetlip. Stay strong. Love you, man."

"Love you," I said.

Jesse arrived with a shoulder bag full of papers. There were prisoners talking to their lawyers in the rooms on either side of us, murmurs floating through the walls. Jesse looked into my eye, shot red through the iris and bruised blue around the socket. She raised a hand, as if she were about to touch my cheek, then let it fall into her lap. She was wearing a ring I had never seen before.

"Are you okay?" she asked.

I couldn't think of an intelligent reply.

"Last night a remand prisoner got jabbed in the eye with an infected syringe." She was telling me as a warning to keep safe.

"Who did it?" I asked.

"He doesn't know. They never know. In prison, people're always attacked from behind. Even when they're stabbed in the face."

I liked it when Jesse acted world-weary and tough.

"The terrible thing was," she said, "he was only in here because he couldn't make bail on a possession charge."

He could have. He didn't want to. He came in to do me, then he would have miraculously raised the bail and got out.

"He lost the sight in his right eye, Chevy," she said.

I was sorry. I genuinely was.

"We're going to get you out of here," she promised.

I smiled, although it hurt me to listen to her. Jesse was a beautiful woman and a lovely person. She was, however, a shithouse lawyer.

The Lion King was naked, except for a dirty towel draped over his crotch. His cell smelled of liniment.

"Take off your pants," he told me.

I looked at his cellie, his biceps built on a construction site, his brow bashed down in a boxing ring. I knew I couldn't fight him, but I might be able to back out of the cell before he could reach me. Then I felt the warmth of a third man behind me. I stepped to the side, to allow him to come past me, but he stayed in position, blocking my retreat.

"Pants," said the Lion King, and wiggled his ring finger.

The third man walked into me, knocking me off balance, and closed the cell door.

I thought about screaming.

"Are you deaf as well as Asian?" asked the Lion King. "Drop your fucking pants."

I felt time slow down, saw my own body from above. "No," I said.

The Lion King laughed.

The third man grabbed me and I threw him over my hip, like a judoka. Something like that only works for you once in a lifetime. His head smashed against the cell floor.

The Lion King laughed again and clapped like a seal. "The slope does tricks!" he cried.

The third man picked himself up, and wiped blood across his forehead. I knew he'd back up on me later, but he'd look weak if it wasn't one-on-one.

"Look," the Lion King said to me, "I just want to see if it's true. Drop your pants for me, and you'll walk out of here a virgin."

I unbuttoned my prison trousers and let them fall. I stepped out of them and turned around.

The Lion King reached out and stabbed my thigh with his finger. "And what the fuck is that?" he asked.

Vasari must've seen it when we showered.

"It's an eco-tower," I said. "It was designed to incorporate elements of Botany Bay's maritime heritage. The twin Ts are supposed to mirror the shape of intermodal container-lifting cranes."

"It's a fucking Tasman Tigers badge," said the Lion King.

"Everyone who worked on the building got the same tattoo," I told him, "the night we won the National Architecture Awards."

"Take it off."

"It's a tattoo," I said.

His cellie pulled a chef's knife from his pants and offered it to me, blade first. "Cut the tattoo out," he said.

I had a visit from Jack Roden QC, man of the people. He arrived in Long Bay with his Zegna suit, acquired ockerisms, and activist credentials. He noticed my limp when I walked in.

"You okay?" he asked, and pointed to my leg.

I didn't know if I was okay. Probably not.

He said he had come to see me as a mate, not a lawyer.

I told him that was good, because I already had a lawyer.

He hugged me when I went to shake his hand. "You've got to dump Jesse, mate."

I did not reply.

"Eh?" said Roden. "Eh? Eh? Mate." He was a brave man, but I had never liked him. "You stay with her and you'll be stuck in here forever." He wanted to refight the Free the Refugees campaign, the best days of his life.

"I'm not a cause, Jack," I told him. "I don't need demonstrations."

Roden leaned forward, as if to confide in me. "Your mates aren't going to let you fuck up your life for Jesse. Not again."

That hurt—the *again* part.

Roden put on his court face. "When was the last time you saw her before this?"

"I don't know," I replied. "A year ago. Maybe two."

"Now she comes in twice a week."

"Sometimes."

"And she gets paid—it's her job—to think about you." Roden did not conclude his argument. He left it to the jury to decide.

Jesse was wearing her grave face—a cute frown, an angry pout. She had interviewed Mrs. Nassoor over baklava and dates. "She said it was you that told her to report Jamie missing. Why didn't *you* report him missing?"

"Do I look like his mother?" I said.

That was a thing Jesse used to say to me, when I left beer bottles on the table, or roaches in the cereal bowl. *Do I look like your mother?* Yes, you do, a little. But you look more like my brother, that beautiful man. *Tim?* No, my brother from a different father. *Show me a picture?* I don't have one. They're all in my head.

In truth, there were plenty of photographs, but when I looked at the first it made me remember the last.

Jesse wanted to go through everything again, from the beginning. I sighed, because it seemed like we only ever had one conversation.

"When did you last see Jamie?" she asked, as if she didn't know.

"Tuesday the sixteenth. In the car park at the New South Wales Golf Club in La Perouse."

"What time?"

"Maybe half eleven," I said. "We'd been drinking and the club had closed."

"Why did you go to the car park? You didn't drive home."

"No," I said. "I left the car there. We went to the car park to wait for a cab."

"What're you not telling me?"

"You know what I'm not telling you."

Maybe she blushed, or maybe I imagined it. "Don't start that again," she said. She fingered the golden Buddha on the collar around her throat.

I wondered if she wanted me to start that again.

"We don't have an extradition treaty with Laos," she said. "You were leaving anyway. I don't understand why you didn't just get on a plane."

"Because I'm innocent, Jess."

She looked at me with eyes that I'd kissed. "There was a camera in the car park, Chevy. They've got film of the two of you fighting."

I'd wondered when they would find that. "We like to fight," I said. "It gives us a chance to touch each other." That was a joke, mostly.

"I've seen it," said Jesse. "You were directly in front of the camera."

"Did you see my left hook? The one that took him down?" That was a great punch.

"He fell to the ground," she said, "and out of the picture."

"And then he got up, got into a cab, and went home."

"Why isn't that on camera?"

"It sounds like the camera was looking at the car park," I said. "The taxi stopped on the road."

"There's a third person with you. Is that Tim?"

"Yeah, he was the referee."

"And where is Tim now?"

"I don't know," I said. "Am I my brother's keeper?"

"Tell me where he is, Chevy."

"He left the next morning. He was going on holiday. I can't remember where."

"Phone him," said Jesse. "E-mail him."

"I have. He doesn't reply."

"Then I'll find him."

"He'll be in the surf somewhere."

"What do you mean by that?" asked Jesse, sharply.

Oh, for Christ's sake! You can't think . . . "I mean he's prob-ably gone surfing, Jesse, that's all."

She wrote the word *surfing* on her legal pad. It was her only note of our meeting.

"Roden came to see me yesterday," I told her.

"I know. I asked him to."

What were you doing when you asked him? Were you lying on your side? "I didn't know you two talked," I said.

There had been a split in the movement, all those years ago. Roden had favored direct physical confrontation. Jesse was more of a Gandhi. Each side blamed the other when we failed.

"We only talk about you," she said. "We think you're not doing enough to help yourself."

We? Fucking we?

I lay on my bunk thinking about Jesse and trying to imagine Vasari away.

I had fallen in love with her when she was a second-year arts-law student and I was studying for a bachelor's degree in building design. We were thrown into a police van at a demo against Pauline Hanson. It was the first time I'd been arrested and the only time I was guilty. The cops offered me a deal: if I agreed to take a kicking, they wouldn't drag me to court. So I lurched out of the cell with two broken ribs and a clean record, and Jesse was released because she gave the sergeant a kiss. Jesse and I got together, but it didn't last. She liked to be dominated but we could only fuck with her on top, because of my ribs. That was the story we told in public—all candid and modern and hip, and maybe even a little bit true—but it was an alibi for a heart full of painful secrets. I could always taste the cop on her lips.

Jesse married a tennis champion, had a baby, and got divorced. She used to joke that she'd mated for eugenic reasons—so that her son Caspar would have his body and her brains. We reduced everything to a formula. Jesse thought I had a dark side—although, God knows, I never showed it to her—but she could change her mind, her mood, and her lover in the time it took to roll off a condom. I used to say I only loved four people—two of them were Jesse, one of them was Tim, and one of them was dead.

Jesse could do almost anything. She sang in a jazz band, played soccer for the district, spoke Russian, French, and German, and wrote like an angel. She chose to become a criminal lawyer because she wanted to help people—like a beauty queen at a bikini pageant—but she only scraped through her exams and anyone could see she was in the wrong job. Roden had become a barrister in the time it took her to finish her articles. Jesse was never going to land a decent case.

Vasari had noticed Jesse among the visitors. He spent the morning drawing sketches of her, legs splayed, up against the wall or down on all fours, and the Vasari character fucking her with his giant dick. In the afternoon he took a nap. I watched him breathe softly as I raised my pillow over his face.

He woke up with the pillow lying lightly over his nose and mouth, and his drawings—all of them, including his stupid grap-hick novel—shredded around his head.

The next day, he put his name down for a transfer to another cell.

* * *

Vasari still passed instructions from the Lion King, but these days he spoke quickly and hurried away to play chess with the rock spiders. My leg had almost healed, but it hurt as if I had been branded. When I came into the Lion King's cell, I stood close to his cellie and waited for him to give me his seat. The Lion King laughed and told his cellie to go to the gym, work out on the heavy bag, and imagine sticking his fists right through my Laotian gut noodles.

"Bloke in here knows you from the outside," said the Lion King, once we were alone, "but he didn't know you were an architect. Thought you were a martial arts teacher."

"That's just something people say about Asians," I responded.

"You used to organize late-night fights in car parks and tennis courts. Like in that film . . ." There was a long silence while the Lion King struggled to remember the name of the movie, and groped for the answer in his pants.

"*Fight Club?*" I asked.

"*Pocahontas,*" said the Lion King.

He could be quite a funny guy, at times.

"He says he's not surprised you knocked a bloke. You used to fight like a werewolf."

I shrugged. "He talks like that because it makes him sound hard."

"You've only got enemies in here," said the Lion King. "The Viets are going to try and get you again. They know about the leg. They reckon you'll be slower now, easier to catch. They heard you didn't cry out when you cut away the skin, so now they think it'll take more than one of them to bring you down." He pointed to an object rolled up in his filthy crotch towel. "You've earned this."

I took it and weighed it in my hand.

"If you want real protection, you can come and work for

me," he said. "I'll make you an honorary Aryan. We can invent some kind of ritual that casts out the slope."

I looked at the newspaper clippings on his walls, photographs of the bodies of his enemies after the Moorebank massacre, and the fourteen-year-old girl who had been killed in the crossfire. Above the head of each Tasman Tiger corpse was written, *Ha-ha!* The girl's epitaph was *Boo-hoo!*

"No," I said.

He flicked a wrist in the air. "Go, then. Fuck off."

I turned my back on the Lion King.

"You're a good-looking boy," he said. "Nice arc."

Jesse turned up in her best lawyer's sweat, a film of condensation on her upper lip, damp patches under the arms of her blouse.

NSW Golf Club spills down to the cliffs of Cape Banks, where formations of lost golf balls rest like banal coral on the bed of the Tasman Sea. A walking track leads from the car park to the cliff edge, skirting the perimeter of Sydney Pistol Club.

"There's a camera on the overhang," said Jesse, "for suicide watch."

When we were students, I reminded her, we'd fought against the surveillance state.

"It picked you up that night," she said, "about ten minutes after the car park camera. The film shows you and another man—it could be Tim—carrying what looks like a rolled-up carpet to the edge of the cliff. You swing it once, twice, three times, then toss it over the ledge."

I scratched my nose.

"What was it that you threw into the ocean, Chevy?"

I told her it was a picnic rug.

"Why would you throw a picnic rug off a cliff, Chevy?"

Why why why.

"You'd believe I'd throw my best mate off a cliff, but not a picnic rug?"

"Christ, you asked my firm to represent you because you thought we could help you. You asked for me—me, specifically—because you said you could be honest with me. You've got to tell me the truth, Chevy. The jury's going to want a motive."

I laughed. "I don't need a motive for throwing a picnic rug off a cliff. It isn't a crime."

Jesse was becoming impatient, unprofessional. "What was in the rug?" she asked.

"You," I said.

I was on the lookout for an Asian, but it was two big Lebs who blocked my way to the yard. One of them was known as the Big Leb, like the Big Banana. He looked like a giant ferrocon-crete statue of an Arab. He said, "We heard you knocked our brother."

Jamie's name was printed in the paper that morning.

"I never knocked no one," I said, like a real crim.

They told me I was dead, but I was used to hearing that.

The Big Leb sent his forehead crashing into my nose. He broke a bone and brought tears to my eyes. As I raised my hands to curb the bleeding, the Lion King's chef's knife fell out of my shirt. The Big Leb picked it up and hurried off.

Then I saw the Viets, mobbed up and moving toward me.

I ran to the Lion King's cell.

A big cock is a status symbol in prison, and there's a thing prisoners do where they sew a marble under their foreskin, to make themselves larger. The Lion King had two marbles, and they must've been dobbers. He was examining them like a jeweler, his right eye squinting, as if into a loupe.

"Grouse, ey?" he said.

The Viets had paused at the end of the corridor, unsure whether to follow me.

"Let me in," I said, "and I'll work for you."

The Lion King looked to his cock for guidance.

"What do you mean?" asked Jesse. "Me?"

"Don't you remember that rug?" I asked, although she obviously didn't. "It's the one we used for our picnic in Scarborough that time."

Jesse's eyebrows drew together. "What picnic?"

"We had a picnic. You made falafel."

"I don't know how to make falafel."

"Maybe you bought it," I said.

"I don't think I ever went on a picnic with you."

This was why Jesse wasn't a good lawyer. She got stuck on the details, couldn't see the bigger story.

"Well, you did," I said. "And we ate falafel and hummus and vine leaves and olives and pita bread. When the food was finished, we fucked on the rug."

"We did not," said Jesse, and put her hand over her mouth.

"Yes you did!" shouted the prisoner in the meeting room next door.

"So I took that rug," I said to Jesse, "and I rolled everything of you inside it—all your pictures and letters, and the James Baldwin books and the Spearhead CDs, and the shirt you bought me in Bali and the shell necklace and the lamp— and I got Tim to carry them with me to the edge of the cliff and throw them the fuck into the ocean, because it's been ten years now, Jesse, and I can't haul them around with me anymore. I've got to let you go."

A tear clouded her eye. I never wanted Jesse to cry.

"So it wasn't Jamie in the rug?" she asked.

"Of course it wasn't Jamie," I said.

My duties to the Lion King were pretty much the same as his cellie's. Basically, I helped him exercise his privileges. I rolled his cigarettes—and the occasional joint—looked after his cell phone in case we got raided, and answered for him and his cellie at the afternoon muster. In the mornings, his cellie answered for me and the Lion King, and I stood like a sentry at his door, because this was his most vulnerable time, when the wing was almost empty. And yeah, I'm ashamed to say it, but I helped him stand over the new prisoners, and ascertain whether they were black, white, or brindle, before he hit them for protection or invited them into his scumbag Nazi gang.

I'd been in Long Bay for three weeks when Jamie rocked up at the Newtown police station, suntanned and smiling and very, very not dead. He did his charm-the-straight-guy thing. He flattered the cops. He'd been fishing, he said, in the Cocos Islands. He'd just got back and heard the news. The sergeant asked him if he'd caught much. Jamie said he'd caught a bonefish as long as your arm. The way he put it could have sounded like a pass if the sergeant had wanted to take it that way.

The cops called in Jesse, she did her thing, and obviously they dropped the blue because you can't have a murder when the murder victim's standing in front of you.

Jesse picked me up and drove me from Long Bay to Sydney Airport.

"So where's Tim?" she asked.

"Turns out he was fishing with Jamie." Imagine my surprise.

Jesse seemed angry. "What was this all for, Chevy?"

Even then, when I looked at her, I felt happy and safe, as if nothing could truly go wrong as long as I had Jesse by my side.

"You got your criminal-law experience, didn't you?" I said. "I'm sorry it didn't go to court."

"Are you mad?"

And, you know, I think I did go a little bit crazy when she left me, because I lost two of the four people I loved, and one of the others was already dead.

I was chewing doughy croissants in the crappy SkyTeam Lounge, wearing an outfit I'd bought in the terminal. I had no luggage, and I was traveling on my Laotian passport. My body was at the airport, but my mind was still in jail.

I was imagining the morning routine. The Lion King had sent his cellie down for roll call. It would be his cellie who told the screws he was alive and, an hour later—after he'd bullied and nuzzled the punching bag—it would be his cellie who told them he was dead. It would also be his cellie who was the first suspect. After all, he had form. He'd killed the girl at Moorebank.

It would be days before they thought of me, a squarehead, an innocent, an architect.

I remembered the Lion King's lazy, startled eyes as I walked into his cell with a razor blade on a toothbrush handle. I'd get no marks for originality, but sometimes you can't improve on a classic. He jumped off his bunk faster than I would've thought possible. When he came up, I caught him with the same hook that had floored Jamie on the CCTV film, but this time neither of us was acting.

I striped the fat cunt like a tiger, the way my half-brother

Trent used to cut up Lions back on Tasman Street, La Perouse, where I was born.

PART II

SEX AND THE CITY

THE TRANSMUTATION OF SEX

BY LEIGH REDHEAD

Parramatta

Every great love affair has its origin story. You know, the thing you tell at couples dinner parties, when people ask: "So, how did you two meet?" And ours is a doozy, although probably a little more R-rated than most.

The day I met Josh my life changed, completely, and the funny thing was that in all my twenty-one years I had never believed in the concept of romantic love, let alone love at first sight. I'd never experienced it, and always thought it was a bullshit scam, laid on by corporations to sell greeting cards and Taylor Swift records. I'd always been kind of cynical, I guess. It started at my country high school where I saw all these smart girls fall for the dumbest boys. Everyone'd be drunk at a party and the guys would tell the chicks lovey-dovey shit—anything to get a blowie or a root—and next Monday the sordid details would be online for the whole school to see; the dude wouldn't even talk to the girl and she'd be so ashamed she'd either OD dramatically on Panadol or enroll in the Christian college on the other side of town. It was pathetic, and it was never gonna happen to me, although that did leave the problem of how to lose my virginity. By the time I was fourteen masturbation just wasn't cutting it, and I didn't like that other girls out there knew something I didn't, so I set about getting that monkey off my back. There was a history teacher I liked at school, Mr. Simms, and as far as I knew none of the other girls had fucked a teacher, so I figured it would be sort of cool, you know?

"OMG," my friend Shona said. "He's ancient. It's gross. He must be at least thirty-five." She needn't have worried because no matter how much I lingered after Mr. Simms's class, leaning over his desk with my top button undone (and I should mention I had the biggest rack in year nine) while asking insightful questions about the impact of European settlement on indigenous people, he wouldn't take the bait. As a young girl everyone warned me about stranger danger, and older men taking advantage, but pedophiles are like cops: there's never one around when you need one.

I finally lost it at fifteen, when a band from nearby Port Macquarie came and played an all-ages gig in the park. Drunk on a four-liter cask of goon. Shona and the other girls were giggling and swooning over the front man, but I liked the bass player who hung back, quietly confident. After their set I went up to him, no giggling, told him I liked their songs, and asked if he wanted a line of speed. He did. It wasn't really speed, just a few crushed-up pills my brother takes for his ADHD, but if you have enough it works. An hour later we were fucking in the back of the band's Tarago. It didn't hurt much and there was no blood, thank god. We were together for a while, after I left school in year ten. Long story short, I ended up with another muso, Matt, who was touring with his System of a Down cover band, and at age eighteen I moved to Sydney to live with him.

All this might make me sound like a bit of a groupie, or hanger-on, but I'm not. I like to have my own money, and my own drugs, and I don't rely on anyone but myself. I'm ambitious, you see, and I think that's for two reasons. One, I've never wanted to end up like my single mother, living dole payment to dole payment and waiting her whole life for a commission flat that never materialized; and two is a book. Now you may look at me and think, *She doesn't seem like much of a reader*, and you would be absolutely right, except for this one book I've read literally thousands of times, ever since I stole it from the Taree Salvation Army thrift store back in 2007. We used to nick clothes, not books, and my friends thought I was mad, but something about the title grabbed me: *Think and Grow Rich*.

In case you haven't read it (and you really should) it was written by this guy called Napoleon Hill, way back in 1937. He basically interviewed all the mega-rich dudes of the time, and came up with "The Thirteen Proven Steps to Riches" which include stuff like desire, faith, auto-suggestion, specialized knowledge, imagination, planning, decision, persistence, the power of the mastermind, and the mystery of sex transmutation. Now, this last one tends to confuse people and it freaks out Americans, probably because of the "s" word, and I didn't get it for a long time, but now I do. Wanna know what it is? Well, you'll have to wait.

So, where was I? Oh yeah, the greatest love story of all time started at a Meriton-serviced apartment in Parramatta that had been rented for a buck's party. I'd been working at the Sefton Playhouse—the strip club near the station—for a couple of years by then and some of the other girls and I were providing the entertainment. You know the drill—warm-up show, vibe show, fruit and veg, and finally the big shebang: lesbian double with vibes. I did the warm-up, which doesn't pay quite as well as the others, but was confident I'd make it up in private dances afterward. When my show was over I went to do another line of coke in the bathroom with my best friend Kailee who was up next, then I found one of those pink Bacardi Breezers that the guys had thoughtfully organized for the dancers, and decided to go out on the balcony for a cigarette.

I was standing there in my bikini, enjoying the warmth of the November afternoon, smoking and looking out over the brown water of the Parramatta River, Sydney Olympic Park, and the city skyline far off in the distance, thinking I'd love an apartment here. Matt and I shared a crappy old house in Lidcombe with his drummer Dave, who was a total sleaze but handy to have around because of his drug contacts. They loved it, thought all the cracked plaster and moldy brown tiles were authentic or something, but I preferred new buildings, like this place. Faux-granite benchtops, gleaming bathroom fittings, and immaculate beige carpet. As I smoked I did a quick calculation about how much money I was going to make from lap dances and had just figured that five hundred bucks was quite achievable when I realized I wasn't alone. Sitting on a chair made of gray plastic wicker, half hidden behind a potted palm, was a guy. Thirties maybe, ordinary looking, dark hair, checked flannel shirt, and glasses. He was listening to an iPod while engrossed in a book.

I nearly laughed out loud. Who in the actual fuck comes to a buck's party to read? I stuck out my leg and tapped him on the knee with the toe of my Perspex platform. He jumped, dropped the book, then took out his earbuds and looked at me.

I get pretty chatty when I'm high, so I said, "Are you actually part of this buck's turn, or just some random who scaled the balcony to find a quiet place to read?"

"Part of it," he sighed. "Wish I wasn't, but my cousin's the buck and my brother's the best man. We've been drinking since ten in the morning and were forced to play paintball. What a nightmare. I'm going to slip away before we end up at a brothel."

"What's the book?" I asked, and he turned it over to show me the cover.

"*The Fall*," I read. "Albert Camus. Any good?"

"Cam*oo*," he said.

"Pardon?"

"It's pronounced Camoo. And yeah, it is good. I'm rereading it for a tutorial I've got on Monday."

"You studying?"

"I was. Finished my PhD and picked up some teaching work."

"Whereabouts?"

"Western Sydney Uni, Parramatta."

"Get out!" I squealed. "That's where I'm going next year."

"Really? What course?"

"Bachelor of Business." This really impressed most guys I met at the Playhouse, but the dude's top lip curled. "What's wrong with a business degree?" I asked.

"Nothing. It's just not really my bag."

The muffled thump of the music inside stopped, replaced by woops and applause. That'd be Kailee's show done and she'd be ready for another line.

"Lesbian double's on next," I teased. "You don't want to miss that."

He groaned and covered his eyes.

I was looking in my purse, checking I still had the baggie of coke wedged behind my Medicare card, when the glass door slid open and the best man poked his bald head out. He wore pressed jeans, a shiny gray shirt, and a cloud of Lynx deodorant so thick it was nearly visible. He briefly ogled my tits, then looking around the rest of the balcony, spotted his brother.

"Josh-o, you faggot. Whatcha doing out here? Dyke show's

about to start." He made a V with his index and middle finger and waggled his tongue in between.

Josh raised his beer. "Just having a quiet—"

"Lap dance!" I interjected, slipping my own fifty out of my wallet, waving it around, then sliding it back in, making out like Josh had just paid me.

I don't know what had given me the urge to save Josh from his brother. Maybe it was because the brother had tried to stick his fingers in when I'd bent over in front of him during my show. Or maybe it's because strippers are like cats. You know how if you love cats, and you're all, *Here, kitty-kitty-kitty,* they'll ignore you? And if you hate them, or are allergic, that fucking cat is gonna be all over you? Well, that's what was happening here, I guess. The brother wasn't looking entirely convinced so I swigged the last of my pink drink, strode over to Josh, planted my legs on either side of his, and held on to the back of the chair. I expected him to flinch, but he was good, hamming it up, saluting his brother with the beer bottle.

Baldy stood there, arms crossed.

"Bit of privacy?" Josh asked. "You watching is uncomfortably close to incest."

The brother snorted and walked back out the door.

"Thanks for that," Josh said. When I didn't move away, he continued, "Uh, you don't actually have to do it, he's gone."

"But what if he comes back? We need to keep up the act. One song. Sit back and think of Camoo."

We didn't have any music, so I grabbed his earbuds, stuck one in his ear and the other in mine. A Nick Cave song started playing—"Are You the One That I've Been Waiting For." It wasn't exactly Lil Wayne, but it would have to do. Then, because there were no pesky bouncers to uphold no-contact laws, I sat on his lap, and the instant the backs of my thighs touched the front of his, the weirdest thing happened. My skin burned with a fierce, inexplicable heat, and buzzed like I was touching a live electrical wire. I jumped up, startled, and as soon as I wasn't touching him my flesh went cold. Too cold. I couldn't bear it so I sat back down and the warmth returned. As Nick sang, *"You've been moving surely toward me,"* I leaned in and slowly rested my lower abdomen, rib cage, then boobs against his torso, and it was the same thing as with the legs: a flood of warmth and tingling that made my heart pound. Sure, I was a little high, but I'm a little high most of the time and nothing like that had ever happened before.

"Oh my god," I said. "Do you *feel* that?"

"Ye-es," he said hesitantly.

I couldn't help it, I leaned in and kissed him. Just a short kiss, more than a peck, less than a porn tonguing, but oh my god. It was like sparks flew between our lips, and my mouth felt like it was stuffed full of Pop Rocks and Wizz Fizz and my brain buzzed like I'd just done an enormous line of the purest cocaine in all Bolivia, even though the stuff I had in the baggie was actually total shit.

Then the song finished and his phone buzzed in his shirt pocket. He fished it out and looked at it, then back at me. He smiled ruefully and said, "My Uber's here."

I walked with him to the front door, the other guys so engrossed in the double show they didn't notice us.

"Well, thanks for that," he said. "It was quite an experience."

I stared at him, desperately trying to commit his face to memory, though it was difficult because he was just an ordinary-looking guy. Average height, dark-brown hair, not ugly, but not even as good-looking as my boyfriend Matt, who had chicks literally flinging their slimy G-strings at him on stage.

A voice in my head screamed, *Kiss me, touch me, don't go!* but all I said was. "No problem, nice to meet you," and then he was gone, and I would never see him again.

Kailee found me in the bathroom, hunched over the sink, grabbing at my stomach which felt like it was being pierced by metal barbecue skewers. She told me later I'd gone deathly pale under my spray tan and she was convinced I'd been raped.

"I feel like I'm going to vomit," I told her. "I think I'm in love."

The rest of the afternoon went by in a blur. I made my five hundred bucks, and when I got home to Lidcombe there was a party going on, like most weekends. I stood at the rusted sink, piled with the usual dirty dishes, and looked out the window. Matt was off his chops, staggering around in the overgrown backyard, attempting to play Rugby League with a couple of friends.

"What's he on?" I asked Dave, who'd sidled up behind me.

"GHB," he said. "Want some?"

"The date-rape drug? No thanks."

"Don't believe everything you read in the *Telegraph*. The sex on G is amazing."

He pushed his groin into my arse and I turned and swatted him away. "Fuck off Dave, seriously."

"You know, Matt plays up when he's on tour. A lot."

I knew, and it didn't worry me. Probably because I met up with the occasional club punter after work, but only if the money was very, very good.

Dave moved in close. He was my height, with shaggy auburn hair and dry lips that collected white stuff in the corners. "It's not fair if you don't get to have some fun of your own."

I pushed him away, took my iPhone into the bedroom, and locked the door. I had research to do.

"So, how's your crush going?" Kailee said. We were in the girls' room at the Playhouse, putting on makeup.

"It's not a crush. This is serious." I wasn't lying. I'd tried to put Josh out of my mind, chalk the whole episode up to a combination of cocaine, Nick Cave, and alcopops, but it hadn't worked. For the last four days he'd been the first thing I thought about when I woke up, and the last before I went to sleep. And then I dreamed about the motherfucker. I was spending more time staring at photos of him on Google Images than I was planning my financial future. I was losing my mind.

"Have you seen him again?"

"No, but I've been checking him out on the Internet. His full name is Joshua Atherton, born October 13, 1979. He's a part-time lecturer at the University of Western Sydney teaching literature and philosophy—"The Ethical Life" and "Philosophies of Love and Death." Lives in a flat in Ashfield he's bought with his fiancée, Kelly Marshall, an academic at Sydney Uni." I turned my phone to show her the picture of Josh and Kelly posted on Facebook a few months earlier, where she was holding out her ring finger to display a vintage rose-gold engagement ring inlaid with, to my mind, a pathetically small diamond. Comments underneath included: *About time, guys!* and, *Nice work Kel—you finally made an honest man out of him!*

"Oh, hon," Kailee said, her mouth turning down and eyes drooping like a sad cow.

"What?"

"I've known you for three years and I've never seen you

go nuts about any guy, even Matt. You're usually so practical. Probably because you're a Capricorn. You know what you want, go and get it, and don't let silly emotions stand in your way. Not like the rest of the girls, always in love, breaking up, getting obsessed, being betrayed. But now you are and it's sweet to see. You're just like the rest of us!"

I doubted that. I was nothing like Kailee with her Tree of Life cushion covers, married boyfriends, and Deepak Chopra books.

"But I'm worried," she continued. "If it doesn't work out," she pointed at my phone, "I'm afraid you're going to take it hard."

I wasn't concerned about the fiancée. I knew from her Facebook status that she was about to fly to New Zealand for a Cultural Studies conference. She'd be gone a week.

"I don't want to see you get hurt," Kailee said, giving me this pouty I-feel-so-sorry-for-you look that made me want to slap her. Instead, I took a deep breath and quoted some Napoleon Hill.

"There is one quality which one must possess to win, and that is definiteness of purpose, the knowledge of what one wants, and a burning desire to possess it."

As soon as I said the words it became obvious what I had to do: go back to the book and apply the thirteen principles. I had desire, faith, persistence, and knew how to plan. Specialized knowledge? By the bucketload.

"I'll be okay," I told her.

Four days later I was at WSU's Parramatta campus—a flat, spread-out place with lots of green fields and jacaranda trees blooming pale purple. Back in the olden days the whole of Parramatta was a gigantic farm which provided food for the penal colony of Sydney, and the university site used to house schools for orphans, a female insane asylum, and a boiler house where the urchins and psychos did laundry, presumably. I knew all this from reading the heritage pamphlet while sitting on a bench outside building EQ, an old-fashioned, two-story job with wraparound verandas where Josh and a couple of other philosophy lecturers had their offices. He hadn't been hard to find. His room and phone number were listed on the university website and it was only a matter of time before he emerged. At exactly 4:36, he left the building in the company of a tweedy-looking older man and I followed them onto a shuttle bus at the entrance to the university. I was incognito, dressed as a student in a denim mini, a striped, off-the-shoulder T, oversized Gucci sunnies, and ballet flats. I carried a bag from the Co-op bookstore. They alighted the bus at the Parramatta City stop and walked toward the railway station, past old sandstone buildings and new office blocks with windows like mirrored sunglasses. I was worried they were going to catch a train together, until they crossed to the Commercial Hotel.

The pub's original colonial façade faced the street, but the inside had been scooped out and expanded to accommodate a bunch of different bars. I tailed them to the beer garden, which wasn't so much a garden as a cavernous two-story atrium with a massive TV screen suspended from one of the glass walls. They bought beers and sat at a wooden table and I nicked into the ladies' for a couple of lines of coke, before buying a Wild Raspberry Vodka Cruiser and parking myself at the next bench, hidden behind a fake hedge. They sunk a couple of beers and then the older guy said he had to run for his train and dashed off.

I approached Josh, who looked up as he drained the last of his schooner.

"Oh my god, it's . . . Josh, isn't it?"

He seemed confused so I leaned forward and whispered, "We met at your cousin's party."

Now he recognized me.

"I'm Lila," I said. It's actually short for Delilah, which is spelled *Darlyla* on my birth certificate because my mum thought it was more "unique." I'd stopped telling people my full name because as well as making me seem like the world's biggest bogan, there was not a man alive who could resist singing the Tom Jones song as soon as they heard it.

"What are you doing here?" he said.

"Picking up textbooks!" I brandished the bookshop bag. "Hey—do you mind if I have a drink with you? I was sitting at the bar, but a couple of engineering students started getting sleazy."

"I was about to leave." He glanced at his watch.

"Just one? I wanted to pick your brain about philosophy. I'm thinking of doing a double degree."

Josh had another beer and I drank a pinot grigio (to look sophisticated) while I asked him questions about the course and philosophy in general. I'd spent the past week researching on Wikipedia, and was familiar with the big enchiladas and main theories of the subject. People think I'm a dumb bitch because I work as a stripper and left school early, but I got a great mark in my Tertiary Preparation Certificate at TAFE, and I'm heaps good at retaining information when I put my mind to it.

Josh had a lot to say on the topic, and as I watched his mouth move and his hands wave around, my pussy literally started throbbing and I had to squeeze my thighs together, tight. I hadn't been mistaken, some irresistible force was attracting me to him, though I never figured out exactly what it was. Kailee, bloody hippie, reckoned we must have met in a past life, but I leaned more toward fate and pheromones. Either way, it was just like the Nick Cave song. He *was* the one who I'd been waiting for. Everything else fell away—Matt, Josh's girlfriend, the chattering pub patrons, and the State of Origin replay on the giant TV. *I'm in love with you*, I thought, and hoped I hadn't said it out loud.

I touched his leg under the table.

He pulled away like he'd been burned. "You'd better not do that."

"Why?"

"I'm engaged."

"Sorry, I didn't know."

His face had a sort of scrunched-up, apologetic expression. "Nothing against you. You're very attractive."

Trust me to fall for the one man in the Sydney metropolitan area who wouldn't cheat on his partner. Still, I wasn't discouraged because I knew he liked me, even if he wouldn't admit it to himself. I also had the words of the good book to back me up. Napoleon Hill says that most people are unsuccessful because they can't come up with a new plan when their original one fails.

I came up with a new plan.

"Oh my god," I widened my eyes, "I completely misread the situation. This is mortifying. I'm *so* sorry."

"It's okay." He leaned over and patted me on the shoulder. The touch of his palm through my T-shirt was so intense I nearly came. I just wanted to push the empty glasses off the table, crawl across, straddle him, and lick his face.

"I am *such* an idiot." I buried my face in my hands, then peeked out at him, cringing adorably.

"No you're not," he said.

"Yes I am. And the only thing that's going to make a dent in this embarrassment is a stiff drink. You like Glenfiddich?"

I knew he did, because I'd seen a picture on Instagram of him and his fiancée at the distillery on a trip to Scotland two years earlier. I hated the shit, but jumped up and bought two doubles. The bartender didn't see me take out the tiny fish-shaped soy sauce container and drip clear liquid into Josh's drink.

By the time the whiskey was finished Josh had started to feel woozy. I suggested that maybe one of the engineering students had tried to spike *my* drink, and offered to help him home. He refused, but I insisted, and held onto his arm as we lurched out of the pub and into a taxi.

It took about half an hour to get to Ashfield, driving down the M4, then Parramatta Road, with the sun setting behind. Before I moved to Sydney I thought the whole city would be glamorous, like the parts you saw on postcards: sparkling-blue harbor, pearly Opera House, the majestic Harbour Bridge, but most of it was dog ugly. Parramatta Road was an endless gray ribbon of used-car yards and service stations punctuated by the occasional McDonald's. Wasn't much different from my hometown, just bigger, with less aboriginals and more Indians and Asians.

Josh's ground-floor flat was in a whitewashed deco building with a cute little burgundy awning out the front. He let himself in, flung his brown leather messenger bag onto the polished wooden floor, and lay down on an Oriental rug. The whole living room was lined with bookcases, all filled with actual books instead of Xbox games and DVDs.

He blinked and half sat up, weight resting on one elbow. "Thanks for getting me home, but you can go now. I think I'm starting to straighten up."

"Want me to call someone? Your fiancée?"

"No! No. I'll be okay."

I looked at him like I wasn't too sure. "You thirsty?"

"Parched."

"I'll get you a drink."

The kitchen was small, but immaculately renovated: stainless-steel appliances, subtle downlighting, and a splashback of tiny blue-and-white tiles. Clean glasses gleamed on the draining board, and a small courtyard with a Weber barbecue and an outdoor setting was visible between the slats of the wooden venetians. I found fresh-squeezed, pulp-free orange juice in the fridge and a frosted bottle of Grey Goose in the freezer and mixed two strong drinks before digging one long acrylic fingernail into my coke baggie and snorting a hefty bump. Taking the soy sauce container out of my skirt pocket, I sized it up under the light. Half full. The initial dose had probably been a little low, so I emptied the remains into Josh's drink, took a second little fish from my pocket, and added half of that. He just needed to relax a bit, let go of his inhibitions, and the G would help. I tried it out myself a few days earlier, and it had worked so well I'd ended up in a fairly revolting three-way with Matt and Dave.

He sipped the drink and made a face. "Does this have vodka in it?"

"No way! Booze increases the effects of sedatives, but the acid in the OJ should neutralize whatever those guys slipped in your whiskey." A druggie wives' tale with zero scientific basis, but Josh believed it and gulped the whole lot in one.

I told him I'd leave just as soon as I'd used the loo, but took my sweet time to give the G a chance to kick in. I peed, did a couple more lines in their modern, white-tiled bathroom, fixed my makeup in the mirror, spritzed a little of Josh's

L'eau d'Issey Pour Homme on my wrist, then slipped off my pink-lace knickers and shoved them in my handbag. I wanted everything to be smooth and cinematic. We deserved it.

Back in the lounge room Josh was flat on his back on the rug, seemingly fascinated by his hand, which he waved around in the air, like a kid sticking his arm in the slipstream out the car window. I stalked the bookcases and found a Bose stereo system and shelf of alphabetized CDs, put on Nick Cave's *The Boatman's Call*.

"I love this," said Josh.

"Me too," I lied. Sure, I liked *our* song, but most of Cave's tunes were too whiny or religious for my taste.

A framed photograph on the mantelpiece pictured Josh receiving his doctorate, wearing a robe and clownish hat. He was flanked by his parents and fiancée, an earnest-looking brunette who could have been quite attractive if she'd gotten a few hair extensions and a decent eyebrow wax. The parents looked fit, self-satisfied, and expensively dressed, and it suddenly dawned on me how Josh and his fiancée had been able to buy this place. Ashfield was close to the city, rapidly becoming gentrified, and the flat wouldn't have left much change from eight hundred grand. You couldn't save that sort of deposit as a sessional academic.

Nick Cave was singing some boring churchy dirge so I fast-forwarded to "Are You the One I've Been Waiting For?" stuck it on repeat, and sat down next to Josh.

"You seem okay now," I said, although his pupils had dilated and his forehead was beaded with sweat.

"I feel reeeeaaaally good," he said.

Bingo, baby. I leaned over and kissed him and, when he didn't resist, I shifted sideways and laid on top, felt him hard beneath his beige chinos, and squirmed around to make him harder. Trouble with G was it could be difficult to come, and I wanted our first time to be perfect, so I reluctantly unlocked lips and slid down his body, unbuckling his belt and opening his fly. His cock sprung free and I opened my mouth and put my "specialized knowledge" to work. You should have seen him, bucking, moaning, fingers all twined up in my hair. When he got close I disengaged, sat up, wiped my mouth with the back of my hand, and took off my top so he could cop a look at my magnificent tits, then I slid down on his cock and OMG. It was nearly too much for me. I'm not talking size-wise, because, to be perfectly honest, it could have been a *tad* bigger, but the feeling inside my pussy was almost too intense to bear. I know this sounds like something Kailee would say, but it was as though his cock was talking to me, communicating with my vagina in some bizarre, otherworldly way. Normally at this point in proceedings I'd be putting on a pretty good show, gasping and thrashing my hair around and massaging my boobs all porno style, but all I could do was sit there, sort of stunned, feeling like I was dissolving into him, surrounded by a halo of golden light. ("Tantra," Kailee told me later. "You were totally having tantric sex.") When I stopped sliding up and down on his dick Josh groaned in frustration, flipped me over onto my back, and climbed on top. I hooked my ankles over his shoulders and as he drove into me, belt buckle bouncing off the back of my thigh, I felt like I was having a kind of continuous orgasm, with no beginning and no end, and the feeling was so overwhelming that it was almost a relief when he made one last deep thrust, emitted a guttural cry, and collapsed on top of me, his chambray shirt soaked through with perspiration. When he rolled off, I realized my cheeks were wet and I thought he'd sweated on me, but no—I'd been crying.

I never cry.

When Josh finally got his breath back, he opened his mouth to speak and I turned to him, eager to hear his first words.

"I feel terrible," he said. "What am I going to tell Kelly?"

This was not what I'd been hoping for.

"Don't tell her anything."

"Lies are the greatest murder," he muttered, staring up at the fringed lampshade. "They kill the truth."

"Say what?"

"Socrates."

"But didn't Camus," I pronounced the name correctly, "write that a lie was a beautiful twilight that enhances every object?"

"Shit." He looked stunned that I knew the line. "He did."

"So stop trying to be the good guy. It's useless. You know and I know this thing is bigger than both of us."

He gazed into my eyes, then completely cracked up laughing. I knew he was high, but for fuck's sake.

"What's so funny?"

"I can't believe you just said that," he said, wheezing like a hyena.

I sat up and crossed my arms. "What about the lap dance? Remember when I asked, *Do you feel that?* You said yes."

"I thought you were talking about my erection!" He broke up all over again.

I stood and walked back into the kitchen, naked but for my denim skirt, semen dripping down my leg. I absentmindedly wiped it with my hand, then licked my fingers. It tasted like warm apple pie, unlike Matt's jizz, which was all asparagus and aluminum. See? Yet another reason Josh and I were meant to be together. If he could just get over all this moral and ethical bullshit. I mixed another screwdriver and my hand was shaking so much the OJ overflowed the glass. Fuck it. I sipped the excess then took the third little fish container from my skirt pocket and emptied the whole thing in. The second was still half full so I added that as well.

He was thirsty after all the exertion, and drank it down quick.

"Are you sure that didn't have any vod—"

"Sssshhh," I said. "Relax."

Our song was still playing on repeat, and Josh closed his eyes and started breathing slow and deep. I laid my head on his chest, slid my phone from my bag, and took a cute selfie of the two of us. Josh fell asleep, but that was okay. I was happy just to lie next to him, pressing my body into that warm skin and inhaling his scent of sweat, washing powder, and Issey Miyake. His breath became shallower, and then it slowed some more. Eventually I crashed out too, and when I woke at two a.m. he was very still, and not so warm anymore. I got dressed, washed the glasses, and wiped down all the surfaces I had touched: the stainless-steel fridge, shaving mirror, and stereo system. Then I let myself out, hailed a cab on Frederick Street, and went home to Lidcombe.

Needless to say, that was the end of Josh, and you'd think I'd be devastated, but I'm not, because I finally understood the tenth principle, sex transmutation. Napoleon Hill reckons that sex drive is one of our most powerful desires and if you can somehow channel this incredible force away from base physical expression into something higher, you can totally achieve anything you want. Famous artists, politicians, and entrepreneurs have used this very principle to create masterpieces, change the course of history, and—my personal favorite—make a shitload of money.

So how have I used it? Well, I took all that powerful sex energy I couldn't use and channeled it into my studies. As a result, I fucking *blitzed* my Bachelor of Business—first class honors—and now I've got a graduate position in asset management at Macquarie Bank. Napoleon Hill was right, but when I try to explain the principles to hipsters at parties (I had to move to the inner east because it was easier to get to the head office in Martin Place), they sneer and accuse me of being a "bread head." I come back by asking if they like Nick Cave (they never say no) and tell them not to put shit on Napoleon because Nick says exactly the same thing in "Are You the One That I've Been Waiting For?" Verse three is about channeling your longing into creating amazing things, and verse four is about identifying what you want and using positive affirmations to go out and get it. *He who seeks finds / he who knocks will be let in.* I didn't understand that at first—I didn't understand a lot of things, until I met Josh.

It's kind of a relief that he's gone, though, because his absence has freed me up to concentrate on my core values and vision. Don't get me wrong, I still love him and think about him (I'm not some kind of monster), but it's funny, he works better for me as a muse than an actual person. He allows me to think, and grow rich.

THE PATTERNMAKER

Julie Koh
Ashfield

I think he's a detective until the night he gets his dick out. He's been hanging around this block of flats all week. Around midnight every night, he's appeared in the back car park, camera around his neck, looking shady. I only noticed him because I've been up late thinking about my runway collection. I've been bingeing on seasons of *Real Couturier* on my laptop, getting myself in the zone.

I've started keeping the lights off so I can watch him from my window on the first floor. He's tall and thin and pale as fuck, with long, terrible hair halfway between orange and brown. I've never seen him walk up the driveway from the street. He just appears. Maybe he's been hiding in the separate laundry room out back. No one's called the police on him yet.

So tonight it's raining and he's standing under the back light staring up at my studio. But this time he's wanking.

I smoke and watch him. When the cigarette's done, I slide the window frame up and stick my head out.

"What's wrong with you?"

"Hang on," he says. "You're not Cathy."

"Why should I be?"

"Is she there?"

"Why should I tell you?"

He puts his thing away, zips his fly. "I want Cathy."

"You and the world. How tall are you?"

"'Bout 180?"

I think, why not? That's a good height. Let's bring this blue dick in from the cold.

He comes up the back stairs, jumper soaked. Smells like a farm animal. But he has a good jawline and frame. Could be a good clotheshorse.

He inspects my studio like he owns it. Walks all the way through without asking. Looks at the rolls of fabric, the cutting table, my little Juki sewing machine, my voodoo pin cushion, all crammed into the living room. He touches Ludmila, my dress form, on the waist. She's just a torso.

"Couldn't afford one with legs," I say.

He moves on to the kitchen, bathroom, and bedrooms, then plonks himself on the couch.

"Happy?" I say.

"I knew Cathy's couch would be red. Cathy wears red a lot."

"It's *my* couch."

"Cathy's really pretty."

"Cathy this, Cathy that," I say.

"Where *is* Cathy?"

"You're the stalker. You tell me."

He looks at the wall, hums some tune.

"Stay for a movie," I say, "and I'll tell you where she went."

I get my laptop and click on a rom-com. We watch the whole thing. Right before it ends, the friends of the main character tell him he's made a mistake. He panics, sprints down streets, knocks over a newspaper stand, finds the girl, gets her back. *I knew you were the one*, he tells her. They kiss at the top of a tower. People clap. Credits roll.

The wanker asks where Cathy is again. I say I'll tell him later.

He says his name is Mugzy. Isn't even a nickname. Is he going to break out into some shitty rap?

No wonder he has to get his cock out in car parks.

Mugzy turns up every night. Stands outside in the same place. Waits until I open the window and call him up.

He's twenty-three. So young I could've pushed him out of my own cunt.

He does what I tell him to do. I say do the dishes, he does the dishes. I say do the ironing, he does the ironing. I send him to Ashfield Mall to buy sanitary pads and Handee paper towels. He stands still for me to take his measurements. He's a perfect robot. He thinks I'm going to give him Cathy's address.

"I like this flat," he says one night while we're at the cutting table. I'm fitting him with a *mino*, a cape I've made of straw.

"It isn't a flat, it's a fashion studio. Downstairs is vacant. You can rent it."

"Got no cash."

Mugzy says he's living in some couple's spare room in Burwood. He's been doing odd jobs—mowing lawns, moving furniture. No one will give him a proper gig.

Mugzy says he wants to become a private investigator to bring in more money. He got the idea when he met me. He shows me an ad he's put up on Gumtree. *Protecting Sydney since 2017*, it reads. He thinks his stalking skills are transferable to this new kind of work. His stalking is all self-directed, he says. He's set himself a lot of challenging assignments.

But all the self-direction is taking up too much of his time. So much that there isn't enough left to fit in paid jobs. He's having trouble making rent. Mugzy says he's a millennial, and that millennials change jobs all the time. When he gets tired of being a shitfuck-famous investigator, he's going to be a shit-fuck-famous street photographer.

"We're gonna be a massive power couple," he says. "Everyone's gonna talk about us all the time."

"I thought you wanted Cathy."

I tell him I'll give him Cathy's address if he agrees to be my star runway model when I get to the final of *Real Couturier*.

"Two birds, one stone," he grins. "Yah, boy."

Mugzy wants to know more about Cathy.

"Nice girl with shit for brains," I say.

Everyone swiped right on Cathy all her life. Pretty, big eyes, midtwenties. An international student from Hong Kong living on her family's money. She went on all the time about her awesome parents but ignored their calls. She made faces at my fashion sketches.

"Too weird," she used to say. "And not in a good way."

She moved out to be with her loaded white boyfriend in his flash apartment on the other side of the bridge.

She met him at salsa class in Darling Harbour. He was wearing a gray fedora, and a pinstriped waistcoat with nothing underneath. His triceps popped, she said. She called him *my man*.

"My man and I are going hiking," she'd say. "My man and I are doing salsa."

I think of her and her man doing salsa and fucking. Salsa, fuck, salsa, fuck, in their boring salsafucking clothes.

"Wearing a hat—it's called peacocking," says Mugzy, when I tell him how they met. "I'm reading it in a pickup book. Girls love that shit. He probably pretended to be interested in her friend first. Probably negged her with backhanded compliments. Works like a dream."

* * *

When Cathy told me she was moving over the bridge, we were having dumplings at Shanghai Night.

"Ashfield never matched my vision of myself," she said, and popped a *xiaolongbao* into her mouth with a fork.

She saw me looking at her shiny pink nails.

"I found an awesome nail salon in Balmain," she said. "Eighty bucks for a shellac mani-pedi. A girl with a good mani-pedi is a girl who is living her best life."

I watched those nails and that fork shovelling *xiaolongbaos* into that mouth, and I couldn't work out what Cathy had that I didn't have. I had a good personality. I was okay-looking. But then again, I didn't have control over my cuticles.

The day she left, I woke up to a pink Post-it on the fridge: *B the change u wish 2 c in the world.*

Lucky I didn't take her advice or I would've slapped that Post-it on her chest and stabbed her through it. Would've left her posted to the kitchen wall, shellacked toes off the lino.

That's a change I wanted to see.

I spend all my cash on a cardboard coffin off the Internet. It comes on a Monday morning. Two guys deliver it. They slide it under my cutting table, next to the couch. The coffin has a wood veneer and gold handles and a white satin lining.

"That looks like a lot of money," says Mugzy, when he comes in that night.

"It's make-or-break time," I say, pulling on the ends of the tape measure hanging around my neck. "Fame is built on sacrifice."

When people push in front of me in lines at the super-market, or expect me to step off the footpath for them in the street, the thing they don't know about me is I'm gonna be famous. Even more shitfuck famous than Mugzy. I'm gonna get out of this hole in Ashfield and I'm gonna go to New York and I'm gonna win *Real Couturier*. And at the final in Vanderbilt Hall, my models are gonna lie in a line of coffins in their shrouds on the runway.

And my favorite judge, Ava Rodriguez, editorial director of *KELLERMAN*, is going to warn me beforehand about how risky my runway collection is.

"Don't make it too costumey," she'll say.

And I'll say, "But I'm drawing on my culture."

And she'll say, "But how is this commercial, Rioko?"

And I'll say, "Just you wait, Ava, I'll show you."

My line is going to transcend all of fashion. It's going to be spiritual. It's going to be Japanese warrior-prince ghost-god, with shrouds and death and destruction.

All the contestants on *Real Couturier* work closely with a key model, and now Mugzy's mine. I'm going to make him into a shinto spirit god from another world. Shinto gods bring blessings. They can't exist without people believing in them. And when we get onstage at Vanderbilt Hall, I'm going to show everyone this new god and send him off in a ritual with all the other models and their coffins.

Mugzy's new cape is already done. Now I'm making him a linen shroud that covers everything except his face. When I send him to the show's makeup team, the look I'm going to ask for is snow white, with pink around the eyes.

The only problem is that the day after the coffin arrives, I get another reminder letter about overdue rent. I've spent my entire design budget on the coffin. I can't afford the studio anymore. But you just have to not give a shit about anything. You've gotta go for your goals with your whole heart. I mean, the day before Cathy went, I lost my job in the city. *Redundant,* they called me. They were taking manufacturing and development to Vietnam. They had no need for patternmakers like me.

It was a sign from the universe. It was a sign I was going to win *Real Couturier*. I took over Cathy's bedroom and turned the flat into a design studio. I bought all these rolls of fabric, and Ludmila. Put a cutting table in. And all I'm doing, day in, day out, while the money drains away, is training for fame.

All my chips are on *Real Couturier*.

Sometimes I duck under the cutting table and get in the coffin for a nap. While I drift off, I think about Nara.

I think of my parents being buried together. Two mounds side by side. People said I was home when they died, but I can't remember it. I was five. After it happened, an older kid on my street asked me how it felt to have had parents with a death wish. There was empty space in my head where the answer should have been.

My grandfather took me in. He did calisthenics in the yard every morning and had a big goldfish tank in his house that had plastic seaweed at the bottom. He called me his little goldfish.

One afternoon I overheard him arguing with his new wife about what they were going to do with me. She didn't like that I never spoke. She'd also found an exercise book that I'd filled with drawings of *oni*—red-faced demons standing in fields of blind snakes.

"This girl brings disaster," the wife said.

While they argued, I went to the tank and scooped up a goldfish with one hand. I took it into the garden and dug a shallow hole and dropped it in. Looking at me sideways from the dirt, its eye was as wide and blank as always. It squirmed and tried to flip. Its lips sucked air. When I was done burying it, I put a rock on top. Then I went back to the tank and did the same with the other fish, one by one, until they all lay in a nice row of mounds topped with rocks.

When my grandfather came out to find me, he went white. He asked me to explain. I couldn't tell him why I did it.

The wife locked me out of the house all afternoon. Then she locked me out of Nara. They put me on a plane to Sydney to live with my mother's sister.

"You are a stone around my neck," this aunt used to say.

I was no one's little goldfish anymore. At school, girls called me a dog. They spread rumors that I didn't wash my hands or take showers.

When I became a patternmaker, the other women at my company avoided me. They never invited me out for coffee, or bought me cake on my birthday.

At work, I had all these big ideas no one liked. I wanted to improve the clients' designs—like add funeral veils to floaty summer dresses.

"Be sensible, Rioko," my manager would say. "It isn't commercial. It's too expensive. The designs are already done. Your role here is to make the patterns."

So I made the patterns. I stayed late most nights because I had nowhere else to be. Sometimes, on the way home from work, I fucked guys. I found them on a dating app. I got them to meet me in alleyways, and we'd fuck against the wall. Once I met up with a guy on a one-way street off Liverpool Road, just past midnight. He showed up wearing a rubber mask. The mask was the face of a rat.

"You're so small I could pick you up," he said.

He grabbed me by my hair, swung me hard against the wall, shoved his fingers between my legs. When he went to unzip his pants, I ran.

"Scurry, scurry, little yellow rat," he called after me. "Let's see you run!"

Lying in the coffin in the afternoon, I'm talking about myself in the third person. I read once on a psychology blog that it helps with performance.

"Rioko had no one," I say. "But she had grit, and that's what counted."

Someone is knocking at the door.

"What would Rioko do? Rioko would see who's there."

It's the old lady landlord. She serves me with a termination notice. Says I'm fourteen days late with the rent.

"But Rioko only got the reminder the other day."

"That was eleven days ago."

The notice says I have two weeks to move out unless I pay what I owe, or agree on a repayment plan.

"Rioko doesn't have any money," I say. "She had to buy the coffin."

"Excuse me?"

"It's the paparazzi, isn't it? They want you to lure Rioko into the open."

"If you can't pay, you'll have to be out by the end of June."

"Rioko will get you that cash," I say. "She's on the edge of glory."

When the old lady leaves, I do five sets of star jumps and some of Cathy's classic Zumba moves. No more time for sleep. My eye is on the prize. I'm going to get that hundred grand and that *KELLERMAN* cover shot. I'm going to take what I deserve. Little landlady will grovel at my feet—beg me to live in her fugly flat in her nowhere suburb—and I'll tell her, *It's too late, lady, you should've been nice to me before I made it big, I own a million-pound converted graveyard in the English countryside now.*

The fashion stakes have never been higher. Every vein in my body is electric. I take my scissors to the linen and cut, cut, cut.

At night, I try out white makeup paste on Mugzy's face, to see how it looks. But even though I'm the one making him into a god, he's still hung up on Cathy. He says he's saving himself for her.

He wants a break. He goes downstairs to wank alone, looking up at the flat.

I follow him down and stand next to him.

"I'm trying to get back to the root of the purity of my love," he says.

He pants and his hand gets fast and furious, and I look up with him at the flat. Then I put my fingers down my underwear and touch myself. I look at him and he looks at me, and I pull my fingers out and bring them to my lips and lick them.

"Fuck you," he says.

He pushes me down onto the concrete on all fours and slides in quick, and while he's fucking me in the driveway like a dog, he says, "I want a nice Cathy the other guys want. A nice Cathy with nice friends. A nice Cathy who goes to the gym every morning, and salsa every week."

We fuck again upstairs on Cathy's red couch. He pees on my chest. I sit on his face and say, "Fuck Cathy. All the pretty Cathys in the world don't want us. Nobody's gonna run back for us through the streets, telling us they've made a mistake."

"Speak for yourself," says Mugzy, when it's over. "Nobody wants *you*. And why would a guy like me want you if no one else does?"

I've got Mugzy into the cape and shroud, and now his entire

face is caked with white. I look at him in the full-length mirror, surrounded by burning incense, and he really is a god. The TV crew is already filming the final episode. They're watching us prep for the runway show and get preliminary feedback from the judges.

Ava Rodriguez is there on the red couch. My grandfather sits next to her, a goldfish suffocating in his hand. He shakes his head at me.

"You're from Nara," he says. "Why do you need this lady to tell you what's good?"

I ignore him. He's only here because he knows I'm about to win. I'll thank him for nothing on the runway.

I tell Ava that my theme is "Ritual and Sacrifice."

"Is it too 'warrior prince'?" Ava says. "Is it too literal, screaming 'the Orient'? Is it fashion-forward enough, or editorial enough? These are the questions I and the other judges have to ask. Do you really have what it takes, Rioko? What if you really are just a patternmaker, and not a real couturier? What happened to Cathy, your original model? Why have you got this dropkick instead?"

"Cathy didn't understand my vision. Cathy was disloyal."

"What?" says Mugzy. "What happened to Cathy?"

"Look out the window," I say. "Behind the laundry. There's your beloved, under the dirt."

He turns and looks where I'm pointing.

"You want to know what happened to Cathy? I'll show you what happened to Cathy."

He's still looking out when I pick up the iron and swing it at the back of his head. I think about Nara, about Cathy deserting me, about that Post-it and how I didn't grab the kitchen knife, I got the iron and flung it at her, then I picked up my scissors and stabbed her to make sure. No more pink Post-its, just like that. I think about how I took her phone and texted her friends to say she was going overseas for a funeral. I texted her salsafucking man, telling him it was time to break up. *It's not you,* I typed, *it's me.*

"What?" says Mugzy. He's standing still, staring at himself in the mirror. The back of his head has caved in, but he can't see it.

He drops forward.

I light a cigarette and smoke it. I stroll around the studio. I look at him sprawled on the carpet. I wash the iron in the kitchen sink. I watch red run off steel. I think, *Well, it was the best I could do under the time pressure.* The styling leaves a bit to be desired, but I can still win this whole competition.

Ava Rodriguez says from the couch, "He would look better *in* the coffin, Rioko, not on the carpet. Remember, it needs to be a complete look."

"You're so right," I say.

I grab Mugzy by the ankles and drag him to the coffin. He's heavy but I lift him in part by part.

"Hngh," he says, all hoarse. "Hnnngh."

I light another cigarette. I hold the orange tip to the collar of the cape. The straw starts to burn. Mugzy panics and squirms. I put my face close to his face, close like the way I look at my pores in the mirror, and I say, "So now you know. Cathy's got no forwarding address."

He whimpers. "Who the fuck ever cared about Cathy? The pickup book was wrong."

Everything smells like blood and incense. I think to myself, *His face shouldn't look like this, what is all this red leaking onto the white? What was the makeup team thinking?* And while I'm pondering the question, Mugzy grabs the ends of my tape measure and twists them tight around my throat. I fight for air. I collapse on him, chest to chest. The little flames lick his shroud, and his hair and my hair, and his face and my face, and then someone taps me on the shoulder and I hear Ava Rodriguez saying, "Congratulations, Rioko, your show was a triumph. You are the winner of *Real Couturier*."

As I relax into black, I hear Mugzy too.

"First time I touched you, little rat," he says, "I knew you were the one."

TOXIC NOSTALGIA

BY PETER POLITES

Bankstown

1.

The city can give you AIDS but the suburbs can make you crazy. I wish I knew this back in the day, when two pin-sized peepers were looking through me, like my twentysomething-year-old body was translucent.

Hendo was sitting cross-legged on the bed. His room was filled with skid-marked sheets, piles of clothes, Sharpies, and used condoms. "Come somewhere," I said. He found a baggie in the sheets and turned it inside out. His tongue rolled into the plastic, lapped up the shards. I jumped up and down on the mattress. "Come with me!" I said. Coins we lost in the blankets rained down on the floor. "It'll be fun! Fun! Fun!" Two hands on his shoulders, facing him directly. "I used to go there as a kid," I said, shaking him back and forth.

Before this time at Hendo's I lived with my dad. I came home late once. Next morning he woke me up by screaming at me for leaving the lights on. So I told him I was a faggot. He kicked me out. I packed up a gym bag of clothes, left the house, and slept on couches of people I knew. Ended up crashing mostly with Hendo. We always ran out of things to do.

Hendo sat in the passenger's side of my car smoking joints. I drove us in and out of the tunnels and yelled out, "Shotty,

shotty, shotty!" He inverted the roach. His head went directly in front of mine. Blew smoke in my mouth.

Back in the day you could get from the inner city to western Sydney in thirty minutes.

I drove down Georges River Road, pulled into a rest stop. Hatchbacks lined up against utes. Next to the parking lot was some scrub. Just beyond it was the shit-colored brown of the Georges River.

Back in the day "a beat" was a three-dimensional version of an online gay sex app. Suss suburban kweens on the down-low congregated around parks.

Hendo and I got out of the car, walked past some trucks. We stepped on condoms. Fingernail-sized pebbles crunched under our soles. We swatted at our ears every time we heard the buzz of mosquitoes. At the edge of the car park, we looked down at the river and saw the outline of two guys sitting on some rocks. We took a path into the bushes. Burrs got stuck to the hairs on my legs.

"Used to know this retail queen that did blue-collar drag," I said to Hendo as we walked among the trees. "Nights he would put on steel-cap boots and work shorts and come down here." When the sounds of cars passing took a break, faint noises of grunts and slurps floated through the brambles.

Men slowed down to pass us. They did the up-down eye scan. Some of them wore too-clean steel-cap boots. Hendo tried to read them. He'd just see a Leb with the angry sands of the desert running through his eyes. I would pay attention to the Lebanese boy with his femme-esque tapered eyebrows. To Hendo an islander in a Dickies T was maybe a shifty cunt, but I'd see a coconut kid who wore big bro's hand-me-downs, soppy brown eyes looking for the love of an absent daddy.

My fingers traced the squiggle indents on the bark of a

crooked gum. Hendo walked ahead. Some overly worked pecs with chicken legs caught Hendo's eyes; he tailgated the guy to the bank of the river. Left me alone. I walked out of the scrub onto the embankment next to the road. I found an old log and sat on it and emptied my mind onto the oncoming cars.

A few cigarettes later Hendo called out to me. I turned around, watched him approach through clumps of grass.

"I have some terrible news," he said.

"What? D'ya get more of the HIV again?" I asked.

"No, worse. He was a sub-bottom that presented masc clone."

Hendo's Nokia went beep. He covered his face with his hands. The Nokia went beep again. He showed me the message: 8===) *now.*

The gay vampire behind the text message was Manco. A Bram Stoker dream with fangs that dripped pure amphetemine base. Failed actor. Never in that wannabe Hollywood way. Television too vulgar for a straw hat–wearing private school boy. At a time when he should have been getting passed over to play the dad in sitcoms he became "that dealer dude."

Manco bandwagoned the drug scene just before the early noughties, just before the outlaw motorcycle gangs took over the club drug trade. It was the bikies and their chrome-mounted skirmishes that made it hard to access a good-quality MDMA. Pills were getting cut with a smacky-type chemical. Instead of inspirational energy you'd get rolling eyes, a desire to park it, cross your legs on the floor while your neck became jelly. Little pills of Mercedes and doves and the blue LVs gone. Poorer customers like Hendo just injected speed. Coke, although off-the-planet expensive in Sydney, was not affected price-wise, proving once again that nothing affects the rich.

Manco kept good clients. Corporate gay drones and the

aggressive young blond ladies in public relations. But the truth about dealers is melancholic. Its illegality creates informal friendships. The kind of upwardly mobile queens who can afford designer chems don't have time for some dropkick peddler.

Manco dealt with the yearns by keeping boys. Boys like Hendo. Money poor, drug needy. Cap in hand. *Sure! But you can pay me back. You got no collateral.* Hendo racked up a debt and then got called in on orgies as payback.

"I don't know what to do. He is ruining sex and my nightclub experience." Hendo rubbed his biceps. Leaned his big head onto me. In front of us cars went down the highway and I patted his arm.

2.

Today I can't remember what Hendo looks like. Then I start with the biohazard tattoo on his arm and there he is. Sitting next to me in my passenger seat. Lifting his sleeve to show me it. His head folds up and down every time he speaks. Skin around his eyes have pavement cracks. Massive pores but always too dry. But I can hear Hendo's voice saying to me, "You are beau-ti-ful."

During those times, men told me a shitty story about myself. They looked at my Mediterranean skin and too-black hair and thought I was something I wasn't. They would sidle up next to me at bars and ask, "Lost your girlfriend?" or introduce themselves with the elegant, "I really like wog boys." Bolder men would say, "Please rape me." Masculine projection was a fatigue. So I'll always remember Hendo leaning his head onto my shoulder, laughing at my jokes, and telling me I was beautiful.

I turned into Deepwater Reserve just as Hendo passed me

the pipe. No streetlights, just a road in a tunnel of trees. High beams lit up a guy walking out of the bush. He was in his fifties, craggy bod, wearing a G-string. Skin like ash. Thin old skeleton with loose flanks of flesh hanging from his sides.

We parked amongst some other cars and got out. Hendo and I walked toward the bank of the river. Across the clearing, we saw an ember of a cigarette glowing. It looked like an alien light from far away, so we went to check out if the dude was fuckable. A young man was sitting on a picnic table with his feet on the seat. His chest was folded over his knees and a pink singlet fell off his hairy skinny bod. He looked up when he heard us coming. The galaxy-black eyes of Lou Marcello.

Hendo knew Lou, they'd killed a million brain cells together and they also used to fuck. But Lou fell in love in the way only lost boys can. Nervous desire. Talking about monogamy but constantly cheating. When they were together, Lou was once rolling around on the grass of a public park, his eyes falling into the back of his head. He latched his hands onto Hendo's calves. "Infect me . . . infect me . . ." Hendo kept walking, while Lou's hands dragged at his calf. "Fuck off, you boring bug chaser," said Hendo as he moved away.

Lou changed after that night. Wore a gold cross around his neck. Decided to shack up with some Turk who had tattoos. They moved in together and played happy families until Lou would show up with an "I walked into a door" bruise. They stayed together. Lou found that familiar suburban purgatory.

But Lou had that Calabrian skin that shone in the dark. He looked up at us and rubbed his neck.

"Did you get an SMS too?" he asked Hendo.

"Manco makes us do things. Weird dodgy shit."

"Not gonna say shit to my boyfriend. I'm scared as . . ." said Lou. The sound of water was lapping at the bank. The river was munching on soil and it was the soundtrack to how we were feeling.

Heard twigs crack. Our eardrums sparked. Sound of footsteps coming toward us. We all turned to face the direction of the noise. Looked to the clearing, expecting something to come through the bushes. Footsteps getting louder. Hendo's body became hard. I put one foot behind the other and raised my fists. The footsteps came closer still. More than one set of feet came at us, started running toward us. Hendo picked up a branch and held it up. Lou put a massive rock in his hand and stood behind me.

The craggy old man in a G-string and sneakers appeared out of the scrub. He saw us and started running. Just behind him was a twink, his face all scratched from twigs. "Cops," said the twink, and ran off.

"Chill," said Hendo. "They are powerless, just a buzzkill."

We sat back down around the picnic table. Two officers strolled toward us. One a solid ranga, the other too much short-man syndrome.

"Gentlemen, how is your evening going?" said Constable Ranga. "We have had some complaints about antisocial behavior."

"Au contraire. We are being extremely sociable," replied Hendo. His voice was pearls hanging against cashmere. The officer had to step back and catch himself from the blow.

"We have taken your number plates down and we will be paying visits to your homes," said Constable Ranga.

"Then by all means, violate as many legal statutes as you can," Hendo countered.

The pair of cops puffed up their chests. Hendo stood up in front of us, putting himself in between us and the cops. He addressed the cops as their badge numbers. He pulled out a

Nokia and made a call, covered his mouth as he whispered into the phone, and then handed it to Constable Ranga. The cop listened and nodded. Handed the phone back to Hendo. The cop looked over at his fellow officer, did a let's-go gesture with his eyes. The other cop was puzzled but followed orders. They walked off. Lou, Hendo, and I folded our arms as they disappeared.

"What the hell was that, Hendo?" I asked. I rubbed the back of his neck and he told me to forget about it.

3.

Lou invited us back to his duplex. The tattooed Turk he lived with was doing a night shift. Hendo walked into the house and looked around like it was a museum. He examined the secondhand IKEA sofa like it had a plaque on it. His hand lifted a Murano ashtray on the coffee table and held it up to the light, looking at the colored glint of the glass. He picked up the remote. The TV with endless channels kept him occupied. An average suburban house was a curiosity for Hendo. Meanwhile, any alone time with Lou and we'd reminisce. That no-good goo honeyed our mind hives.

I'd met Lou at a house party down the road from Bankstown Maccas. We were both teenlings. He was there with some fire-twirling twink and I was there with some straight boys. Me and my boys entered the house from the driveway. In the backyard people just stared at us. Some of my boys tried to talk shit with the girls and we got pushed out of the party. We were all stoned, all in Adidas. I sat on a car out front of the house and Lou passed me a flask. Same deal. Both wogs. He Italian, me Greek. Both out of place. His dad was Lucky Marcello, in jail for a hit on a business deal that went kerplunk. Mama and Nonna and a herd of older sisters kept him out of trouble.

For us there was a window for sex. The window closed and love cemented. I was happy for him. He got out. Found a man who kept him. His job was to clean and keep it tight. Barrels of protein powder accessorized his kitchen.

Lou wanted to complete the 2.5 gay dream with a puppy. Said something about a French bulldog. I told him about a childhood pet goat that I'd had. She was the color of the dirty sea foam, so we called her Afroditi.

Afroditi climbed trees. She'd get up there and sometimes couldn't get down. Afroditi would find herself up in trees. She would holler in distress. Sounded like a toddler being murdered. Then me or Dad would have to find a way to get her. Sometimes I would get a ladder and wrestle her down. Sometimes I'd put her over my shoulders and hear her cry. One time my dad got fed up; he was sick of getting her down. We were standing in front of the olive tree and she was high in the branches. Dad ran into the house and came out holding his double-barreled shotgun. As he marched he put shells in the barrel. Cocked the gun. A failsafe way of getting her out of the tree. I ran and pushed the shotgun down just as he was about to shoot. The shot fired. My eardrums burst and the grass exploded below us.

4.

Back in the day, peak Sydney was interchangeable with being gay. The highways from the suburbs into the city were like our own yellow-brick roads. Some nightclubs were tiny holes in the walls. The international superclub fad had kicked off, places that were three stories high, dedicated gay venues that played handbag house upstairs and underground electro downstairs. The City of Oz, with its emerald jealous streets and amyl nitrate scent, was—once—a playground for Dorothy's friends.

Hendo, Lou, and I became a trinity. Summer Sunday-night dancing became ours. We hit the strip. One of the clubs was a chemical dungeon. Descend downstairs and everyone who was too ugly to fit into mainstream land, too drug-fucked to hold down a job, too loose to care, too chemically washed out, would come together. The four-four drum led a coven of people. Pozbears praising Dionysius in a sweat frenzy.

The most common phrase I heard was, *Just go home, you're trashed.* Hendo or Lou would defend me. On long weekends, we would laugh at all the suits feigning bohemia before they went back to their office cubicles.

Sunday club bond was our breaking bread and Lou partitioned himself—his new suburban house husband life vs. his old chems club kid past. On Sunday nights, he'd pop by at six p.m. Straight-to-our-heads champagne and we'd drink it out of plastic flutes and jars. Allowing the ingredients of alcohol to prolong casual touches. Once Hendo placed a hand on Lou's leg and Lou got up and mumbled something about his tatted Turk husband waiting for him at home.

They left me at times. Manco would call them in. He wanted a night. I wanted a room to myself and they'd go hesitantly. From the window, I would watch them go down the street. Two men who were boys walked off with heads bowed, making for the world they wanted to leave behind. They passed people in the street: happy couples, corporate gays, women with prams.

That night, I picked out Sharpies from Hendo's sheet ball and curled up. Round midnight the bedsheet filth made me itch. I woke and Hendo and Lou hadn't returned.

5.

Hendo slept the big chemical coma. Someone once said that dead men are heavier than broken hearts.

Lou told me how it went down.

They'd both arrived at Manco's building. Buzzer pressed, indecipherable static answer. Cheap foyer, up a mirrored elevator. Hendo and Lou were testifying to each other. "Something gotta change, something has to become new, I can't do this." They arrived at the apartment and inside were three fit-looking finance-sector bodies in their work uniforms. Manco handed them knee pads. Lou started to put them on. Hendo said the color didn't suit him.

Hendo. Dry mouth. Feelings from zero to a hundred thanks to his IV habit. Riled up. Lou saw it, saw what was coming, and split Hendo and the host. Took Manco into the bathroom. Lou tried telling Manco how it was going down, that this was the last of their debt. But Manco wouldn't hear it. He put a vial to his nose and snorted gelatinous confetti.

In the bathroom, Lou was teary and he started to plead. Told Manco about the new man, about being a hausfrau, about a new start. Hills hoist and gardens. Pot plants. Orange-colored cookware. Maybe a French bulldog as a pet.

Manco just pawed at Lou's pecs. "Interest . . . interest . . . you boys gotta pay the interest," he kept repeating.

Lou was at his end. He threatened an anonymous tip to the cops. They were always looking for the next bust. A big fag dealer with off-the-books cash and lots of drugs. Bye-bye loft apartment. Hello concrete cell. Manco fell still. Asked Lou to fix himself before he exited the bathroom, told Lou that he didn't want to use tears as a lubricant again.

When he went back into the living room he saw Hendo sitting on the black leather sofa. All the men were standing around him. They had their shirts open and weren't wearing any pants. The pale-blue office shirts contrasted against their pink skin. Hendo was putting a syringe into a little baggie of speed and water. The men all looked down on Hendo, licking their lips.

One of the men took the syringe off Hendo and shepherded him to a room with a swing. That was the last time Lou saw Hendo.

Lou was crying when he told me. We knew that Hendo was gone. Hendo wasn't a poem that I wrote and lost. He was just a rich-kid fuck-up. Lou wrote himself into me. On him I saw the same dark Mediterranean skin. In him I saw the potential for a good life; at least one of us could be saved.

6.

Sometimes I take the long way home. Suburban streets lead to the highways and they lead to the city like a river does to an estuary. I drive down Oxford Street. The road is wet, streetlights expose its emptiness. Under a rainbow flag I make out two emaciated figures that sway. They wear mesh singlets and huddle in each other's arms. Those cold lost boys could be a memory of me and Lou.

Lou and I kept hitting clublandia. We had a strong three-horse race with Hendo. When he was gone, we became crutches for each other's mourning. On dance floors, the baby gays scoffed at our dated looks and melancholic energy. A generic twink put his pink fingers on the collar of my jacket and looked for a label. He gasped when he saw it was from Kmart. Lou kept spilling drinks on his pants so the exits looked appealing. We wandered out into the street and huddled under a rainbow flag, almost falling on the wet concrete.

There were headlines when Hendo died. "SENATOR'S SON DEAD, GAY SEX SANDWICH." I learned more about Hendo from that headline than he'd ever told me in life. Explained how his rent was always paid and he never worked.

Made me reflect on that moment in the park with the cops, how Hendo spoke to them with a string of pearls in his voice. I reflected on his anthropological analysis of Lou's suburban home. The headline made me realize that people like me and Lou were just subplots between the first and final acts of Hendo's life.

The only reasonable response was to boycott Hendo's funeral. Said to ourselves, *Nah, just nah.* Too many jerk-off journalists. Too many judging eyes. We kept on seeing the newspapers lining pavements with sordid tales of the senator's son. So we avoided going out. Avoided cafés, train carriages, anywhere we might find a paper.

Lou's house was in the outskirts of Bankstown. There was a sea of grass in the front yard. Roses not in bloom. Rusty old hills hoist. Paint flaking off Corinthian columns. As evening set in we lay on banana lounges in the front yard next to a kiddie pool. I put the whole of my hand in the kiddie pool, mosquito larvae swam between my fingers.

Eventually tatted Turk came home. Around a laminate table, Lou served us lasagna. Dutiful wife he was. I was hush-hush, watched Lou as he fussed pouring wine and filling side plates with salads. Easy conversation. Tatted Turk was a security guard, a late-in-life gay but a kid from a rough home, desiring a simple life. Part of me just called him ride-a-motorbike-and-drink-protein-shake dumb. Part of me called him solid, unpretentious.

The tatted Turk husband went to bed early that night. We were in the kitchen when Lou received an SMS from Manco.

Lou's eyes were open fully. "If Manco tells tatted Turk about my old life, he'll leave me. I'll have nothing. I wish someone would do something," he said, and his eyes were like big wet frying pans. Rock-hard tears next to Tupperware and laminate tables. His body folded and he took long breaths; I came from behind and hugged him.

I put my palm on Lou's back and started rubbing it while he sobbed. That night I told him it would be alright and for the first time in my life I felt like a father. I realized that this is what a father should do. Protect. Help. Solve. Have dominion over a son and not in that gay-daddy kind of way. Eventually I lifted Lou up, pulled his arm around my shoulder, and put him to bed next to his boyfriend.

The next morning before anyone got up, I drove to my dad's. I waited for him to leave the house. In his Stalinist-cell bedroom and behind the door there was a case with a weapon. I pulled out the sawed-off double-barrel. It was heavier than I'd expected and the glint from where it was sawed gave it a sense of menace.

Took the bullets out of the breech and put them back in the case. Wrapped the gun in a towel and slipped it in a gym bag.

I had no money and Lou needed a problem resolved. Manco had a stash of cash and drugs. Problem crushed.

6.

The apartment hallway had the sterile nothing of a medical center. My knuckles hit the laminate door three times. Manco opened the door. He was in his sixties, bald, wearing jeans and a faded black T-shirt. His round wire-rimmed glasses were a hint of intellectual and creative pretension. I was carrying the gym bag and I held it low to the ground. Told him that Lou had sent me, that I was going to be the payment today. He put his hand up on the doorframe, blocking the entrance. His gaze started at my feet, scanned up, and when he reached my neck, he muttered an, "Oh you'll do," and waved me in with his hand.

I followed him into the apartment. Went past a marble kitchen with stainless-steel appliances. I took deep slow breaths that filled the pit of my stomach. The rubber soles of my shoes squeaked against the polished concrete floor. The living room had a TV against a wall of glass that looked out over the city.

"Nice view," I said. He asked me if I needed to use the bathroom to freshen up. I held my gym bag low, tried to make it a discreet thing that I was carrying.

In the bathroom, I opened my gym bag and unwrapped the double-barrel from the towel. There was a weight to it that seemed new. I looked at myself holding the gun in the mirror. Angled my head low and put the butt in between my arm and torso. Creased my forehead and eyebrows, practicing a look of menace. I entered the living space holding the gun. Manco was sitting on the sofa with his dick out. He stood up and put the pink thing back in his pants. He raised his hands up in the air, his palms facing me. His lips pressed together like two cars in an accident. I took one step toward him and pushed out the gun in front of me.

"We need to talk about Lou," I said. My voice was lower than a sewer. Told him that Lou's debt was fully paid, otherwise he would see me again. He gulped and nodded, knew exactly what I was saying.

I asked him where his stash of cash was and where all the dope was. A single drop of sweat ran down his face. He directed me to a kitchen cabinet. I walked over to the marble kitchen; my shoes made a squeaking sound that echoed throughout the apartment. I bent my knees and squatted. Opened a cupboard. Kept the gun straight as I pulled out a container full of chems. I snapped open the lid. There were caps of MDMA, blue LVs, and doves. All the pills were in sandwich bags, neatly arranged.

"This is a nice little system you have here," I said, and put the container on the kitchen bench. "But I'm gonna need cash too."

Manco pointed to the top cupboard; I reached up and pulled out a tin box. I put the tin box on the bench, ready to open it.

There were three knocks on the door. I turned around to face Manco with the gun. His lips were gray, two thin slugs coated with saliva. The front door flew open and two cops came into the apartment, their guns in their hands. They saw me with the stash of drugs in front of me, holding a double-barrel pointed at Manco.

Manco was smarter than I was. His organized pills were part of a system. His life was part of a system. Dealers needed a series of checks and balances. And what I didn't know then is that many fresh-faced boys with threats had been there before me. Many fresh-faced boys trying to make a forced withdrawal. Manco had a failsafe. At an allocated time, if he didn't send an SMS to a person and confirm that everything was good with his guest, they would call certain police officers—slightly dodgy and on the cut—who were intertwined with Manco. They would come. Scare the shit out of the person causing trouble. Make it seem that it was a legit arrest, when they were just clearing the scraps.

"That's him, officers," said Manco.

The cops ordered me to drop it with booming voices. They held their guns with both hands and arranged themselves in a pincer movement around me. I put my gun on the bench in front of me. Gently resting it—the sound of metal clinking on marble. I put my hands in the air. A blue uniform came toward me and twisted my arm, forcing me to turn around. I felt a big hand push me on my back and I was up against the glass wall. My chest was pressing against the cool.

I looked out over the city and the skyscrapers were dead-eyed monuments. Behind me the two cops and Manco muttered while my arm was twisted. The pain made me shut my eyes and when I opened them again, I looked over the cityscape, saw the skyscrapers as concrete pillars that were a bulwark to suburbia. Beyond them were the fringes of a landscape that had houses with red roofs, dead-end streets, nature strips, and parks. There were fringes of green trees. When I squinted I could almost see an olive tree and there was a goat stuck in its branches and underneath a father and son fought.

THE RAZOR

BY ROBERT DREWE

Lavender Bay

One humid Sunday morning when the scent of frangipani hung heavily in the air, Brian Tasker stood in his yard overlooking Lavender Bay while his mother-in-law shaved his body.

Sunlight bounced off the fence of oleanders and frangipanis and flickered through the native fig trees clinging to the cliff behind the house. The cliff marked the boundary of Luna Park, the harborside fun fair, and between the loops and slopes of the dormant roller coaster that came to rumbling, screaming life every sunset, a mirage quivered on the surface of the bay.

While Dulcie Kroger was kneeling and spreading shaving cream over her son-in-law's legs, he tried to concentrate on the way the mirage lapped like a windswept lake on the boat shed roofs across the bay. But once his mother-in-law began wielding the razor, working upward from his size-thirteen feet, up his shins and calves to his thighs, he found it difficult to maintain interest in an illusion.

During dinner the evening before, he'd mentioned something Don told him at training.

"Guess what?" Brian said to his wife Judy and her mother as he dug into the five courses Dulcie had served him. "The Yanks have had a bright idea—shaving their bodies before a race."

"Seriously, Brian?" Judy's eyes twinkled. Even after six months of marriage he still found her wide-eyed look and little-girl giggle appealing, even provocative. "Shaved all over?"

A delicate creature to look at, but her chirpy laugh, blond bob, bright nails, and arms like twigs hid her intensity. Though full of energy, she seemed to hardly eat. Compared to his meal—tonight it was chicken soup and thickly buttered bread, six lamb chops and vegetables, a plate of potato and egg salad, a dessert of sliced bananas and ice cream, and cheese and biscuits, washed down with two glasses of milk—hers was miniscule: a single chop, a smidgen of mashed potatoes, and a smattering of peas to push around her plate.

"*All over?*" her mother repeated.

"*Shaving down,* it's called," Brian explained. "The whole body. All the exposed parts anyway. They reckon it makes them swim faster."

Don Wilmott, his longtime coach, had picked up this intelligence from an American friend who'd observed a training session of the swimming squad at the University of Southern California. "Shaving down eliminates drag," Don told Brian as he dried off after his afternoon of one hundred laps in the North Sydney Olympic Pool. He'd been Brian's coach ever since Junior Dolphins, where he'd recognized the talent of the skinny nine-year-old who was swimming to help his asthma. More than a coach, really. A mentor, almost a father figure. Then through all the high school and district victories over his teenage years, and the regionals, and his successes at state level. And now, if all went to plan, to the nationals and the selection trials for the Australian team.

"We'll give it a shot," Don went on. "They say you feel transformed. Smooth and slippery like a fish. The psychological effect alone is supposed to make you swim quicker."

Brian didn't need reminding that he had to swim faster. To be transformed. As Don repeated, unnecessarily, the Melbourne Olympics were only nine months away, in November. The Australian team would be selected in August, after the national championships. And there was another Sydney swimmer, Murray Rose, dogging his heels. Rose's times for the 400 and 1,500-meter freestyle almost matched his. Worse, they were improving, and he was still only sixteen.

This boy Rose was a handsome wunderkind, a blond prodigy who defied swimming's traditions. For a start he was thin, rather than conventionally barrel-chested and broad-shouldered. And he trained in Sydney Harbour. *The harbor? With its tides and waves and oil spills and flotsam?* Moreover—veteran sports writers shook their heads in wonder—the kid was a vegetarian.

They struggled to recall any top athlete who'd been a vegetarian. The papers set up photographs of wet-headed, muddy-footed young Murray standing on the harbor shore after training, towel looped around his neck, skinny ribs poking out, happily munching a carrot or a stick of celery.

Brian knew Melbourne was his last chance to make the Olympic team. The combination of his BSA Gold Star with slippery tram tracks on the Lane Cove line led to a broken elbow that had ruined his chances for Helsinki in '52. So he'd sold the motorbike. No more physical risks. He'd be twenty-four by November, twenty-eight, positively elderly, by the 1960 Olympic games.

"Get out the razor this weekend," Don had said. "We'll do a time trial on Monday."

Brian thought he'd surprise Judy with his new smooth body when she came home from Mass at St. Francis Xavier that

Sunday. Surely anyone could put a new blade in their safety razor and shave themselves down? But standing there in the sunny yard in his skimpy racing costume, cursing with the effort, he found it surprisingly tricky. How to shave the backs of your thighs? How to avoid nicking the tender skin behind your knees?

The grunts, the near-naked contortions: a neighbor or passerby might have wondered what was going on behind the frangipanis and oleanders.

Dulcie was watching this comedy through the kitchen window and she came out into the yard. She was wearing a swimsuit too: pale blue and strapless, in some sort of elasticized satiny material.

"Come here, furry boy," she said, and took the razor from his hand.

It was like a mild electric shock at first. As she scraped the razor up his shin and thigh to the edge of his swimsuit, his focus on the wavy roof mirages of Lavender Bay began fading fast.

"Relax, kiddo," Dulcie said. "I used to be a nurse."

This was evident in her proficiency: in her frowning attention to her task and the frequent pauses to rinse the razor in a pot of water to keep the blade keen.

Brian stared out across the bay. Dulcie kept on shaving his thighs while he fought the reaction of his body and mind: somewhere between excitement and fear, stimulation and embarrassment. This woman kneeling before him, her head abutting his groin, strands of her auburn hair brushing his skin, her tanned cleavage looming below his eyes, was his mother-in-law!

After she'd finished shaving his thighs, she rose to her feet, rubbed more shaving cream on his stomach, and, as a tremor ran down his whole body, she performed a professional depilatory operation on the furry track of his abdominal hair.

Brian was blinking rapidly by now and finding it difficult to regulate his breathing.

"Don't worry, I've seen it all before," she said. "I've done this a thousand times."

Nevertheless, in her competent hands he felt ridiculously young, a self-conscious adolescent. His heart was still hammering when she rinsed the razor again and attacked the curly hairs on his chest. As she worked, she hummed a sentimental song from the hit parade, "Oh! My Papa."

In a greater effort to distance his mind and body from Dulcie's busy razor work, Brian lifted his gaze to the sky where a pelican was hovering over the bay, higher than he imagined possible for such an ungainly-looking bird. Then, as his mother-in-law glided the blade carefully over his pectoral muscles, gently circumnavigating the nipples, the pelican became a tiny soaring white blotch.

The sun beat down. *"Oh, my papa,"* Dulcie hummed. In the fig trees on the cliff, a flock of black cockatoos clumsily rustled and fed. Brian closed his eyes on the sky, and orchestrated shapes like dew droplets or oil globules began to float in patterns behind his eyelids; he could feel the sun's rays on his upturned face.

The chest-shaving continued. "Head up, tiger," Dulcie said, standing on tiptoe. In four strokes she swept the razor from collarbones to chin. "Right arm up," she ordered. Brian's arm hung tentatively in the air, trembling slightly, until she held it steady and shaved his armpit. "Now the left one."

Unhindered now by hair, a trickle of suds ran down his chest and stomach. Eyes still firmly shut, he heard the cockatoos continuing to squawk and eat, and half-gnawed figs plopping on the ground, and a train clattering across the Harbour Bridge toward the city.

By now the breeze felt overly intimate on his exposed skin. His whole body seemed disconcertingly sensitive and electrified and he was light-headed from the female smell of her olive skin and her satiny swimsuit, giddy with his intimate proximity to a semi-naked, mature woman on a summer's day.

Dulcie took up his right wrist again, held it steady, and swept the razor up his forearm to his elbow, then along the triceps to the shoulder. She paused there and put her free hand on his right shoulder and clasped it for a few seconds, and closed her eyes as if considering its muscles and tendons, reflecting on the hard exercise that had gone into its formation: the hundreds of miles it had swum.

Time stopped. Then she shaved the other arm, and for a moment she closed her eyes and squeezed this shoulder too.

"All done, Johnny Weissmuller." She dropped the razor in the pot of water and ran both hands over his chest. "Smooth as a baby's bottom."

When her second husband and Judy's stepfather, Chief Petty Officer Eric Kruger, had shipped out for nine months' duty on the destroyer HMAS *Warramunga*, a month before, Dulcie had moved in with her daughter and son-in-law. The Australian navy, the *Warramunga*, and, by extension, CPO Kruger, were assisting the British navy in maintaining the security of the Federation of Malaya against Communist insurgents.

The arrangement suited both households. Dulcie gained company while Eric was away, and the young couple benefited from her help around the house, and especially from her assistance with Brian's Olympic preparation.

Soon after their marriage, Brian and Judy were delighted

to find and rent the terrace house above Luna Park. A two-bedroom, nineteenth-century workman's cottage, its sandstone walls and narrow back garden surrounded by oleanders and frangipanis, it suited the newlyweds' romantic mood. Importantly, it was a mere hundred yards from Don Wilmott's coaching headquarters at the North Sydney Olympic Pool, and only two train stations across the harbor from Judy's nightshift copytaker job at the *Daily Telegraph*.

Brian, meanwhile, worked as a phys ed teacher at North Sydney Boys High, a welcome job for an amateur athlete. The pay wasn't great, but the school was just a mile from their house, easy jogging distance, he had use of the gym, and the hours suited his early-morning and afternoon training sessions.

What he most welcomed about his mother-in-law's presence was her cooking. His fuel requirements were huge; five miles twice a day in the pool, plus his weight training, burned up mountains of protein, carbohydrates, and calories. And frankly, Dulcie was a better cook than his twenty-one-year-old wife.

In any case, Judy's new nighttime job absented her at dinnertime during the week, so Dulcie's cooking had become crucial. Only on weekends did Brian and Judy get to eat meals together. Or, for that matter, retire to bed at the same time.

Their clashing personal schedules were the only impediment to marriage harmony. While Brian rose at four thirty for his five a.m. laps, and usually fell asleep by eight thirty at night, Judy's shift at the *Telegraph* ran from four p.m. to midnight, the newspaper's busiest hours. When Brian arrived home from school she was going to work, and he had to immediately leave for the pool. And after catching the last night train home from Town Hall station, Judy invariably fell exhausted into bed around one a.m.—her head ringing with domestic crimes and gang stabbings and gambling-den raids.

From Monday to Friday, Dulcie prepared Brian's evening meal. After dinner, in deference to her excellent cooking, her role as Judy's mother, and her status as an elder relative (she was forty-four), he'd chat politely with her over a cup of cocoa. Then, as his eyelids began to droop, he'd stretch his weary limbs, say good night, climb the stairs, and hit the sack.

On Sunday mornings, Judy hurried home from Mass so the young couple could make up for their love drought during the week. As Sunday was his only break from a four thirty rising, Brian was excused from church, allowed to linger in bed, catch up on sleep, and wake refreshed for her return to bed at eleven.

On this particular rest day when she returned home from church, Judy was puzzled to find Brian not in bed as usual but sitting in his bathrobe in the backyard, drinking coffe and reading the *Sunday Telegraph*. Recalling the shaving-down conversation of the night before, she peeled back his bathrobe to inspect the transformation. His hairless chest looked strangely pale and vulnerable, and his back was striated with scratches.

Shamefaced, he said, "My first try at shaving myself."

"Idiot. I would've done that for you." She stroked his wounded shoulder blades. "Poor baby."

In the kitchen, her mother was making a din with pots and crockery, noisily preparing food and impatiently switching radio stations back and forth: from a haranguing evangelist on the *Worldwide Church of God* to a country-and-western couple yodeling competitively. The radio was hopeless on Sunday mornings.

"What's up with her?" Judy murmured. She picked a pink

frangipani blossom and put it behind her ear. "Back to bed, smooth fish," she whispered.

As he trudged upstairs behind his frisky wife, she continued to scold him. "Fancy trying to shave your own back. You don't grow any hair there, thank goodness."

It wasn't only the lazy mornings that Brian relished on Sundays. At around one thirty, the couple would rise languidly, put on their swimsuits, and head to Bondi Beach. Dulcie sometimes joined them, and this particular afternoon she was keen to do so.

After his hundreds of pool laps during the week, it was a luxury for Brian to swim purely for pleasure, to catch waves, enjoy the ocean. Today the salt water made his shaved limbs tingle and his back sting in an unfamiliar, sensual way.

Indeed, after a surf, a milkshake, a meat pie, and a hamburger, sunbaking on the sand with Judy and Dulcie stretched out on either side of him, Brian felt sated, pampered. Like a sultan. Judy's hand rested openly on his newly sensitive left thigh. And as Dulcie turned on her back and wriggled and adjusted her swimsuit to expose a fraction more chest to the sun, her knee or foot kept brushing his right calf.

The sea, the warm rays, and the tasty takeaways were such great revivers of a top young athlete's body and spirits that the sultan was soon speculating on the week ahead, suddenly a bewilderingly different and arousing week, beginning with this evening when he and this slender blond girl presently stroking his left leg would be in bed again.

When this did occur several hours later, however, a loud knock on the bedroom door interrupted them. Judy groaned. How long had Dulcie been standing there, within earshot?

"What's the matter, Mother?" Judy called out. "We were

fast asleep!" Clearly false, but difficult for an eavesdropper to contradict.

"I've brought you some cocoa."

"We don't need cocoa!"

"Brian always has a cup of cocoa at this time. It's part of his training diet."

"God! Leave the cups outside the door then."

"I can't. I'll spill them."

Brian's back was smarting. He was suddenly exhausted.

Judy rose, strode naked across the room, and opened the door. The women faced each other. Neither was smiling.

Judy took the cups of cocoa. "Thank you," she muttered.

"Put something on," her mother said.

Judy shut the door on her and returned to bed. Brian's eyelids were drooping as the couple lay waiting for Dulcie's footsteps to go downstairs. In the long silence, Judy thought she could hear her mother breathing outside the door. Eventually the stairs creaked and shortly afterward plates and cutlery were clattering and cupboard doors were banging in the kitchen.

"Where were we?" Judy whispered to Brian. He was nearly asleep but he rallied valiantly to the cause.

On Monday afternoon, when Don Wilmott put his 1,500-meter specialist through a time trial, the newly shaved-down Brian Tasker swam the distance 3.5 seconds slower than in his natural hirsute state the month before.

"Heavy weekend, boyo?" Don asked, shaking his head. "What happened to your back?"

Brian shrugged. "Shaving-down," he said.

For punishment, Don made him swim an extra three miles, made up of ten 400-meter swims within an hour, with an average time of four minutes and forty-five seconds, representing about 90 percent effort.

As if the shaving-down and its sexual aftermath had never happened, the week passed as it had before Dulcie's Sunday-morning razor work.

There was no real reason for Brian to shave down the following Sunday; the point was to shave just before a big race, so your body felt the difference—the physical transformation—and reacted accordingly. But as soon as Judy left for church, Brian was in the back garden with the shaving cream and razor.

Under low humid clouds the day headed sullenly toward a thunderstorm. Cicadas buzzed a monotone refrain in the trees and a mirage already juddered across the water. Brian watched the tiny Lavender Bay ferry steaming through the harbor: the illusion was of two mysteriously joined boats, the regular ferry and, over it, another ferry that churned boldly through the air, above the water's surface. For some reason Brian thought of his nemesis, the up-and-coming young harbor swimmer Murray Rose.

Soon Dulcie joined him. She'd changed into her blue satiny swimsuit and heat seemed to radiate off her flesh. With a frown, she examined him. Only a shadowy stubble showed on his limbs and chest but she lathered his body and shaved him anyway.

Although the westerly breeze from the harbor was warm and humid and carried smoke from a far-off bushfire in the Blue Mountains, Brian shivered. The air was pungent with the smell of burning eucalyptus and the drone of the cicadas was almost deafening. As the two conjoined Lavender Bay ferries approached Circular Quay, they slowed, then docked, and their images merged back into one small boat.

"I need to be thorough," Dulcie said. When she finished, she ran her fingertips slowly over his body. Neither of them had spoken until that moment.

As she drew him into the house and upstairs, he asked, "Have you trimmed your fingernails?"

Her glistening eyes aroused and slightly unnerved him. She didn't answer.

There was an abrupt change in Brian's weekday routine. Now when he got home from his afternoon pool laps, still damp-headed and smelling of chlorine, Dulcie was waiting by the door to take him directly upstairs to her bed. Afterward, she served him his customary big dinner and bedtime cocoa.

Once only, starving after training, Brian suggested dinner before bed, but then fell deeply asleep the instant they'd finished having sex. It was difficult for Dulcie to wake him, drag his heavy body out of her bed, across the landing, and into his own.

"Come on, Ross!" she'd urged him. It was nearly midnight and she was beginning to panic. "Christ, Ross, wake up!"

"Ross?" Brian had mumbled sleepily. Ross Gooch had been Dulcie's first husband. A front-rower for Randwick Rugby Club, and Judy's father, big Ross had died of a heart attack at thirty-one.

As for Sundays, Judy was slightly mystified that Brian now waited in the shade of the frangipanis and oleanders for her return from church. And that he'd always shaved himself again—even attempted to shave his back. They'd head upstairs of course, but Brian seemed wearier these days.

"Poor boy, has Don increased your training load?" she asked one Sunday.

He shrugged. "We've had to step it up. The Games are getting closer."

Her heart went out to him: her champion. Usually he thrived on tough training, and he'd worked so hard for this. Ever since she was sixteen and he was eighteen, high school sweethearts, he'd had this grand ambition of the Olympic Games. As the Games drew closer it was understandable that he was feeling stressed.

He'd even lost interest in their Sunday-morning pillow talk. After they'd celebrated her return from Mass—although not as playfully and energetically as they used to—Brian just wanted to go back to sleep, whereas in the past they'd lie there chatting about the past week's newspaper gossip.

As a *Telegraph* copytaker, she was well up on the local news. When deadlines drew closer, reporters out on the road would phone in their stories to the copytakers. Sitting there with her headphones, or typing up the paragraphs they dictated from the nearest public phone, she'd get the latest news from the law courts, police beats, and crime scenes even before the editors did.

A recent story she'd wanted to cheerily discuss with Brian was a case of thallium poisoning on the North Shore. On discovering her husband Keith's extramarital affairs, Thelma Teasdale, in the *Telegraph*'s words "a respectable Roseville housewife and a regular finalist in the Royal Easter Show's cake-baking competition," had put rat poison in his breakfast cup of tea.

As the paper's science reporter, Warren Baxter, a lugubrious fellow known in the newsroom as the "Undertaker," wrote in a rider to the Teasdale murder trial, "Known to the police as 'inheritance powder,' 'wives' revenge,' and 'the poisoner's poison,' one gram of odorless and tasteless Thallium sulfate in cakes or scones, or mixed in hot drinks, can slowly and subtly kill an unsuspecting victim."

The Undertaker added helpfully: "*Thall-Rat*, the brand favored by Thelma Teasdale for poisoning her husband, is freely sold in hardware stores nationwide."

Thelma Teasdale's crime was only discovered because her husband's brother Raymond was a chemist. Keith's dizziness, stomach pain, and nausea were at first put down to Christmas and New Year's overindulgence. But when followed a few days later by pains in the hands and feet, agonizing leg cramps, and complete hair loss, Raymond looked up his old pharmacology textbooks. When Keith died at only forty-two, Raymond declined Thelma's offer of tea and cake at his brother's wake and went to the police.

It was the sort of juicy crime news Brian usually enjoyed. But he showed no interest in the Thelma Teasdale story so Judy didn't pursue it.

However, when she arrived home from her next shift, she called his attention to another news story, waking him with tearful ferocity at one o'clock. Bursting into the bedroom, she smacked a first-edition *Telegraph* on the bed and pushed the offending page, smelling of fresh ink and still warm from the presses, into his sleepy face.

With the copytakers' room envious of Judy's marriage to a handsome swimming champion, an older unmarried colleague, Cynthia Jackson, had hastened to point out the story to her. "Look at these bitches cuddling up to your hubby!" Cynthia said, frowning sympathetically. "He doesn't look too upset about it, though."

The photograph and accompanying caption in the sports pages showed three grinning female swimmers, slippery as seals in their wet racing costumes, stroking Brian's muscular bare chest and shoulders. Brian was flexing his right bicep and beaming back at them.

Super-smooth Olympic 1,500-meter hopeful Brian Tasker proves popular with the girls as he displays his new shaved-down physique at North Sydney Olympic Pool.

Coach Don Wilmott is recommending this innovative trend from America for his entire male swim squad. "For extra speed, even a fraction of a second, my boys will be shaving down before big events," Wilmott says. And distance specialist Tasker looks enthusiastic. "I'll try anything to give me an edge," he says.

The girls (from left)—backstroker Rowena Flynn, 18; breaststroker Maxine Vanderhaag, 19; and up-and-coming freestyler Carole Sinnott, 17—certainly endorse Brian's sleek new look!

Dazed and defensive, Brian sat up in bed. "It was a posed picture, a setup by the photographer," he protested. But his heart was racing. He didn't recognize Judy's fierce tortured face, the bared teeth and projectile tears. "Just a bit of fun. Some girls in the squad fooling about for the camera."

"You're a married man," she sobbed. "It's awful and too intimate. And I suppose you're sleeping with them?"

It was his turn to be indignant. "Don't be ridiculous!"

She ran out of the room, crying, "I never want to see this disgusting sort of thing again," and slept on the couch downstairs.

When Brian returned from his early-morning training at seven, Judy was sitting with Dulcie at the kitchen table with the offending sports page in front of them. Both women were smoking cigarettes and drinking tea, and they fell silent and glowered at him as he entered.

"You're up early, love," he ventured to Judy. He was exhausted from exercise, sleeplessness, and emotion. "What about your sleep?"

She drew on her cigarette, said nothing, and stared at him with tragic possum eyes.

"*Popular with the girls,*" Dulcie quoted. She gave the newspaper a disdainful backhand slap. "Surely you can't expect your poor wife to be able to sleep after that?" Her eyes were glistening.

That afternoon at training, the swim squad passed around the paper, laughing and teasing each other over smooth Brian and his "fans," and the girls all complaining, ridiculously, that they looked fat in the photo. Shortly after, Brian's next 1,500-meter time trial did not go well. He'd lost another 6.08 seconds.

Don frowned and looked anxious. "What's the matter, son?" he wanted to know. "You look buggered. Everything alright at home?"

"Sure."

"Well, take ten minutes to rest, you bloody slowcoach, then I want another 800 at 90 percent effort." And Don stamped off.

Dusk was falling and dozens of nesting swallows flitted about the pool's cornices and skimmed over the water's surface. On one side of the pool, commuter trains rumbled home over the Harbour Bridge; on the other, the eyes, teeth, and lips of Old King Cole, the giant grinning face at Luna Park's entrance, suddenly lit up, scaring the swallows perched on King Cole's eyelashes. Little ferries steamed back and forth across Lavender Bay.

At twilight the ornate art deco fixtures of the stands, gyms, and changing rooms, built when the North Sydney Olympic Pool proudly hosted the 1938 Empire Games events, seemed more gloomily ornamental to the swim squad than they did to their sleepy eyes at dawn training.

Ever since Don had moved his team from the Drummoyne pool to North Sydney's superior facilities two years before, Brian had been a little in awe of this place, the venue for an extraordinary eighty-six world record–breaking swims. As he recovered his breath, his eyes followed a flight of swallows to their nests above the topmost stands. Sitting in the back row was Dulcie, staring down at him.

When he arrived home an hour later, she met him at the door. Oddly, for this hour, and the evening temperature, and indoors, she was wearing her satiny blue strapless swimsuit.

She pulled him toward the stairs. She had applied fresh makeup and her body was shiny with perfumed lotion. He noticed her eyes had that eerie gleam.

"I don't think so," he said. "Not anymore. Why were you spying on me?"

"In order to check on you with your young girlfriends, you cruel bastard. You'd better come with me so I can punish you."

He was speechless. Her urgent tugging released the now-familiar warm scent of womanly flesh, and the satiny fabric of the blue swimsuit brushed against his face with its own erotic smell, and his anger, bewilderment, and weakened resolve had no resistance.

Afterward, thanks to her wild fingernails, his back was scratched even more painfully than usual.

When Dulcie greeted him at the door the next evening, he managed to avoid her embrace. That she was wearing her swimsuit, he found alarming.

"I saw you watching me at the pool again," he said. "I

can't do this anymore. Seriously, it has to end now."

She smiled coquettishly. "I have to make sure Johnny Weissmuller is behaving."

"Everything is peculiar about this," he said. "Being shadowed by my mother-in-law is very weird behavior. I'm twenty-three. I've got a marriage to think of, not to mention the Olympics."

"I'm too old for you now, is that it? And I'm weird!" She began to weep. "You lead me on, and now you prefer your teenage sluts."

He groaned. "They're not . . . I don't . . . Jesus, I'm calling a halt for the good of everyone."

Dulcie wiped her eyes and sighed theatrically. "Sure you are, you monster. Come and sit down for your dinner then."

She spun on her heel and he followed her swimsuited backside and bare thighs toward the kitchen. In the doorway she turned abruptly and kissed him hard, and pressed her body against him, and he followed her upstairs once more.

Afterward, she said to him, smugly, "I bet those girls aren't as good at this as I am."

Speechless, he just shook his head. His shoulder blades had left spots of blood on the sheets.

Brian and Judy walked hand in hand through Old King Cole's monstrous mouth. Luna Park was Sydney's traditional Saturday-night entertainment magnet for young couples: for boys treating their girlfriends to a night out, and for both sexes hoping to meet someone. It was so close to home yet this was their first visit there since moving to Lavender Bay.

It was Brian's idea. So was leaving the house quietly, without involving Dulcie. "We need some time alone," he'd said.

They strolled along the boardwalk past the Wild Mouse, the Spider, and Dodgem City. The roller coaster rumbled overhead, the night regularly punctuated by customers' screams. A breeze from the bay ruffled girls' skirts and blew ice cream wrappers across their path.

Outside Dodgem City, four young sailors were chatting to three women. The sailors were egging each other on with nudges and winks, and smoking flashily, with tough-guy hand gestures. They wore their caps so jauntily far back on their heads, behind waves of pomaded hair, that the caps seemed to defy gravity. Sparks flew over the dodgem cars and the air smelled of electricity.

Brian felt Judy's grip tighten and her shoulders stiffen as she urged him away.

"What ride would you like to go on?" he asked her. "The Big Dipper? The Ghost Train?"

"Did you see those girls?"

"The girls with the sailors? Yes, why?"

"What did you think of them?"

"Prostitutes, probably."

"Attractive? Your sort of girls?"

"Hardly! What's this about?"

"I'm trying to work out what sort of women you go for."

"*Your sort*. Jesus, Judy!"

"Come home then, and show me how you really feel."

As they walked back through Old King Cole's mouth, two incoming teenage girls, heavily made up and no more than fifteen, elbowed each other, giggled, and the bolder one called out, "Hey, aren't you Brian Tasker?"

He nodded in polite acknowledgment, but Judy glowered at them, her mood worsening when she heard the girl mutter, "The lucky titless bitch!"

At home, Dulcie was sitting in the dark garden. She looked pale and jumpy and her hair was awry, as if she'd been pacing in the wind. She was underdressed for the cool night and had a frangipani flower stuck behind an ear.

"There you are!" she said, too brightly. "The two love-birds!" She raised her voice over the rumble and screams of the roller coaster. "I'm having a sherry. Will you join me?"

"Not in the mood, but thanks, Mum," said Judy. "We're off to bed."

When Judy returned from Mass the next morning, Brian was sitting in his bathrobe in the garden again, sipping a cup of cocoa and staring sleepily across the bay.

She pulled open his robe. "So you've shaved down again!" she said, and slowly shook her head.

"I need to be transformed," he replied. He reached a languid hand out for his cup but misjudged the distance and his hand fell short. "Sit down and have some cocoa."

Dulcie was watching from the kitchen window. "There's no more cocoa, Judy," she called out. "I'll make a pot of coffee."

Brian looked toward his mother-in-law. "I'd like a coffee too—thanks, Dulcie. Everything's a bit blurry this morning."

Judy said, "I've been worried about your cuts and scratches. Sitting out here among the oleanders. They're highly poisonous, you know."

It was during his next 1,500-meter time trial on Monday that Brian Tasker collapsed at the 1,350-meter turn and became tangled in the lane ropes.

Still holding his stopwatch, Don Wilmott jumped fully clothed into the pool, disentangled him from the ropes, and held his head above water. But by the time Brian was hauled from the water, laid on the pool deck, and resuscitation was attempted, he was dead.

At the inquest the city coroner found that, tragically, repeated severe exertion had further damaged the clearly genetically defective heart of a gifted athlete.

His grieving widow attracted wide public sympathy after the *Telegraph*'s pictorial coverage of the funeral service at St. Francis Xavier, attended by top athletes from a wide range of sports, including the up-and-coming swimming star Murray Rose.

Two years later, Judy Tasker, only twenty-three, married the *Telegraph*'s young police reporter, Steve McNamara. By this time, after winning three gold medals at the 1956 Melbourne Games at the age of seventeen, Murray Rose was a national hero.

In April 1958, when CPO Eric Kruger and the *Warramunga* left for six months' exercises with the Far East Strategic Reserve, it was convenient for all concerned for Dulcie to move in with her daughter and her new husband.

PART III

CRIMINAL JUSTICE

RIP-OFF

BY TOM GILLING

Sydney Harbour

I t was Haklander who gave me the passenger's name: Ramirez. He told me Ramirez was flying in from the States and would need a ride into the city. Usually I sat on the airport rank with the other drivers, but Haklander said I could make a bit extra by picking up Ramirez in person.

"You don't have to go looking for him," he said, tossing me the keys to the taxi. "Just hold up a sign with his name on it. He'll find you."

Haklander was Dutch, or maybe Belgian. You had to listen hard to catch the accent. He owned half a dozen taxis. Four times a week I paid him $120 for the privilege of spending twelve hours in a Ford Falcon with illegal tires, a clapped-out gearbox, and nearly 200,000 kilometers on the clock. I drove days: three in the morning until three in the afternoon. The money and traffic were worse but there was less chance of being beaten up. Haklander must have paid a quarter of a million each for the plates, but thanks to Uber they were practically worthless. Haklander already had his eye on other ways to make money and upgrading his taxis wasn't part of his business plan.

"Is this guy Ramirez a friend of yours?" I asked.

"No," said Haklander. "One of the other drivers told me about the job. He couldn't take it himself so I'm giving it to you." He paused. "If you're not interested I can give it to someone else."

The details sounded vague—deliberately vague. It wasn't exactly a dream job: forty dollars max. I was probably better off taking my chances on the rank. But I spent too much of my life sitting on ranks. I told Haklander I'd do it.

"Ramirez. R-A-M-I-R-E-Z," he said. "The commonest name in Mexico."

"Someone told me Rodriguez was the commonest name in Mexico."

"Is that right?" Haklander replied without interest.

"That's what they said."

Haklander held my gaze for a few moments. "Just make sure you're on time." He wrote down the arrival time and held out his hand for the cash. "By the way, the oil gauge isn't working."

"I told you that last week," I said, as Haklander's phone started ringing.

He waved me out the door.

The flight must have landed early because as soon as I held up the sign with Ramirez's name on it, he walked straight up to me. Or maybe he'd caught a different flight, I thought.

"You're Mr. Ramirez?" I asked.

He nodded a bit too eagerly. "Ramirez. Yes."

He was young, early twenties. He had bad skin and teeth that had never seen a dentist, but his Nike trainers were brand new. When I asked where he'd come from, he said, "Miami, Florida." It sounded rehearsed, a phrase he'd spent time practicing in front of a mirror. As I threw his suitcase into the boot I noticed a half-torn tag on the handle from Bogota, Colombia: *Aeropuerto Internacional El Dorado*. Suit yourself, I thought. None of my business.

"You're going to the city?" I asked, since that was what Haklander had told me.

Ramirez—if that was his real name—looked momentarily confused. Then he showed me a scrap of paper with an address written on it: *Park Regis Concierge Apartments, Cremorne.*

"Are you sure?"

Ramirez pointed to the address on the paper.

"Okay," I said. It didn't matter to me where I took him. Besides, I'd make twenty dollars more by driving him across the harbor. I got in and started the meter.

"Long queue?" I asked.

He looked at me blankly.

"Customs," I said. "They've been on strike. It was chaos yesterday."

Ramirez held the scrap of paper in front of my face.

"Park Regis Apartments," I repeated. "I saw it the first time."

I told him he had to wear the seat belt. He pretended not to hear, just sat there clutching a bag from Downtown Duty Free.

"Mate," I said, "I'm not copping a fine because you refuse to wear a belt." I tugged at the inertia reel to show him what I meant. He showed me the address again. I decided it wasn't worth the effort.

Ramirez wasn't a talker. That didn't bother me. You get used to all sorts: the ones who won't shut up, the living dead, and everything between.

The traffic on Southern Cross Drive was a nightmare— two lanes closed, police cars and flashing lights everywhere. I warned Ramirez the trip was going to be expensive but told him there wasn't much I could do about it. I turned on the radio: Ray Hadley. I wouldn't want him sitting next to me in the cab but on the radio he's alright. You can always switch him off.

I asked Ramirez if he had Australian money. I've had people try to pay me in rupees, pesos, cigarettes. He didn't understand. I rubbed my finger and thumb together. Ramirez pulled out his wallet. He must have been carrying a thousand dollars in new fifty-dollar notes.

"Bridge or tunnel?" I always ask. Some passengers think it's a trick question. Lion or tiger? Chicken or egg? I know one driver—Iranian, used to be a dentist—who refuses to use the tunnel. It's the lights. They remind him of the months he spent in one of the Ayatollah's prisons. I've never heard of a driver who won't use the bridge. You can't drive a taxi in Sydney if you're scared of crossing water. If the passenger doesn't have a preference, I always take the bridge. I've never liked the thought of all that water above my head. Once I picked up an old bloke who had worked all his life as a bridge painter. His skin was gray from all the paint in his pores. He told me he had talked seven people out of jumping; he still remembered their names. There was one he couldn't stop—it was the one name he'd forgotten.

I waited for Ramirez to answer. He was staring straight ahead, both hands gripping the duty free bag in his lap. I pointed out the Opera House. You'd be surprised how many people don't notice it, especially traveling north. Ramirez shook his head, as if I was trying to sell it to him.

By the time I pulled up outside the Park Regis Apartments, the meter showed $137.30. Normally I'd knock a few dollars off to make up for the traffic, but this time I didn't. Ramirez pulled a bunch of fifties out of his wallet. I took three and tried to give him the change but he wouldn't take it. I didn't offer him a receipt.

He stayed in the taxi as I walked around to open the boot. A police car with flashing lights was parked fifty meters down the road. The cops had pulled over a P-plater in a black Audi TT. The driver looked about seventeen, black singlet, tattoos down one side of his neck.

As I popped the boot, Ramirez got out of the taxi and started walking away. "Whoa, mate!" I shouted. "Don't leave this behind." He looked back. For a second I thought he was going to make a run for it. Then he came back for the suitcase. The cops were still dealing with the P-plater, who was leaning against the Audi with his arms folded.

I left Ramirez standing on the porch of the Park Regis Apartments, hitting the numbers on his phone. It was only later, as I vacuumed out the taxi for the night driver, that I noticed the plastic duty free bag lying under the driver's seat.

Inside the bag I found a bottle of Gordon's gin and a Seagate computer hard drive. It would have taken me half an hour to drive back to the Park Regis Apartments. I called reception and asked if a guest checking in this morning had reported any missing baggage. The woman who answered had just started her shift. She put me on hold for a couple of minutes. Then she came back on and said, "Nobody checked in this morning." I thanked her and hung up. It was just after three thirty p.m. I called the taxi controller. No one had reported losing a duty free shopping bag.

I took the gin and the hard drive out of the bag and stuffed them in my backpack. As I walked down Foveaux Street, a dero in an army coat asked me for money. I gave him a handful of coins and dropped the empty bag in a bin outside Central Station.

As soon as I got home I put the chain on the door. Ramirez's story—the version Haklander had given me—didn't add up. Haklander had told me just enough to get me to take the job but not enough for it to make sense. Ten to one Ramirez was Colombian, not Mexican, and his name wasn't Ramirez.

The silver seal on the Seagate box was still intact but when I unwrapped the hard drive and plugged it in, nothing happened. A sticker underneath said, *Made in Thailand.* I used a kitchen knife to pry the plastic case apart. The circuitry and components had been stripped out. Inside the case was a vacuum-sealed slab of white powder.

I sat for a long time in silence. I remembered Ramirez's reaction when he saw the police car parked across the road from the Park Regis Apartments, the way he started walking away without his suitcase. It dawned on me that Ramirez had panicked at the sight of the cops and left the duty free bag behind on purpose. Luckily for me, he had paid in cash and hadn't taken a receipt. Chances were, he hadn't noticed my license number. However, my face and that stupid sign would be all over the airport CCTV. What I wanted to know was, did Haklander know what Ramirez was carrying?

Haklander lived in a 1930s mansion in Bellevue Hill with stone lions on the front porch. I had been there once for a barbecue. Usually I called him at his office in Bondi Junction. I dialed the number.

"Hello, Mr. Haklander," I said. "I picked up your friend Ramirez."

"Who?"

"Ramirez. The guy you asked me to pick up at the airport."

"Oh, yes," said Haklander.

"I took him across the harbor, like you told me to."

Haklander didn't correct me. Maybe he'd forgotten telling me that Ramirez needed a ride to the city. I could hear him breathing on the other end of the line. I had the impression he was waiting for me to say something else. When I didn't, he said, "I hope he made it worth your while."

"Sure. Mr. Ramirez gave me a big tip."

"I'm glad to hear it."

"By the way," I said, "one of the rear door handles needs fixing."

"Leave it with me."

I knew what that meant.

In the corner of the room was an old pair of Tannoy loudspeakers wired up to a secondhand amplifier that no longer worked. I pulled the front off one of the loudspeakers, unscrewed the bass driver, and pushed the slab of cocaine into the cavity.

I was living in a run-down art deco block in Potts Point. My apartment was on the top floor, facing the back, with a bay window that offered glimpses of the Finger Wharf and the rust-streaked warships in Woolloomooloo Bay. It cost me $525 a week, which was less than it was worth but more than I could afford. I sold a bit of weed to make ends meet.

Six months earlier a neighbor had collared me on the staircase. He lived in the apartment below mine. Heavyset, careless shaver, always wore a crumpled sports coat and Hush Puppies. He wore a wedding ring but lived on his own, did his laundry on Saturday nights, and rarely bothered to pick up his mail. We'd nodded to each other a few times but never had a conversation. I knew his name—Fowler—from the intercom list beside the front door.

I was pretty certain I had seen him at Haklander's barbecue but Fowler would have been too drunk to remember. I had assumed he was another of Haklander's drivers. Haklander liked to have more drivers than taxis for them to drive; it kept everyone hungry. It turned out that Fowler was a detective at Manly. It was possible he moonlighted as a cab driver. Plenty of cops did.

He stopped me on the stairs and said, "Quite a social life you've got going up there."

I didn't reply.

Fowler leaned forward until his face was a few inches from mine. "I know you're dealing."

"Not me," I said.

"Don't fuck with me."

"I don't know what you're talking about."

Fowler stood aside courteously to let another tenant pass us on the staircase and waited while she let herself into her apartment. When she'd bolted the door behind her, Fowler asked, "Do I look stupid?"

I've never been good with rhetorical questions. What was the right answer? That he was stupid and didn't look it or that he wasn't stupid and did? "What do you want?" I asked.

Fowler reached into his coat and took out a packet of cigarettes with a picture of a gangrenous foot and the words, *Smoking causes peripheral vascular disease.* He shook a cigarette out of the packet and offered one to me. I told him I didn't smoke.

Fowler followed me upstairs. I kept my stash under a loose floorboard in the second bedroom. There was a small chest of drawers over it. As Fowler helped himself to the stash—and eleven hundred dollars in cash that I was going to use to pay the rent—he said, "You should be more careful."

I wasn't sure which of us was more pathetic—Fowler for shaking me down or me for letting him do it. The bastard walked away looking smug but he missed out on another five hundred I kept hidden behind the microwave.

* * *

An hour after my conversation with Haklander, I heard a fist banging on the front door. It was Fowler. This time he hadn't brought his manners with him. I had to let him in before he broke the door. He pushed past me and went straight to the spare bedroom. I stood in the doorway while he shoved the chest of drawers away and pulled out the loose floorboard. He lay on the floor groping between the bearers. "Where is it?" he demanded.

"Where's what?"

Fowler got to his feet and said, "I could arrest you now."

"On what charge?"

He didn't answer. I knew what he was after, but who had told him about it? It had to be Haklander. Fowler let me stew for a while. Then he said, "The Colombian. I know he left something behind."

"Did he?"

Fowler walked toward me. "You're out of your depth, son. Tell me where it is."

I hesitated. I had allowed him to rip me off once but I wasn't planning to let it happen again. "It's somewhere safe," I said. "Not here."

Fowler stood so close that I could smell the lunch on his breath. "Don't play games with me, son."

"Fifty," I said.

His mouth fell open. "What?"

"Fifty thousand. The stuff's worth two hundred. All I want is fifty."

For a while Fowler stood there wheezing like an old Labrador. Then he started laughing. On his way out he said, "You've got some balls."

My mobile was ringing. I looked at my watch. It was just after ten in the morning. I had drunk too much gin. The sun was blazing through the broken blinds. I rolled over and picked up the phone. It was Haklander. He said we had to talk about something, the oil gauge or the broken door handle on the taxi. He sounded flustered. I said, "I'm not driving today. Can't it wait?"

Haklander said he needed to come and discuss it in person. There was a pause and then he asked me for my address.

"My address?"

"Yeah," said Haklander. "Where do you live?"

I sat up. Haklander already knew where I lived, although he had never been inside the apartment. It sounded like a warning. I had the feeling that somebody was with him and telling him what to say. Ramirez? Or the people Ramirez was working for? I wondered how long Haklander had been dealing with the Colombians. Was it cocaine that had paid for that mansion in Bellevue Hill?

Suddenly the phone went dead. Haklander's visitors must have realized what he was up to. I doubted it would take them long to get what they needed. I threw on some clothes, grabbed the cocaine from the speaker cabinet, and stuffed some spare clothes in a holdall along with whatever cash I had in the apartment. Then I put the radio on and left. I was watching from the laundromat on Macleay Street when a silver Subaru WRX pulled up outside my apartment block. I saw two men get out, a dark-skinned Latino in jeans and a white T-shirt and a younger man in a leather jacket. Fifteen minutes later only the Latino came out.

There was a public phone in the laundromat, although the sound of the machines made it hard to hear. I rang triple zero and told the operator I wanted to report a break-in.

* * *

I agreed to meet Fowler at nine p.m. at a self-storage depot on the industrial side of Chatswood. I thought Chatswood was all apartments and Chinese restaurants; I didn't know there was an industrial side. According to Fowler he'd been renting a storage unit there since his divorce. He said it was cheaper than an extra bedroom. The kids were grown up and none of them wanted to stay with him anyway. He hadn't spoken to his eldest since she was sixteen.

I arrived twenty minutes early but Fowler's ten-year-old Magna station wagon was already in the car park. He had promised to come alone but I could see someone sitting beside him. I drove around the car park and back onto the street, parked a couple of blocks away, and walked back.

The roll-a-door to Fowler's lockup was half open. I had to bend down to get under it. As I straightened up Fowler said, "This is Mr. O'Connor. He's offered to come along. For security."

O'Connor was sitting on a fishing chair in the corner. He was smartly dressed in chinos, polo shirt, and a blazer, but he had a boxer's busted nose. He was smoking a cigarette.

"It was supposed to be just you and me," I said.

Fowler said, "Fifty thousand dollars is a lot of money. We don't want anything bad to happen."

"Is he a cop?"

Before Fowler could answer, O'Connor said, "We're golfing buddies."

Fowler shifted awkwardly in his Hush Puppies, eyes downcast, like a man who knew he'd made a bad call.

I figured that Haklander and Fowler had ripped off the Colombians. Fowler must have arranged for the uniformed police to be outside the Park Regis Apartments. He and Haklander would have known that at the first sign of trouble the delivery would be aborted. They had to take a chance on what

Ramirez would do next, but it was a fair bet he would leave the cocaine in the taxi. Fowler had ripped me off once and thought I'd let him do it again. Paying me off would not have been part of the plan yet it still left them a nice profit. So where did O'Connor come in?

The lockup was full of old tools, rusting tins of paint, boxes of bathroom tiles for a renovation job that Fowler had never gotten around to. There was a men's bicycle hanging from a hook on the wall but it was hard to picture Fowler ever having ridden it.

While O'Connor explored the pockets of the fishing chair Fowler said, "Give us the gear, son." It was more like a plea than an order.

"Who's got the money?" I asked.

"You'll get the money," said Fowler. "Just hand over the fucking gear."

I remembered him warning me that I was out of my depth, but if anyone was in over his head, it was Fowler. I watched O'Connor playing with an iridescent fishing lure he had found in one of the chair pockets.

Fowler pointed to my backpack and said, "Open it."

O'Connor dropped his cigarette and extinguished the butt delicately with the toe of his shoe. Then he put the fishing lure back in the chair pocket and stood up. "Let's get this over with," he said.

His hand went into his blazer. When it came out there was a gun in it. He took a silencer out of his pocket. I thought he was going to shoot me. Fowler must have thought the same thing; he told O'Connor to put the gun away. O'Connor fired once. The bullet went through the pocket of Fowler's blazer and left a crimson stain. Fowler was dead before he hit the concrete.

O'Connor frisked the body for a weapon, but Fowler had

come unarmed. Corrupt but trusting: a fatal combination. O'Connor asked me politely for the cocaine, then sat back in the fishing chair. I handed it over. He made a small hole in the shrink-wrapping and took some of the powder on his index finger and rubbed it on his gums. Then he took my car keys and gave me Fowler's. "There's a gym bag on the backseat," he said. "Bring it here."

I could have tried to make a dash for it but I didn't trust O'Connor not to shoot me in the back.

The gym bag contained a hundred meters of nylon rope, a box cutter, and a car battery. O'Connor had come prepared. He told me to lash the car battery to Fowler's corpse. "Make the knots good and tight. We don't want him coming back."

It was after eleven when O'Connor told me to go and fetch the car. We bundled Fowler into the back of his station wagon and drove through silent North Shore streets to the Tunks Park boat ramp. Tinnies and a handful of larger boats were chained to a row of metal stands near the top of the ramp. O'Connor chose a dinghy with two paddles stored inside the hull. The padlock wasn't even locked.

The wind had come up. Yacht masts jangled as we paddled past the point into Middle Harbour. As the Spit Bridge loomed out of the darkness, O'Connor put down his paddle and said, "This'll do."

We heaved Fowler over the side. There was a splash when the body hit the surface, followed by a stream of silver bubbles while it sank to the bottom.

I watched O'Connor light a cigarette. His complexion looked darker in the moonlight, his features more Mediterranean. He didn't look like an O'Connor. Who was he working for—the Colombians? Haklander? Or was he just another opportunist out for himself?

In the distance a fishing boat was chugging slowly out to sea. Getting out of Sydney seemed like a good idea. I tried not to think about the money. Fifty thousand dollars was an awful lot of money not to think about. I'd had sleepless nights thinking about a lot less. I left O'Connor standing on the boat ramp. He made a gun out of two fingers and fired.

For some reason I hoped Haklander had talked the Colombians out of shooting him. As for Fowler, I didn't believe his body would stay hidden. He'd be on the move before long, dragged up and set adrift by a carelessly thrown anchor. Where would he end up—Balmoral Beach? Rushcutters Bay? Or bobbing among the pylons at Manly Wharf?

The harbor always gives up its secrets in the end.

SLOW BURN

BY GABRIELLE LORD

Clovelly

The great thing about retirement is that it gives you time to do the things you enjoy, like fishing off the rocks at the point near Clovelly Beach. Which is what I'm doing right now, standing on the point, line baited for bream, watching the sea roll in and the big green swells lift the seaweed around the rock shelves where the dusky flatheads like to lurk. It's a relaxing way to spend a morning. Gives me time to think too. Time to think about vengeance. The Lord is reported as saying, "Vengeance is mine," but in this, as in all things, it's my belief that the Lord sometimes needs a helping hand.

It is a perfect blue and white Clovelly day as the small breakers fall away from the rocks in sheer white waterfalls and my companion jerks his gear back after a bump on his line, hoping to jag a flattie. "Got one!" he yells.

I remember catching a big old duskie some years back who had four rusted hooks along his jaw. Out of respect, I cut him free, removed the hooks, and sent him on his way with good luck wishes, one old survivor to another. Now, I studied my companion as he played his catch along—giving the fish some slack, then hauling back on the line, bringing him in closer each time. It could be a big duskie, I thought. Or a skate.

They say it's dangerous to go rock fishing alone, so I almost always have a companion. My usual fishing buddy, also a retired cop—we worked together in homicide years ago—is currently traveling the east coast in a fancy caravan with his missus, and over the last couple of months I've been fishing with this new fellow, and not just for bream or flathead. He thinks this came about because of the casual camaraderie that sometimes develops between the normally solitary men who fish off the rocks. We've never got round to introducing ourselves and just call each other *mate* on the rare occasions we need to speak. He knows nothing about me but I know a hell of a lot about him.

He has no idea that for nearly two decades, I've been planning to destroy him. His name is Ronald Leslie Twigg and there he stands, a few meters away from me with his canvas hat and his gear baited for flathead, playing his catch, looking south, not taking much notice of me. I've been keeping tabs on him since I was a senior sergeant in traffic, and he was a young thug, the baby in a family of thugs, part of the 15 percent of the population who harass the rest of us, one way or another.

Now Twigg is a weathered fifty-two, with a permanent scowl on his face and carrying too much weight. But I don't want him to cark on me, dying of a stroke or a coronary. I want Ronald Leslie Twigg to live for many years to come. Many years.

I've been waiting and watching for the right opportunity. Just biding my time for the possibility that all the ducks might one day line up. It's a big ask, and I'd almost resigned myself to the fact that it might never happen. One duck has been in place for some years, in the person of my clever young daughter Kerryanne, who works in the New South Wales Police Force in forensic services. So imagine my elation when out of the blue, a second duck settled into position. Some months back,

Twigg left the inner-city boarding house he'd been living in and came to live in Clovelly, several streets away from our place, renting a shed in the backyard of a house whose owner is currently overseas. When that happened, I dared to be hopeful that there was now a real chance that our long-discussed plan, sometimes seeming like a fantasy that we'd been telling ourselves for all these years, might actually materialize. It was as if Fate had delivered him into my hands.

Some evenings, I walk past the vacant house with its blinds pulled down as the interior lights come on automatically at six thirty p.m. and I head around the block to the back lane, and peer over the fence, noting the dim light in the shed inhabited by Twigg, hearing only the sound of a TV and the occasional clink of bottles as he drinks alone. Outside the shed in a sagging box, I've sometimes spotted a cat, tucked up in the dodgy shelter, with a bowl of curdled milk nearby.

I've followed this man now for nineteen years. Unlike his older brothers, he was acquitted of a particularly brutal crime, in which a young man was almost beaten to death and then had his throat cut. This young man had been on his way home after having dinner with his family to celebrate successfully completing the first four years of a pharmacy degree, when the three thugs jumped him, threw him to the ground, dragged him into an alley, and went to work—took his wallet and phone and continued bashing him until they were interrupted by some people who heard the commotion. But it was too late for the victim, who died of massive blood loss and a heart attack in the ambulance.

I try not to be too obsessed, but it's hard. *All we need*, I'd say to myself, *is a violent crime in the area*. But realistically, how likely was that? That's the really hard part in a place like Clovelly: quiet, gentrified, with constant renovations and rebuilding going on; artists and journalists moving in over the last couple of decades and almost no serious crime to speak of. We just don't have violent crimes in Clovelly, with its family-friendly beach and village atmosphere, open football field and coastal walks. Until—but I'm getting ahead of myself.

Claire and I bought our cottage in Clovelly over thirty years ago from her parents when you could pick up a nice little place for a hundred and fifty thousand—a fortune to us then; you'd probably have to pay twice that as a deposit for anything in the vicinity these days. We liked the safe little beach with its breakwater where our kids could play and swim without fearing any dangers from rips or sharks. We also liked the ocean swimming pool—washed out and topped up by the tides every day—where Claire swims her laps most mornings. A couple of other retired cops live in the area and we sometimes get together to revisit our times on the job, sitting around on the concrete terraces and steps near the pool, swapping war stories, reminiscing about the crims we helped lock up. And, less frequently, of the flatheads and crims who got away. It's a sad fact that a lot of crims do get away with crime. Our statistics might suggest otherwise, but then, as the saying goes, there are lies, damned lies and statistics. Many crimes are never reported and policing is mostly bluff—just enough to keep a civil society behaving itself. Also, nearly 85 percent of crime is committed by around 10 percent of the population. The other 90 percent police ourselves.

Clovelly is a coastal suburb of Sydney and used to be called Little Coogee years ago because Coogee Beach is just around the corner to the south. It was also known as Poverty Point because back then it was mostly inhabited by battlers, Italian and Greek migrants trying to settle into Sydney after the war. In those days, the buildings were fishing shacks or humble semi-detached cottages. The surf life-saving club is over 110 years old and all our kids started their beach lives as Clovelly Nippers, racing in the sand, practicing with the old-fashioned line-and-reel surf life-saving equipment, learning how to bring a person in distress to shore. I think of those days a lot. Life was simpler and the job wasn't so complex.

My daughter Kerryanne is a senior police officer now, team leader with the forensic services group. She's among those called out to any major crime scene around the eastern beaches. A lot of crime scene work can be undertaken by specialists who aren't sworn officers, though murder is always handled by the police forensic teams. Murder in Australia is not a common crime, averaging a fairly stable sixty-odd per year. Around Clovelly and Sydney's other eastern suburbs it is extremely rare. Cops fight to get onto a team investigating a homicide; it's so infrequent and everyone wants a part of it. Most of the time round here, it's routine work—hoons who race down the hill in stolen cars, the occasional brawl at closing time at the pubs, and drug arrests. They do district patrols around the beaches and keep a lid on alcohol-fueled antisocial behavior.

Kerryanne often drops by to visit us. She knows that with Tim away in the west, and our Anthony gone forever, she's the only one now who can do that. Over a cup of tea, we chat. Last time she dropped in I said, "You've got soot or something on your face."

"Oh, have I?" she said, looking at herself in the mirror in the hall and rubbing the smear, making it worse. "I've just come from a job with the fireies. Fire investigation unit. Arson job, with the shop burned almost to the ground. The owner thought he'd get away with it because there he was, thirty kilometers away, sleeping the sleep of the innocent beside his loyal wife."

As we walked into the kitchen, she put her bag down and pulled out her camera, switching it on. "See what he used as a wick? We lifted a bit of masonry from a corner and look what we found. He thought it would all be destroyed by the fire. But part of the collapsed roof had covered this corner and kept the ash intact."

I looked at the screen on Kerryanne's camera and saw the outline of a perfect spiral in ash. "Ha! He used a mosquito coil!"

"That's right. A nice slow burn. He lights it, and it burns away for hours until it reaches the middle of the spiral where it was linked to combustible material and containers of petrol. The place would've gone up like a bomb. And he thought he was being very clever, buying hours and hours for himself to establish an alibi."

"He was very unlucky that it wasn't destroyed in the general fire mess," I said, looking at the fragile damning evidence.

"Sometimes the angels give us one like this, Dad," she responded, smiling.

I nodded, remembering a rapist who'd dropped his wallet at the crime scene. We'd driven around the corner and arrested him.

Kerryanne put the camera away, washed her face and hands in the bathroom, then joined me for a cuppa and one of her mother's famous Anzac biscuits.

After she left, I leaned back in my kitchen chair and thought about what I'd just seen. The slow burn of an arsonist's wick which had exploded into a destructive fire. *I've been burning for nineteen years*, I thought. And all this time I've been just waiting for the explosion that will destroy Ronald Leslie Twigg.

* * *

My daughter has known for years about the man I've been fishing with lately, and she looked at me with her wide gray eyes when I told her he'd moved into our area and said, "Dad, this is good news, but we still need one more factor—and that's the tough one."

She was right, but if the gods are with us, she'll alert me when the right conditions arise and then we'll have the duck trifecta. Maybe they never will, and I might have to change my mind about murder; a quick shove one day when the seas are treacherous—Old Testament style, a life for a life. My fishing companion got away with murder, cutting that young man's throat nineteen years ago. How do I know? I have an old acquaintance—can't really call him a friend, but for many years he was one of my most trusted informants. Although I don't see much of Stanley these days, seventeen years ago, not long after the end of the trial that resulted in my fishing companion's acquittal, he asked to meet me. He told me he'd been drinking with a group of men at a pub in Glebe—ex-jailbirds from a halfway house in the area—the night young Twigg was celebrating his acquittal.

"The bastard was bragging about it, Chief Inspector," Stanley had said. "And that's not right. Gloating, he was. *I got away with murder*, he was saying with every drink. *Cut the bastard's throat like a sheep.* He spent the whole time boasting. Big-noting himself. Little prick. If my situation wasn't how it is," he'd shrugged, "I'd swear it in court. But you understand, given the work I do . . . I can't do that."

I did understand, and that was when I swore I'd get this bastard one day. Stanley's moral code has always been ambiguous, but even a gig has his standards. And the deliberate murder of a defenseless man, already bashed into unconsciousness, was obviously something that offended his particular standards.

* * *

My fishing companion is a piss-weak swimmer; sadly, we've lost several rock fishermen along this stretch of coast over the last few years—and it would be easy to just shove him into one of the big swells we get along here when the weather rolls in with powerful waves, but I have other plans for him. Murder meant nothing to him; in fact, he was a gratuitous murderer, cutting his victim's throat just to show his brothers how "tough" he was. To me, as to the law, murder is the ultimate crime—the taking of a life and all its potential, the young man's future, the wife and kids he never got to have, the grandchildren—a whole family tree cut off. So I have other plans for Ronald Leslie Twigg. The Latin motto on the New South Wales Police Force badge underneath the sea eagle translates as, *Punishment swiftly follows crime*. My companion's punishment has not been swift because it's taken almost two decades for a suitable incident to arrive, yet punishment will certainly follow. The vengeance I'm planning isn't simple revenge; it's applying the law. Belatedly, because the law failed nineteen years ago.

"Fuck!" shouted my fishing companion. "Bastard!" The flat-head he thought he'd hooked had bitten through his line, which now drifted around as he reeled it in. He swore some more over the loss of his flathead rig and I suppressed a smile.

As far as he's concerned, I'm just a retired bloke who likes to fish. I was not involved in the investigations or the following trials, which sent his brothers away for life, yet acquitted him. I saw him once or twice in court, but I was just one face in a packed public gallery.

The evidence of the eyewitness to the attack was hazy. She'd only seen the two older brothers in the streetlight near her window. Nor was there any physical evidence to link him to the crime. None that couldn't be explained away by the defense lawyer as transfer DNA from the other two men, his brothers. Nothing conclusive to put him at the murder site. The grub wore gloves. Didn't want to get blood under his fingernails.

My companion was clearly calling it a day. Or at least a morning. He packed up his gear, grunted about the poor fishing—"Not enough to feed the bloody cat"—and started walking away, toward the beach and the parking area. I packed up too. I already had everything I needed, and unlike my companion, I'd caught two nice-sized bream.

I was making my way back to the car when I took a phone call from my daughter.

"I'm calling from Pigling Bland's phone," said Kerryanne. Immediately I knew she was speaking from a public phone, which she always did when she wanted a secure line; in fact, I even knew which public phone. When the kids were little, there'd been a fading advertisement on the wall of the long-gone corner shop for Pinkerton's Brand Dyspepsia Mixture. Kerryanne, as a little one, had thought the sign was about the character in a Beatrix Potter book.

"We've got one, Dad," she said. "Reported earlier this morning. And it could be the one we've been waiting for. The story should break within the next few hours. So far, the press isn't onto it. But that won't last. I'll be going out there shortly."

"What do you need from me?" I asked, adrenaline shaking my hands.

"Anything helpful. I'll be searching the exhibits and doing some of the analyses. I'll report on what I find. That's my job. And the people at Lidcombe will do the rest," she said, refer-ring to the government laboratories. My daughter's sharp intake of breath came down the line. "Dad, we've been waiting for so long. We might never get another chance."

"I know, honey. I know. Okay. I'll gather up the doings and leave it in the designated spot."

This was in the boot of my daughter's car. I held a spare key to that as well as a key to her house.

"I expect to be called out any time now. The local uniforms have called in the homicide people and they'll call me. It's down on Vale Street. I'm just finishing another job but I'll take my car home and pick up some extra gear on the way there."

I could barely speak. "Yes," I finally croaked. "You do that."

Over the time I've been fishing with Twigg, I've gathered up a bloodstained rag from when he'd cut himself on his knife while gutting a fish, and I also have an old chisel that he'd used on his catch, whacking them on the head with a killer blow. He thought he'd lost the chisel when a big wave broke over the rock ledge we were fishing from. He doesn't know that I dropped it into my tackle bag.

Over the years, Claire, Kerryanne, and my surviving son Tim, now away in the west with his wife and family, had discussed the plan with me until there was no further doubt in anyone's mind that what we were formulating was morally acceptable, if not legal. There is a higher law, as Claire had once said. "So we're all agreed?" I asked, last time we got together to talk about it.

They'd all nodded and Claire wiped away a tear. "It's the right thing to do," she said, and I put my arm around her.

I turned to my daughter. "Kerryanne, you realize the risk to you? You could be prosecuted. You would lose your job and you'd never get another job anywhere in your field. You could face prison for perverting the course of justice. You're the one facing the biggest risk."

"No one will find out, Dad," she'd said. "How could they? No one here will speak about it, and no one else knows. And I won't be conspiring to pervert the course of justice. I'll be doing the opposite."

Back home, I washed up, cleaned the two bream I'd caught, and put the bream, minus their heads, loosely covered into the fridge. Claire was making my favorite, macaroni and cheese, for lunch.

"Kerryanne called," I said. "I need to duck out now." I took a deep breath. "Today's the day."

Claire looked up from grating cheese, fixing her brown eyes on mine as the significance of what I'd just said hit her. "What will I do if you two end up in jail?"

"Not going to happen, love," I said, kissing the top of her head. "Kerryanne knows her job. She'll do the job and do it well. And she'll make sure she does it in a way that's unde-tectable. I'll suggest to her to make sure the items are in situ when the video unit people start. Or she'll do the photographic work herself."

"But what about the other one? The real perpetrator?"

"Kerryanne and I will work something out."

I had wrapped the bloodstained rag and the small chisel very carefully without touching them, using my fish-scaling gloves. I knew that I'd need to be quick now.

The drive to Kellyanne's only took nine minutes. Her station wagon was parked in her driveway and I quietly opened her boot, putting the items in their paper bag safely inside. She had a lot of gear stacked neatly in the boot: heavy-duty exhibit bags, reels of security tape to seal these with and sign, and several large cases with cameras and other equipment. I closed the boot and looked around. There was no one about and my daughter's driveway is shaded by interlocking trees. I drove home and washed up.

The story broke on the evening news. A man had been found murdered in a house in Clovelly. Channel 9 cameras showed a neat little 1920s bungalow with crime scene tape sealing off the area around it and several uniforms and a detective standing nearby. Police had cordoned off the area, the newsreader said, and were talking to local residents. Little detail was released. Police were "continuing with their inquiries."

I couldn't sleep that night. I wondered about the victim, who'd killed him and why, though that was no longer my job anymore. I lay awake, hoping that everything was working out as we'd planned. That Kellyanne had been able to do her sleight of forensic hand and that she'd come away from the crime scene with two separate exhibit bags, one containing what she'd found at the scene of the crime, the other containing the material I'd given her. I felt I'd lit the wick and now I just had to wait.

The following morning, Kerryanne came over for breakfast. Claire had cooked grilled tomatoes and sausages and I poured tomato sauce all over mine.

My daughter grimaced. "That reminds me of yesterday's crime scene."

"So what was it? What happened?"

"A guy with his head bashed in, in his kitchen. The back of his head completely stove in, like he'd been hit with a sledgehammer from behind and a little to one side. Most of his brains were on the floor." Then she smiled at me and added,

"Curiously, there was an old chisel with a rag around it, which wasn't the murder weapon from the look of the injuries to the skull. But Jeff down at the morgue will no doubt let us know more about what kind of weapon was used. And it's possible that the chisel could have been used to break in."

"It'll have to be accounted for," I said, grinning back, spearing a sausage, while Claire looked first at me and then at her daughter.

"So it appears to be two offenders," Kerryanne said.

"What do we know about the deceased?"

"Name is Dudley Russell O'Dea. Released from the Bay about a month ago after doing time for GBH. He was living with his elderly sister on Vale Street."

"And the sister?" I asked.

"She didn't hear a thing—she's deaf and she'd gone to bed early. Poor old thing, she's very shaken up. The kitchen was accessed through the back door. There's some indication of a forced entry. Could've been that chisel," Kerryanne said, glancing over at me as I stabbed the last bit of sausage. "Two killers, eh? Could be something to do with payback for a jail altercation."

"Nasty," I said, getting up and clearing my plate away.

Claire looked at me and asked, "So it's in the bag?"

"I wouldn't say that," Kerryanne responded, "but it's in the trap, Mum. There's a ways to go yet. Once the DNA analyses are processed, things will be clearer. Whoever did this will almost certainly have form and they'll be in the database."

I kissed my daughter on the cheek as I removed her empty plate and stacked it in the sink with mine. "See," I said, turning around and leaning back against the sink, "my fishing companion has kept out of trouble for the last few years, but he's got previous violent form. And he got away with murder nineteen years ago."

"And he'll never plead guilty to this crime," said Kerry-anne. "He'll be screaming blue murder how he didn't do it! The judge won't like that at all."

"And he didn't do it," I said. "Not this one, anyway." I was smiling as I washed the dishes. I was determined to be there when the warrant was served. I wanted to see this for myself. And then I wanted to go to the trial and hear the sentence. I hoped it would be long. I wanted that man in prison, somewhere tough, where he could stew about the terrible miscarriage of justice that had sent him there. But it wasn't a miscarriage of justice. It was the rectification of justice delayed. He'd pay a debt that he owed the state and the society he lived in. Not to mention his debt to us, murdering our eldest son. That dreadful night is burned into my memory, the cops coming to the door. From their faces, I knew it was death. I'd delivered those death notices myself years ago, and it was the most difficult part of the job. I knew before they spoke that it would be Anthony because the other kids were safely here with their mother and me. I remember my legs buckling and how I had to lean against the wall before I could let them in. Then Claire's terrible screams.

"Better get to work, Dad, Mum," Kerryanne was saying, kissing us both. "I'll let you know what's happening."

A week later, the story was all over the evening news again, with more detail. Police were now searching for two men whom they hoped would, help them with their inquiries. I wondered if an anonymous tip-off might be in order concerning the whereabouts of my fishing companion, but I decided against any further involvement. The plans that I'd been making for almost two decades now were coming to fruition and I whistled as I tended the veggie garden, pinching out the laterals on my young tomato plants and staking them to keep them upright and healthy. I felt that I could enjoy my retirement more now that justice was about to be done. My whistling stopped as I approached the *Banksia serrata* we'd planted in memory of Anthony, a huge gnarled tree now where lorikeets and honeyeaters feasted when the banksia cones were fresh and green. "We're getting justice for you, son," I whispered to the tree. I stood a moment in the garden, watching a lone bee zigzag around the basil plants, then went back inside.

Kerryanne dropped by briefly on her way to her boyfriend's place and I made her a cup of tea. "Twigg's DNA and his fingerprints were found at the O'Dea crime scene, Dad. The other accused has latched onto the notion that someone else was involved, and he's screaming that he's innocent of the murder, that it was the other guy who swung the murder weapon. Which hasn't been found yet. Probably chucked into the ocean the same night."

"Couldn't have wished for a better outcome, darlin'," I said as I poured her tea into her old bunny mug that she still liked to use.

"Me neither. It's very satisfying."

"Any regrets?" I asked.

My daughter shook her head. "Not one. It's like a transferable ticket. He skipped out of one murder but he's going to be in the frame for another one. You do the crime, you do the time. Even if it's been billed to another account."

A week later, my insider from the homicide squad tipped me off: "They'll be serving the warrants for the arrest of the two men wanted for the murder of O'Dea. Later on today. Can't give you an exact time."

Later on today was good enough for me. I wanted to be there; I wanted to witness the beginning of the end of the slow burn; and I wanted to somehow convey to him—while remaining unidentifiable—that this wasn't a random mix-up, this wrongful arrest. I wanted to link it back to what happened to our son, so that Twigg understood that the lady with the blindfold and the scales had finally caught up with him.

I hurried to the vacant house on foot and turned onto the lane behind it to check the shed. I didn't want Twigg going out somewhere because that way I'd miss seeing the third last chapter of the retributive justice plan enacted, the second last chapter being his trial, and the final chapter being his incarceration for a very long time.

I peered through a crack in the fence. The old cat was stretched out there in the sunshine with ants clustered on the bowl of curdled milk and I could see that he needed a good feed but at least was getting a nice snooze in the sun. The shed door was closed though a piece of fabric draped over the inside of the window had sagged, allowing me to see Twigg moving around inside. My mobile chimed and I grabbed it. My friend on the inside, alerting me that the arresting officers were on their way.

I didn't have long to wait. I saw a tall guy in uniform and a middle-aged detective walking down through the garden, from the front of the property. The cat sat up as the two men made their way through the long grass, watching warily as the uniformed officer rapped on the door. Twigg opened it, his scowl speed-changing from irritation to disbelief. Before he could speak, the uniformed officer grabbed him and cuffed him while the detective presented the warrant for his arrest in the matter of the murder of Dudley Russell O'Dea.

"What are you talking about?" Twigg yelled, struggling.

"Murder? I don't know anyone called O'Dea! There's been a mistake. Get your hands off me!"

They dragged him out of the shed, easily managing him between the two of them. Twigg was yelling, "You've got the wrong man! I don't even know him!"

"You know him well enough to leave your fingerprints at the crime scene, Ronny," said the detective.

The cat suddenly bolted around the shed and disappeared into the long grass, frightened by the yelling.

"You can't just haul me off like this. Who'll look after my cat?"

"Stuff your cat, Ronald," said the detective. "That's the least of your troubles."

I jumped onto a bin, climbed over the fence, and dropped to the other side, taking the police and Twigg by surprise. "Stay back, sir," said the detective. "This is police business."

"Sure," I replied, "happy to comply. But I just wanted a word with my fishing mate before you take him away. You're worried about your cat, Twigg? Probably kinder for it to be put down. It's not in a good state."

Twigg paused in his struggles, trying to make sense of what was happening. Then, with all the years of pain, rage, and frustration concentrated into one laser-like beam of fury, I said, "If you're so worried about your cat, why don't you just . . . cut his throat?"

For a few long seconds I stared at Twigg's face before hauling my bulk ungracefully back over the fence. Then I chinned myself up and looked at Twigg being dragged toward the front of the property.

He had twisted around between the two officers and when he saw me his face registered shock and bewilderment. He tried to jerk away from the arresting officers, screaming his head off. And I knew then that he was desperately scanning his memory, trying to place who it might be among his jailbird mates to whom he'd so foolishly big-noted himself when he was a stupid kid, who'd set him up like this, and trying to work out how the man he'd been fishing with seemed to know about a nineteen-year-old murder. I also hoped that years later, if he ever worked out who I was, the prison officers would say, *Sure, Ronny, pull the other one.* In that moment, I felt the deep satisfaction that, although a long time coming and in a very elliptical fashion, justice had finally been done.

I went home with the cat under my arm and I put him in the laundry with some water, a dirt tray, and a nice bream fillet. I thought I could hear him purring as I closed the laundry door.

BLACK CUL-DE-SAC

BY PHILIP MCLAREN

Redfern

It is around two a.m. and dark; council workers stopped replacing streetlights in this narrow alley behind the old Chippendale brewery years ago, it is simply too dangerous. Stoning outsiders is commonplace for the youth down here in the slums, and good sport. The same goes for most other cul-de-sacs in the aboriginal enclave of Redfern at night: black.

Pools of several too-bright LED flashlights survey the area adjacent to the bloodied, spread-eagled body. As police vehicles arrive, headlights are left on as well as the rotating red, white, and blues, and wipers—the autumnal tropical deluge has been bucketing down for days.

I push past the first line of cops, flashing my ID card as I go, sheltering under my large golf umbrella. I am the first person police call regarding black deaths; it's protocol. I'm black. I'm the aboriginal liaison for this region; a politically appointed watchdog, I watch cops and how they deal with aboriginal people. The history of black deaths in custody sparked a demand for oversight. The lifeless man lying in the alley is also black.

I'm from the Kamilaroi Nation. Both my mum and dad are Kamilaroi, from Coonabarabran and Gunnedah in the western region of the state, but I was born in rundown Redfern thirty-two years ago. I still live here but on the other side, it's not as tough over there, went to school and university just up the road, played all my football here.

The middle-aged plainclothes senior detective at the center of the group looks up as I approach. Dicky Henderson is his name, Tricky Dicky, looks like Nixon too.

"Hey, Craig, good to see you. Now I can go back to bed." He is only half-joking. He puts on that counterfeit smile. He knows it annoys me. Fuck!

"G'day." I force a phony cheery note into my voice.

"You reckon this is a good day? It's a bit fucking wet."

I ignore him. I walk to the body and flash some LED of my own. So much blood and so much money, fifty-dollar bills all strewn about, then I see the battered face. "Oh shit."

"Know him?"

"Yeah . . . I know him. He's my cousin."

"Sheeet, all you guys are cousins."

There is much to irritate me in this man's voice. "No, really, Dicky." He hates me calling him that. "He's my first cousin. I saw him last night at my aunt's place." I pause and lower my voice. "His name is Lally Cameron. He lives . . . *lived* a bit farther up this street, over there, second house from the end." I point to the house.

All the residents of the street are looking on, mainly black faces, while kids and adults are being interviewed by uniformed cops.

I sit on my haunches for a closer look. Fuck! He's been seriously bashed, very seriously bashed, something solid has been used on his head and upper torso, a tire iron maybe. His skull has been cracked open and pieces of his brain sit on the wet asphalt, his half-empty cranium is full and spilling rainwater; some teeth cling to his gums. A nauseating odor comes from the mess.

"Sorry, mate." Dicky's speech is muffled. He is one of those old codgers who barely moves his lips to talk. "Were you close?"

"Yeah, kind of, there were Christmases and holidays. We grew up together."

Dicky looks up the street as I speak. I guess he is trying to figure out who Lally's family are from the drenched rabble.

"Yeah, he lived with us for a while, just him, for a whole school term, don't know what was going on in his family at that time. He was five years older than me. There's a big Coonabarabran mob here in Redfern, all related. A few other Coonabarabran families live on this street as well as the Camerons."

Just then the FSG—forensic science group—arrive and shepherd us away from the body. A taped-off no-go zone is being established. I push up against the high brick wall of the brewery; Dicky follows suit. The rain continues.

"Do you want to work with us on this or . . . ?" He leaves the question dangling.

"If that's okay?"

"Good, yeah, fine, let me know when and for how long."

"I'll talk to you, maybe at the debrief, whenever."

"Right, say at ten this morning?" Dicky is eager to pass this mess onto me to sign off on. Black deaths in this town can have unforeseen consequences.

"Yeah, ten is good."

We both fall into a pact of silence and listen to the waking city as early-morning workers start to fill its arteries.

Last week Lally had come to the door of my aunt's small two-up two-down terrace house on William Street. I was sleeping on her couch while I looked for another flat. They were pulling my old place down. Progress. Lots of "progress" going on in Redfern lately, politicos are adopting the successful New York "broken windows" theory. Repair the architecture and the crime rate drops. Lally lived about a mile away. He'd been doing some serious drinking. He was almost incoherent. My aunt wouldn't let him in.

"Come on, Auntie, come on, just tonight. I'll sleep on the floor, it's pouring out here. You won't even know I'm there."

"No, Lally, go home." Auntie Joyce spoke with her cheek up against the closed door.

"They won't let me in down there."

"Of course they'll let you in."

"I'm telling you, they won't let me in, Aunt . . . not when I've been drinking."

I was sitting at the dining table and didn't want to intervene but was compelled to call out from the next room. "Go home, Lally!" I shouted in my deep other voice.

"Craigie? Hello, Craigie . . ."

"Go home, Lally," Auntie Joyce said again softly.

"Drugs, Auntie."

"What?"

"Drugs, I'm off my head, Auntie—drugs, lots of drugs, I'm using and can't go home. Just need to sleep."

She let him in, filled him with hot coffee, and an hour later he left, sheltering beneath her floral umbrella. He was singing "Rocky Mountain High." We could hear his voice fading off as he staggered up the middle of the narrow street: ". . . *going home to a place he'd never been before . . . He left yesterday behind him . . . you might say he was born again . . . born again.*"

I stay behind after Lally's body has been removed from the alley and all the cops have left. I want to see his mother and her family at her house. By this time the rain has eased a little.

"I'm sorry, Auntie," is all I can say, all I can get out. I pull her to me.

"It's okay, boy," she whispers as we hug. "The poor little

bugger done a lot of bad things, but he didn't deserve this."

"That's right, Auntie, you're so right," I mumble. I'm hopeless, anything I think to say sounds trivial. Usually I say as little as possible.

In the room are Lally's three sisters, all red-eyed, all stunned to silence. Auntie sits down and a tabby cat leaps onto her lap. She strokes the cat and it purrs. I ask what anyone knew or heard; shaking heads, nothing, no one heard or saw anything. Someone pushes a cup of tea in front of me and I drink it as we take turns recalling funny incidents involving Lally and we laugh. Relief. It's funny that, about grief.

Tucked away at the back of the morgue, the FSG crew has worked overnight. The evidence has been meticulously tagged, arranged, and spread over five stainless-steel trestles. Very anal-retentive people work in forensics. They are startled as I come through the automatic sliding doors into the great room at the center of their complex which butts up to the autopsy theaters next door.

"Woo, you're early . . . too soon!" says Matthew, the senior officer. The other two in the room just smile. "Nothing yet, I'm afraid."

"That's okay, I'm just on my way home, thought I'd pop in here first on the off chance."

The team resumes their work, which of course is more important to them; visitors are given second rank here. I admire the work ethic but the staff are difficult to engage.

"I'll take a look around, if that's alright."

"Goodo . . . but don't touch or move anything," Matthew says without looking up from the skull fragments and tissue that are placed like a hundred-piece jigsaw puzzle on his smaller bench. The pieces of what were my cousin's skull and brain. Matthew has an angioscope and a larger microscope—both have computer monitors linked to recording and printing devices.

I watch him work for a short time, fascinated. Ten minutes later I leave, uttering a polite goodbye. No one responds or even looks up.

Even though I am tired, I decide to walk the mile and a half to Auntie Joyce's place, through the university grounds and across Victoria Park. A couple of derelict men are there, sleeping rough.

You've never had to sleep rough, boy, my dad said to me a few years back, during a playful argument. He and my mother had slept under a tarpaulin hitched to a horse's sulky for the first two years of their married life. He worked as a boundary rider, fixing fences on large sheep spreads, out of town for weeks on end, sleeping rough. I told him that I had, many times—he knew very little about my hitchhiking, backpacking days. My thing between rides was to find a school as my overnight camping spot for when it got late. The old country school houses all had verandas, I slept on them. But my dad was right. I never had to, it was a choice that I made.

I arrived at the debriefing at the Redfern police station precisely at ten. The place was full, maybe fifteen detectives, some were chatting, someone laughed. I looked across. Must have been a joke. Dicky came in and all settled down, just a few muted whispers hissing about the place. In turn, everyone read from their notes. The upshot was nothing. There were no leads.

Dicky came up to me. "It'll be hard shit, this. Anyway, I got someone for you from downtown, you know, for you to work with."

"Who?"

"Brian Lynch."

"Lynchie the ex–footie player?"

"Yeah. Here's his number. Hook up today. Okay?"

"Right, okay."

I waited until I was outside to phone Lynchie. We got on well straightaway, we talked mostly about football. We laughed a bit. Over the following weeks I phoned him twice a day, but there were no leads.

We moved into winter in a blink. I braced against the cold wind as I walked out of Long Bay Correctional Centre after visiting a couple of blackfellas and headed for football training. It's Tuesday. I play in a semi-professional rugby league for the Redfern All Blacks, the local aboriginal team. It got harder to get fit once I hit thirty.

The Redfern All Blacks Rugby League Club advertised in the local newspaper, calling on those interested in playing in the upcoming season to register now. Last week me and two of my first cousins decided, over a beer, that we would roll up again. The reality of the hardship of preseason training didn't occur to us at the time.

Training is on Tuesday and Thursday nights, at seven, all winter. I arrive early. I like to kick the ball before training. The coach honks his horn and calls to us from his car as he arrives.

"Laps!" he yells. "Laps!"

There is the usual groan from the men as we form one large pack and set off on our four-lap warm-up run. Calisthenics and wind sprints follow. Then the coach forms us into our playing positions, working on coordinated plays. It takes an hour and a half in all. The Railway Hotel, the club's sponsor, is full of footballers by nine. It is our duty to support our sponsor, some club wit once said.

* * *

After another two weeks of training I feel a real physical difference, I'm more energetic, more alert than I've been for
years. But I won't give up the occasional beer, my card games,
or betting on the horse and dog races—and especially not my
nights out with my mates.

It's the first game day of the season. The C Grade, our
under-eighteen side, are playing as I arrive at the grounds.
Inside the dank dressing room, men's voices go up a few deci-
bels and down a few octaves, echoing through the communal
shower recesses. These are tough rugby-playing men, you can
tell just by their voices.

"You fucking blokes know what to do with these cunts.
Hammer them up the middle. I don't want any fancy stuff,
just hammer them. For the first twenty minutes just fucking
hammer them. If they've got the fucking ball . . . hammer
them. If we've got the fucking ball . . . hammer them. Don't
run around them. Run straight at the cunts!" The tall, thin,
red-haired coach pauses for breath. "What are we gonna do
to them?" he asks.

"Hammer the cunts!" the men shout in response.

"The big men up the middle for the first twenty . . . Okay?"

"Okay!"

"Pass back inside, okay?"

"Okay!"

"Hammer the cunts, right!"

"Right!"

"Say it! Hammer the cunts!"

"*Hammer the cunts!*"

The shouted strategy continues in the Redfern dressing
room, back and forth, until a few seconds before the game.

* * *

Two hours later we are back in the same stinking, steam-filled dressing room. We won 22 to 7. We, me included, had well and truly hammered the cunts. The defeated C Grade boys joined in the celebrations and led the singing of our club's victory song.

"Hey, uncle, you got the bastards who bashed Uncle Lally yet?" It was one of the younger players from the C Grade.

I'm on my back on the floor. "No, mate, still looking, lots of cops on it though. Me and Lynchie liaise, have catch-up calls most days. You know Brian Lynch?"

"No, I don't know him, never met him," he smiles, "but everyone knows Lynchie."

"Yeah, best halfback Australia ever had."

"Yeah . . . look, I heard something, uncle." The kid looks serious. "Cowboy Cassidy drank with Lally every morning at the Anchor, the early opener. Cowboy's a dealer. He's a bad cunt, uncle."

The Anchor Hotel is one of five Sydney early-openers that cater to the inner-city blue-collar shift workers. Of course there are the twenty-four-hour clubs, but Lally would never be allowed in those because often he'd arrive loaded. The Anchor was his favorite, according to his mum, and the closest to their place.

A barman is flushing the exterior walls and footpath of the Anchor with a garden hose as I approach. These types of places are tiled inside and out, like bathrooms, easy care, as often patrons could not keep their drink and fatty pub food down.

"Yep, I know Lally," the slim barman replies to my question as he keeps flushing. "Haven't seen him for a while. Is he okay?"

I tell him.

"Fucking hell!" He shakes his head.

"Do you know a bloke called Cowboy Cassidy?" I ask him straight-out.

"Cowboy?"

"Cowboy Cassidy."

"Oh, I know Cowboy pretty well, from the bush, a rodeo rider."

"Is he a dealer?"

"Yeah, but you didn't get that from me."

"Was Lally dealing?"

Slim turns the hose off and looks at me like I'm a kid. "D'you know Lally at all, mate?"

"He's my cousin."

"Ya cousin?" He stares into my face in disbelief, and speaks softly: "He's been dealing for fucking years, mate."

"I knew he smoked a bit . . ."

"Smoked? He was into fucking everything."

I watch his lips move as he rattles off the range of merchandise that Lally handled, which included handguns. I didn't know my cousin at all.

Slim tells me Cowboy comes in every day around eight. It's seven. I have an hour to kill. I slip him a twenty and we part.

I walk the few blocks to the busy wharves at the quay. The ferries are unloading their people cargo in the center of the city. The sun is shining. It is a crisp winter day. I sit near the jetties, mesmerized, watching the sparkling sunlight on the surface of the water, eating hot chips from a cardboard carton. I wonder what life would have been like for the blacks living here before the British landed. Aboriginal people claim they've always occupied this land and never migrated here, as most academics say. The blackfellas simply reverse the logic—if people could walk south over the so-called land bridge which joined Australia to Asia, then surely they could also have walked north. After all, the most ancient evidence of human habitation has been found right here.

Just then, an unassuming aboriginal man carrying a long, elaborately painted didgeridoo takes up a position next to me. He peels off his shirt, reaches inside a carry bag, and pulls out several small jars of body paint. A few people stop to watch. He applies the paint in long stripes, first to his torso then to his arms, crimson oxide, yellow ochre, and white. The crowd swells to more than twenty. Now he paints his face using colored dots and concentric circles.

The crowd has increased to around fifty. He slowly secures the paint jars, takes up his instrument, and begins to play. The droning music from the hollow log reverberates through the quay. He closes his eyes, totally absorbed in the melancholic drone, oblivious to the coins and notes being placed in his large upturned cap.

I finish my chips and walk behind the busker and across the historic cobblestone road back to the Anchor Hotel. It is five after eight.

I perch at the end of the bar away from a pack of noisy desperates arguing with each other, barely able to sit. The thin barman recognizes me, acknowledged by a head nod, then he comes down.

"He's not here yet. Want a beer?"

"Yeah, sure, Tooheys New, a schooner," I say without meeting his eyes. I am busy looking about.

I pull out my phone.

"Hi, Lynchie here, mate."

"I'm following a lead, a name, meeting with a bloke that might know something."

"What's his name?"

"Cowboy Cassidy . . . Do you know him?"

"Never heard of him. Who's the informant?"

"A young kid from the football club."

"What's the connection?"

"Drugs, he says."

"Okay . . . get back to me after you talk to him."

As I hang up, Slim arrives with my beer and spins away without breaking stride. I glance about the bar. It is dim, hard to tell what time it is, not much daylight in this place. It is 8:20. The television is tuned into a sports betting channel; somewhere in the world there is always a horse or dog race to bet on, to lose your money on. Most pubs in Australia are licensed to take bets on any televised event. I couldn't help watching, there's something about a live race. I choose horse number two as they jump out of the starting gates; he settles behind the leading pack of five bolters, makes a race of it, down the final straight, he charges at the leaders, shit, can't quite make it, comes in third.

Slim slides off his stool by the cash register, looks my way, and rolls his eyes at the double doors. The short guy who enters is not what I expected. He is gray-haired, wears a long winter coat two sizes too big with his sleeves rolled up; he is tough-looking, a pug, an ex-boxer for sure, but you know, really, he is an old man, seventy easily, maybe seventy-five. He takes a stool at the bar near the rabble. I sort out my options, how to play this, writing scripts in my head like I'm in a movie. He takes a beer from Slim and makes his way down the bar to me.

"You looking for me?"

"Maybe, yeah. Are you Cowboy?"

"That's right."

"I have a small location that I want to enlarge."

"I'm not into real estate, sorry." He turns to walk away.

"Me neither. I have a good few medicinal patrons in my location."

He stops and shoots me a smile. I try not to stare at his rotting yellow-and-brown teeth. "Where is your location, mate?"

"Redfern."

His eyes narrow. "Don't I know you from somewhere?"

"I don't think so."

He takes a deep breath. "I got weed, hash, ice, all kinds of uppers and downers. It's good Aussie weed, I know the growers, from Griffith." He pauses. "What do you need?"

"I'll take your weed to start with."

"How much you want?"

"How much will two thousand dollars buy?"

"A suitcase will set you back two. That's for twenty kilos. It'll retail for four after you rebag it."

We have an agreement within a minute. I'll bring two thousand, he'll bring a full suitcase. He wants to meet that night at one a.m. in the cul-de-sac at the back of the Chippendale brewery. Oh shit.

He walks away, didn't drink his beer, not one sip, leaves it on the bar. He waves at Slim and is through the double glass doors in double-quick time.

I call Lynchie straightaway to bring him up to speed.

"So you want to meet with him, do the deal?"

"Fuck yeah!"

"Okay, just asking. You reckon he'll be alone?"

"My feeling is yes, but I'm not ruling anything out. This bloke works for the Griffith families. He can't fuck up."

"But he might only be interested in your cash with no trade . . . freelance."

"That occurred to me too."

"And two thousand dollars is chicken feed, surely."

"Yeah."

Lynchie goes into cop mode: "Okay, I'm gonna get there early, about eleven, and blend into the end of the street. And I'm gonna sign for a pump-action, just in case. I'm not fucking around with this bloke."

It's after one a.m. I caught four hours of sleep and now I'm standing at the corner of the Chippendale cul-de-sac under a streetlamp. I see Cowboy coming toward me wheeling a big tourist-style suitcase. I nod as he gets closer, then I walk up into the alley. I look at the pile of trash at the end of the lane where Lynchie is hidden, nothing suspicious there. Cowboy stops ten paces from me.

"You got the two thousand?"

"Yeah, it's right here." I pull a bulging envelope from my coat as Cowboy steps away from the suitcase.

"Put it on the case," he says.

I move the few paces to the case slowly, not taking my eyes off him. Immediately as I place the money on the case, he lunges at me with a steel pipe in both hands, gripping it like a baseball bat. The sucker punch. First swing, he breaks my arm as I shield my face. I fall. I yell. He is quick to belt me on my shoulder and up the side of my face. He belts me again on my neck. *Fuck, I've had it here!* I think, or maybe I say it.

"You cunt!"

He runs at me with the pipe over one shoulder. I can only put both arms up to shield my head and kick at him, then *BLAM!* The whole alley gets lit up from the explosion rushing down the barrel of Lynch's shotgun. *BLAM! BLAM! BLAM!* Cowboy falls to one side midstride; his chest is ripped open and blood gushes through his shirt. I pass out.

* * *

Next I'm being treated by medics. The alley is filled with police cars and lit by their headlights plus the red, blue, and whites rotating, plus an ambulance and coroner's van. Lynchie is sitting on the ground, spent. He is being interviewed by cops.

I call out, "It was a justified kill." I say this over and over. "It was a justified kill." I'm in shock. "A justified kill."

It is around two a.m. and dark behind the old Chippendale brewery, back to normal. It is simply a dangerous place to be at night. The same goes for most other cul-de-sacs in the aboriginal enclave of Redfern at night. Black.

CHINAMAN'S BEACH

BY P.M. NEWTON

Mosman

A text message: *WE MUST TALK. COME TO MY HOME. NOW. PLEASE.*

It's the *please* that stands out.

The old man never says please. You've spent a lifetime lifting rocks just to see what crawls out, cramped nights in cars watching the windows of his house, afternoons following him round the bookmakers' ring at Randwick, pressing up behind him, so close you can hear the click of his tongue when he settles on a bet, and yet you've never heard him say please. Not once. Not to anyone.

I sit at the traffic lights and stare at my phone. That *please* sits mute and strange. A horn blast from the rear tells me the lights have changed. A slow grind forward, but we don't go far. The rat run past Military Road on a Saturday morning is as choked with traffic as the main road. I come to a halt, still sandwiched between a Range Rover and the horn-happy bald bloke in an iridescent-red convertible. Sunlight catches Mr. Convertible's Ray-Bans, classic Aviators of course, and bounces off the helmet of perfect blond hair on the woman next to him.

I know what I should do. Call it in. That'd be the sensible, proper course of action. I even snap to my contacts, scroll through, and hover, but then I let the phone drop back into my lap.

Almost make it to the bottom of Spit Road before the bridge goes up. Nothing for it but to switch off the ignition and wait. The deck swings open. The tips of masts glide through the gap. All those oversized yachts heading out for a day's racing on the harbor. Never into boats, the old man. Middle Harbour Yacht Club almost on his doorstep and he'd never spent a cent buying friends and status down here among the deck-shoe mob. That's what racehorses were for. A more forgiving crowd at the track. More fluid. Punt up, pay up. Buy fast horses. Win big races. And watch the doors fly open all over this town.

Great place to give your money a tub too. The track, that is. A rich man once likened yacht racing to standing under a cold shower tearing up hundred-dollar bills. The track and the bookmakers, well, they're a lot kinder to money that might have a bit of dirt under its nails.

The Saturday Spit Road traffic inches down the hill to merge and crawl across the bridge. High sandstone and scrub to my right, a deadly drop down to blue water on the left. A crane, tall enough to build an office tower, rests on a platform of concrete just off the footpath. It lowers the makings of a new harborside palace down the escarpment like a big metal bird lining a big metal nest. Cost of a suburban Sydney apartment right there just in the tool hire. Weekend rates too.

The switchback off Parriwi, past large old houses with larger leafy gardens, safely enclosed behind walls of stones and security cameras, runs down to Cyprian and into McLean. The road cuts back and forth, revealing glimpses of tennis courts, pools, rockeries, and ferns.

The old man had gone for something more classic than a glass-and-pile shard clinging to the side of a cliff. A big house, behind a big electric gate, at the end of a cul-de-sac. I like to think I sent him here. The old mansion in Balmoral was where I'd sat outside and watched him from my car as he'd go from room to room, shuttering the blinds against me. He'd been well-settled there in Balmoral. Christmas drinks with the neighbors by invitation only, grudging respect turning to abject envy once they spied the jade, the silk rugs, the museum-worthy antiques. Hard-earned, that respect. I'd chipped away at it. Evidence to various commissions, the ones that compel you to talk then lock you up for lying but rarely, oh so rarely, ever charge anyone with the dirt that gets uncovered. Reputation ruiners, coupled with the odd drop of gossip to a hungry journo. Auto-da-fé by headline. No smoke without fire. The RSVPs dwindled. And then the old man who never said please sold up and moved.

It was still Balmoral. Technically. A little pocket of park and beach and a thin golden strip of sand washed by the tide of Sydney Harbour. Safe for toddlers and waders. Quiet. Secluded. Chinaman's Beach.

The subbies had had a bit of fun with that. If you look on a map, *Cobblers Bay* is written over the blue bit, *Rosherville Reserve* over the green bit, but everyone knows the yellow bit in between it is Chinaman's. There'd been market gardens back in the day, parkland now where dog walkers and fitness instructors drill their charges. A perfect little piece of paradise, where the neighbors keep their thoughts to themselves and the old man keeps himself to himself, and that's how everyone likes it.

The old man's security gate is metal of some kind, the color of sand, inobtrusive. A security camera looks on as I roll down the window and press the intercom. The gate melts away. A walled driveway curves to the left, trees and undergrowth block any other view. The seclusion of the rich and the dangerous. I raise my foot from the brake and the car rolls through in automatic, starts dragging itself forward over the gravel. The gates swing shut behind me. Silently.

Last chance to call someone. But I dismiss it. Call who? Say what? *Hi, thought I should let you know I've accepted the invitation of the crook I've been stalking for close to twenty years?*

The move to Chinaman's hadn't changed that, my stalking. Not once I found the ruin. Great old house caught up in family hatreds. Millions of dollars' worth of art deco and views left to molder while relatives brawled over the estate of an old woman in a dementia unit. Chain wire around it. Graffiti on every wall. It was a top spot for young Balmoral kids to hide their bongs and dream of putting on a dance party.

For me, the climb up the once-grand, now-slimy concrete staircase to the turret provides an excellent view of the old man's hideaway. Those walls. That driveway. The shrubs and trees lull him into sloppiness. A pair of binoculars and a night-scope borrowed from a tactical unit who'd left their kit bag unattended, and I can watch the old man shuffle around his back terrace in his slippers, hawking a night's worth of phlegm into the gardenias. When his son visits, they sit for hours at a time beside the pool, papers and laptops spread around them. Occasionally the old man jumps in and strides up and down, performing some kind of angry aquatic tai chi. He's built like a wiry old piece of teak, the kind of body that speaks of harder violent times. The old man's wife is rarely more than a shadow moving behind curtains. Only the presence of the son ever draws her outside, to deliver tea, water, to rest a hand on his shoulder, to stand behind him stroking his head. I've never seen her touch the old man.

Magpies and currawongs call warnings and threats to each other from the trees when I get out of the car. The cedar door opens immediately and the figure behind it beckons me in. First time I've seen him up close without the benefit of a search warrant, a courtroom, or a commission, a wall of lawyers.

He's older. Smaller. Bare-handed. In his thin knit sweater and light cotton trousers he looks ready for a round of golf.

"Thank you for coming so promptly, detective. Please come into the lounge room."

First time he's ever spoken to me, directly. Formal and polite, he ushers me into a light-filled room where a small woman sits on the edge of an antique ebony Chinese stool. She faces the door, a small automatic pistol in her hand, pointed at us. The gun looks heavy. She looks tired. I freeze in the doorway.

The old man's voice comes over my shoulder, reassuring, soothing. It's like the *please*—it doesn't fit. "I do apologize, detective. But my wife is not feeling very well. I assure you that if you do what she asks, you—that is *we*—will come to no harm."

I risk a glance back at him, the question, *What do you mean* we? forming. Sweat beads his upper lip and his forehead, and there is a small tremor in his hands as he smoothes down the sides of his pants.

I focus again on the woman. She's sitting primly, neatly dressed in a suit, stockings, high heels, makeup in place, knees pressed together. She's got the gun in both hands, which rest on her upper thighs. She sits on her stool, on either side of which sit two large suitcases.

I try for an unthreatening tone, inquiring, not interrogating: "What's the problem, ma'am?"

The woman turns her beautifully outlined eyes on me. Behind the makeup they're not so young and they're filled with pain. "My son," she says, and gestures with the gun at the suitcases.

"You're leaving him? To go to your son?" I do my best to

ignore the gun, hope she just wants a lift, but the woman looks at me uncomprehendingly.

The old man clears things up: "My son is in those two suitcases, detective. My wife found them at our front door this morning. She opened them. It has . . . disturbed her mind."

What I'd taken for shadows in the pattern of the rug around each suitcase I see now as dark stains spreading across the thick silk.

"What does she want?" I whisper over my shoulder.

"My wife has been a very unhappy woman for very many years. I have caused that. She has never been," he pauses to choose the right word, "comfortable with my business interests. This morning she tried to shoot me. She has decided that it all finishes. Now. She wants us to walk out of this house and leave it all behind. She wants me to tell you everything in return for protection and immunity. She wants us to leave with you, now."

I disobey every instruction I was taught at the police academy and turn my back on someone with a gun.

Something green and glassy lies splintered all over the floor behind the old man. There's a toppled wooden pedestal and a telltale hole in the white plastered wall at head height. A matching pedestal, still upright, flanks the other side of the doorway; a giant jade horse still prances on it, intact.

I wonder if the old man has thought to count the shots.

"Your wife arrested you?"

"She convinced me I have no immediate alternatives. She has not convinced me that we have a long-term chance."

That *we* again. The old bastard's casting me as his fucking Tonto.

"What do you mean?"

"Those who killed my son are powerful. You may know

that. I thought I could control them but there are bigger play-ers in the game than I assumed. A miscalculation of risk on my behalf. It is my belief that I have become irrelevant, there-fore redundant. If we can make it out of this house, detective, then maybe we have a chance."

Put like that, it sounded almost noble. But killing the son, chopping him up, and sending him home? That was just flam-boyant. An MO that fit the old world and the new.

My sources had kept me briefed. The son with his plans to expand. The old man with his old world ties to triads and tongs and tradition, he was just slowing a young man down. Old-fashioned thinking. A biz needs fresh blood if it's going to grow. A couple of paparazzi shots in the Sunday papers of the son riding a Harley, a custom number, throbbing up Campbell Parade for a lunch at Bondi Icebergs even gave it all a touch of glamour.

In reality, various deals with various devils on moving mountains of meth, and it'd all come down to a couple of suitcases bleeding on a silk rug.

Time to make a call. The crafty old bastard's right. A bunch of cops, armed response, a heavy presence, and we just might make it out.

And then?

The return of the lawyers and the commissions and the deals and the negotiations.

I take another look at the woman and ask her, "What do you want?"

She stares at the old man. The gun propped between her thighs, barrel centered on his body mass. It strikes me that I've never heard her say a word. Even the rare occasions we bugged the office or the car. Not a sound. Maybe she doesn't speak English.

"I want him to pay."

Her voice is calm. Unaccented, stripped of emotion. Translucent. But I recognize myself in the eyes that meet mine. We can do business.

"Okay. Let's go."

"Please, detective, we will take my car, I think it is a little safer. There are certain design features, you understand." The old man trying to keep control.

The woman gets to her feet and gestures toward her son. The old man takes hold of the suitcases, places them into a small elevator. She prods him with the gun until he steps in. The doors close and we look each other in the eye.

I wonder if she recognizes me. The stalker in the car across the road. The cop with the warrant who turned up on their wedding anniversary. I've grown old watching them. Maybe she doesn't recognize me at all.

I almost tell her. Right then. Just the two of us, as the elevator takes the old man and his son down into the garage. I almost tell her what he did. And why I couldn't—can't—stop. But he's sent it back up; the doors open and we step in. The hand with the gun drops down at her side. I make no move to disarm her.

The Mercedes fills the garage. I've tailed it often enough to know it like it's my own. Tinted windows, bulletproof so the story goes, and bodywork that only hints at the depths of protection.

The old man pops the locks on the Merc, but as he lifts the first suitcase into the boot, his wife fires a shot into the wall behind his left shoulder. She doesn't flinch. My ears feel like they're hemorrhaging. The old man swings the bag out again, shuffles to the side of the car, and sets it gently on the backseat, places the second one on top. The woman climbs in alongside, rests one hand on the stained tan hide, and follows her husband's movements with her gun hand.

The old man slams the boot shut and moves to the driver's side, stopping to shut his wife's door. She fires another shot through the gap, vaguely aimed at his feet; it ricochets; the old man skips and jumps, but doesn't bleed.

"The detective drives."

The old man climbs into the front passenger side and I slide in behind the wheel, adjust the seat. The engine turns over like a big cat being stroked. The old man rummages for the garage remote. There's a beep from the backseat and the door opens soundlessly.

We roll out into the sunlight and I accelerate smoothly down the drive. The front gate swings open to another beep from the backseat and McLean Crescent opens up before us, houses to the left, Rosherville Reserve to the right. Barely eleven a.m., croissants and coffee still being dawdled over on the next-door balcony. A dog and kids bounce out of a car and make for the beach. In the park, flush up against the old man's fence, a fierce game of cricket breaks out between a bunch of big blokes with tattoos. A row of motorbikes line the boundary.

By my right temple, a corner of the driver's window crystallizes. A fine webbed tracery appears as if by magic in the dark glass, a complex mosaic of radiance and black.

No sound but the crack of bat against ball, or a sniper rifle with a suppressor from among the trees on the other side of the park.

I brake.

The old man touches me gently on the forearm. "The bulletproofing on this car is very good. It's working as it should."

I release the central locking, lean across him, and open his door.

"I needn't detain you any longer. Your wife, unfortunately, I'll need to charge with certain firearm offenses, but I think after a medical examination they may not proceed."

The old man looks at me, unguarded. He forcibly regains control of himself. "What do you mean?" He doesn't move.

The cricket game in the park is getting rowdy. Howzat!

"Condolences on the loss of your boy. We'll need a statement but there's no rush. You, sir, are free to go. Now."

"You can't do this. I came to you for protection. I want to speak to someone in charge. I want—"

"I made him call you," the woman says.

I lean over, unclip his seat belt, and shove. He's old but he's strong. He resists. Wraps his fingers around the seat belt.

"I wanted it to be you," she says, and slides forward in her seat, jabs the muzzle against the old man's fist, and squeezes the trigger.

The echo of the shot swallows his shriek. He tumbles out onto the driveway.

"I knew you'd know what to do," she says, letting the acceleration push her back into her seat. I put my foot down. The car door slams shut of its own volition as I power out of the drive.

I see the old man in my rearview mirror, scrambling on all fours across the gravel, tugging to close his gates, the remote in his wife's hand locking them open. There's a rumble like thunder as half a dozen Harleys sidle through the gate and I turn my eyes to the road.

McLean sweeps left back into Cyprian. We glide up Parriwi but I don't stop until we reach Military Road and the safety of the Saturday gridlock.

I turn in my seat to look at the woman. She leans forward and places the gun gently onto the center console. A small patch of her husband's blood is smeared over her chin. I use my thumb to wipe it off. She reaches out and pushes my hair back behind my ear. Like a mother would.

"I always wanted a daughter," she says and sits back, her arm draped around her only son.

GOOD BLOKE

BY PETER DOYLE

Edgecliff

I t was the usual thing: nine in the morning, Di settled behind the reception rostrum at New Beginnings Self-Care Center, the ambient playlist (Celtic harp today) murmuring in the background, a crystal wineglass of chilled Pellegrino with a sprig of mint and a slice of lemon. At thirtysomething, or maybe forty, Di looked healthy and elegant—*balanced*, you might say—and not like she had to work at it.

New Beginnings took up three rooms on the top floor in the rear of Riga House, a squat blue-gray box on noisy New South Head Road, opposite Edgecliff Station, which may have been a smart address once, back in the days of brown pebblecrete and white stucco, but nowadays, as the real estate guy had said, it was all about affordability. Di had opted for the second-most affordable suite in the place, nearly at the end of the corridor, beyond Competitive Dentistry and LaMarque Depilations but not as far back as the mysterious Just in Time Credit Solutions. Right opposite her was the frosted-glass door of Good Bloke Labor and Logistical. Contract laborers, warehousing services. The business, if you could call it that, run by Justin, her ex. A whole other story.

Despite the general seediness, Di had done the best she could with New Beginnings—potted palms and silk grass, a nice lounge, a small, not-tacky fountain, and simple consultation rooms at the back. The way she had it, she could sit at reception and do her work, see the customers coming down the hall, and have a nice smile ready for them before they even noticed her there.

When she'd arrived that morning, Timmy had been skulking near the lift doors, chatting with her two practitioners, hired just for the day. Charming them. He'd given Di his lost-boy grin. The lank hair over one eye, tat-shop leather coat with frayed lining trailing halfway down his thigh over battered jeans, all made for a nicely achieved vagabond look (or was it bold musketeer?), which worked on her a bit, she had to admit, but not that much. Di had headed straight into New Beginnings, the practitioners, Maddy and Kim, behind her, and in the absence of an invitation to come inside and wait, Timmy had shuffled back into the lift.

At nine thirty the first appointment, a mother and daughter from Bellevue Hill, arrived. Di sat them down in the lounge area, made a pot of lemon ginger tea, and while it was drawing discreetly texted Kim, waiting out the back, who appeared a moment later with Maddy. Kim was scheduled to do a myofascial release for the mother, and Maddy an essential oil emotional support session for the daughter. Later, when they'd finished and the credit cards were out, Di would give them all, practitioners included, caramel truffle tea.

Back at her perch, confirming appointments, booking practitioners, processing a few late web payments for tomorrow night's seminar ("Women's Financial Mindfulness"), she saw Bec, the receptionist at Good Bloke, come hurrying out of the lift. She waved absently at Di, unlocked the Good Bloke door, darted inside, barely a minute ahead of the Two Stooges. No friendly waves from them.

Five minutes later the lift bell rang again and Dave stepped out. Tall, okay-looking. He called hello to her, in his clear voice. That nice smile, the manners and looks, definitely enough to cast a spell. She could see it. But there were things there not declared. Seemed so, anyway, but she kept that to herself. Try not to judge, right? Dave, like her, like all of them, even the Stooges, staying clean a day at a time, trying to be open to whatever changes they might have to go through, agreeing maybe not in words exactly that they were all kind of on the same team. None of them was perfect. None of them even *adequate*, really, if it came down to it. But recovering. The line she recited often to herself.

Justin was last to arrive, via the stairs, a Fitness First back-pack on one shoulder, not carried loosely. Anything but. He slowed as he approached, peered through the door into Good Bloke to see who was there, then glanced at Di, nodded, gave a quick smile. He had that elsewhere look that she knew well. They'd been separated for four years now, though there was always stuff to deal with—who was taking Mimi to ballet to-morrow, to piano on Friday, to the weekend playdate—and they'd turned a corner this year, had mostly gotten past the embittered-ex thing, becoming whatever they were now. Friends. Wary friends.

But they never talked about the business, Justin's business— Di had drawn the line there. Not to say she didn't know a fair bit anyway. There was plenty of talk. At meetings, at the coffee shops. People weren't happy. She understood that. The hydroponic—okay, people could sort of accept that. But pow-ders were different. Thing is, as Di had said more than once, what do you do, form a lynch mob? Anyway, like they'd told her at the Al-Anon meetings she'd gone to when she was breaking up with Justin, ask yourself, *Is it my business? Is it really my business?* It was maybe a yes to the first, but definitely a no to the second.

Two minutes after Justin went in, Bec tottered out, holding her phone, cigs, and lighter, heading for the lift. She looked at Di and eye-rolled, came over to the door, and stage-whispered, "Fuck. It's all going on today."

Di nodded slowly.

"Something to do with—" and nodded in the direction of the lift.

Di knew. Timmy was in the shit. That much was obvious. Plus, she'd heard something yesterday. And there was that Fitness First backpack. Which she'd have rather not noticed.

But that was all the time Di had to give it: a Double Bay woman, hefty, arrived for her consultation. Di, all smiles and gentleness, ushered her into the free room, sat her down, poured her a tea. "Okay, so, let's talk about raw diets . . ." and as she closed the door caught a glimpse of a distressed, harried Andy bustling into Good Bloke.

Dave got himself a Diet Coke from the fridge in reception, plonked down in the armchair in Justin's office, and watched them all take their places. Awkward, bumping into each other. Justin came in, slung the backpack under the desk, shut the door, took the big chair, sat back, scowling.

Dave tried not to look at the backpack at Justin's feet. But he felt its radioactive force. The rest of them had all been heroin junkies, and for them okie-doke was just a little extra fizzy thing they did from time to time. But cocaine had been Dave's drug of choice. It didn't exert the same pull on him now, but still, he *felt* its presence.

The others felt it too: the excitement of the whack-up, the largest batch so far, the most pure, at the best price yet. The supply side was mostly a mystery, all they knew was it came from a Korean guy. They sort of knew it came on boats, and that the Koreans kept changing the method, and that had kept things reliable. So far.

This business with the powder had just more or less happened, when Justin's Korean mate approached him, and Justin had approached them, and they in turn had each spoken to one or two people *they* knew. By then their circles consisted of other former drug addicts. So it had come about almost by accident that the stuff was sold mostly by addicts who didn't use dope anymore. No one really planned it.

Dave had been the first to get the tap on the shoulder. He had sought counsel on the matter, confidentially, from Mac, who wouldn't make a yay-or-nay call on it, just put the responsibility right back on Dave: do whatever you do, he said, just be prepared to deal with the consequences, whatever they may be. So Dave in the end decided, fuck it, come this far, go with it.

But it was still too new a thing for him or for any of them to really weigh it all up: for one thing, they were making good money, so far expressed in new cars, better threads, jet skis, and holidays in Bali. But not quite at the level of real estate yet. And there was the anxiety, though they had their ways of dealing with that. They all knew, too, but hadn't discussed together the fact that people, their friends, took a dim view. But they, people they knew, didn't want to condemn or moralize either. None of them had ever met a recovering addict who actually supported drug prohibition—the addiction isn't in the substance, it's in us, in me, in you. Maybe it's like the ex-alcoholic who runs the bar, right? In fact, look at it this way: who better to sell drugs? No one was quite convinced by that line, but that was the sort of shit swirling around in their heads, understood between them, mostly unspoken. So far, though, so good. Maybe it was meant to be?

But the whack-up would have to wait. There was an emergency.

Justin leaned forward and, no smile, glanced toward tough, wiry, agitated Andy and said, "So?"

Andy sighed, searched out Justin's eyes, which remained distant. He looked at the floor then back at Justin again, then put his head down, apologetic. "So, yeah. It's what I thought. Timmy's been using."

"How long?"

Andy shrugged. "Couple of months."

"Our stuff?"

Shook his head. "Smack." He looked up, faced Justin. "But paid for with our stuff."

No one moved.

"He blew the lot."

"Smack from . . . ?"

Andy shrugged. "Don't know, mate. From the Cross. Lebs, whoever. I'm fucking gutted."

Another silence.

"What's he into us for?"

A pause. "Ten."

Head shakes and slow exhalations around the room. Next thing was obvious to all. The way drugs were dealt the world over: get a bag up front, bring back the money, and you get another bag. Fail to bring the money back and get a flogging. Then you're given time to make good. And if you don't make good, there's another flogging, only worse. The iron law. Timmy was due for a hiding.

The Stooges would arrange it. That's what they were for. Except none of them had dealt with this in recovery before.

Dave sat watching. Andy was scared, but not groveling. Justin kept silent, then swiveled around and peered through the window. An outlook, not much, back toward Paddington, a corner of Rushcutters Bay Park, but no harbor view from this angle. Turned back and looked at Andy, very directly now. Getting ready for the hard bit.

"He still using?"

"Been to detox. Got out two days ago. He's back at meetings."

Justin nodded this time.

"Slimy cunt," Stooge Brett muttered, then looked up, his mouth open. "Fuck. Sorry. I know, I know. But, fuck. You know?"

Justin turned to Dave. "What do you reckon?" with a little upward nod on the *you*, part challenge, part real question.

Dave inhaled quickly, let it out slow. He and Justin had a bond. They'd jailed together. For Dave, the last three years had happened way too fast for him to keep up, to understand: a bit of dabbling, for show, to fit in, a few more lines, and a few more, then finding out too late his interest in the stuff was serious, and that he'd already crossed over, but had no one he could really confide in, go to. Then the bust, the forced detox, a charge of deemed supply, then suddenly, real jail. He was out of his depth, scared. He did his best not to be noticed, hiding away in the gym. His sports background helped, but he was rugby union, eastern suburbs, private school, and inside it was all rugby league, western suburbs, public school. Dave had started using in jail—a suicide move, and he knew it. Sometimes he worked out with Justin, who was doing two years for the hydro crop, but who had gone into jail straight, and was staying clean inside. Knew the ropes, had respect. Not running any sort of obvious manipulation, invited Dave to tag along to a jail meeting. Dave went, pretending to be open, but inside sneering at the sharing, the stories, the earnest bullshit.

Then something in him worked loose. He started listening in a different way. He still felt like a fake, but bits of what he heard applied to him, no denying it. Justin continued to show kindness.

Then later, on the street, paroled a week after Justin, he kept up the meetings. That fraudulent feeling never really faded, though he got used to being there, got used to hanging out, taking it a day at a time, not using. He made friends. He talked to newcomers, even visited jail. When Justin started the labor hire business, he kept Dave in work, mostly the better jobs. When this other thing started up, Dave was the first one Justin invited in.

Now, the rest were waiting for him to speak. Dave felt himself torn in three different ways. What was the right thing to say?

But before he could speak, Andy blurted out, "Thing is, I feel responsible."

All eyes back to Andy now.

Andy looking from one to the other. "He fuckin' wasn't ready."

Still watching.

"We put him out there too early."

Justin nodded and looked at Dave again, still waiting.

Those few seconds had been enough. "Andy's right. We should've looked after him better. He can be a bit . . . flaky, we knew that. Our responsibility." Dave sat up a little straighter. "We deal with the consequences. All of us. So, I say no flogging, but obviously he can't sell gear for a while."

"Not ever," Noel speaking quietly. "He's a liability. In other ways."

A silence.

"I mean, that we don't know about."

"He didn't get busted," said Andy.

"Not that he told you."

Justin, looking closely at Noel now: "Something from your guy?"

Noel's *guy* was a cop. They'd gone to school together, played third-grade league together. The guy was bent, cheerfully so, always had been. These days Good Bloke bought him a regular drink in return for access to the police computer system and for whatever snippets he could pass their way. Other than Noel, none of them, not even Justin, knew who he was. He was reliably crooked, though, which in their game was gold.

Noel nodded. "Timmy was pinched for racking two months ago. Department stores. Sports gear. Cameras and shit. Hasn't come up yet. He's still on remand. Matters pending."

Heads shaking around the group, Brett muttering, "Jesus *fuck!*"

Andy went pale.

"Keeping that secret from us?" said Brett. "From everybody? I mean, how did he manage that?"

The thought in the room: what if Timmy *had* turned dog?

"He's downstairs now," said Andy. "Waiting. He wants to do the right thing."

"So he reckons."

Justin nodded. "Okay," he briskly reached for the bag at his feet, put it on the desk, "we better do this now, so we can all fuck off. Timmy's out of the rort. He's got to square up. Straightaway. Alright, Andy?"

Andy nodded gloomily. "He hasn't got a zack."

"How you cover it, that's your business."

A slow nod from Andy.

Justin unzipped the backpack and brought out a lumpy Coles plastic bag, set it on the desk. From that he took a flat package wrapped in clear thick plastic, like a packet of Chinese noodles, neatly taped at the ends, and carefully put it down on the desk. Then the small scales, no bigger than a phone, accurate from .01 up to 500 grams, the aluminum foil, the sandwich bags.

"Alright. Let's fuck this puppy."

Suddenly laughter. Relief, to be getting on with it.

Later in the morning, during a lull, Maddy and Kim out fetching sushi, Di glanced out the small back window toward Darling Point—cloudy, no rain—and then down to the little lane that ran beside the building. There under the scrappy paperbarks, Bec and Timmy. Bec puffing on a ciggie, looking at her phone and talking to Timmy at the same time. Bloody long ciggie break. Or maybe Justin had told her to clear out until further notice.

Di looked across the hall toward Good Bloke. The front door still closed. Maybe sometime someone had cold-called the business to get a worker or two to unload a semi, or drive a forklift, or something. And maybe a laborer of some sort had gone out to do the job. But the punter would've received no encouragement to call back, and as far as Di knew, Bec—who'd just turned up one day and asked for a job, and Justin had let her stay, why not?—dealt with the legitimate side of the business pretty much singlehandedly, ringing this one or that one, anyone she knew was looking for a day's work, and get him to bring a mate if necessary. They might've made enough money that way to cover the rent.

She looked out the window again. Bec was chatting to another woman now: young, light hair. Timmy was walking away, ten yards down the lane. Was he picking up pace? A green car parked there illegally.

Then the ding of the lift bell, and footsteps coming up the stairs at the same time. No one due for another half hour.

Inside Justin's office, each one had his sandwich bag, tightly rolled, a rubber band around the outside. Different amounts—forty grams for Andy, a hundred each for Brett and Noel, eighty for Dave—the biggest whack yet. And the cleanest shit yet. But no money in the room. That was another iron law: never the drugs and the money in the same place at the same time. That too was a benefit of them sharing that atmosphere of trust: you didn't have to act like it was total dog-eat-dog, you could count on an honest square-up later on.

Next everyone was standing up, ready to piss off. Each to make up his own smaller deals, grams or caps or whatever. Noel to Canberra, where he knew people, and where prices were better than Sydney. Brett to a pub in Chatswood and the university. Dave to Bondi. None of them to the Cross, though, where things were just too harsh. Andy was gloomy, but he had his stuff and now there was work to do.

Dave, with his deal double-bagged and stuck in his jeans pocket, was looking at his phone when they heard the knock at the door. Surprisingly gentle and tentative. Justin glanced through his office door toward the frosted glass. A single pro-file there.

Noel and Brett looked at each other and then without a word moved toward the unused second office, where there was another door leading into the back hallway and the fire stairs. Andy and Dave stood still. With Bec not there to field whoever it was, Justin strode over and opened up.

He knew the detective, MacDonald, standing there grin-ning. There was no shouting, no guns, no battering ram. Just MacDonald, who said, "Gooday, pal!" like a postie about to ask him to sign for a package. "Coming in, mate, alright?"

And then the room was full of men and women. Andy on the floor, the Stooges back in the room after being ambushed at the other door. Justin was whisked into the back room. Dave into Justin's office. But still not much noise.

Everyone knew the drill. Cops asked first if there were any guns, then asked each one to hand over the drugs, while in the very act of thoroughly searching each one of them. The boys had too much form to break down or blather—say nothing, they knew that—but there was despair on every face. Andy looked at Noel: *So what about your fucking mate, wasn't he supposed to warn us about shit like this?* Noel's return look: *I don't fucking know. Ask Timmy.*

The packets of drugs they'd just so carefully weighed out were lined up on the reception desk. Appreciative whistles from the cops. Next to them the pocket scales, nearly as important as the dope itself, which would help prove the intention to supply. The cops miffed, though, that there was no money.

The whole time MacDonald was friendly, conciliatory, like a favorite uncle who'd dropped by unexpectedly to take the kids to the pictures, but maybe had to clear up this little misunderstanding first.

It all went on for an hour. The boys were separated, then all brought back together in the reception area. Justin, Andy, the Stooges all in a line, handcuffed, forlorn. Except for Dave, who was still being questioned in Justin's office.

Then pairs of cops took each one of them in relays to the cars downstairs. Here in Edgecliff the cops knew to keep it low-key.

Di watched it all, half hidden behind the palm in New Beginnings. Her heart beating fast, even though it was not her business (*really* not her business).

When the mob of jacks had come pouring out of the lift and off the stairs, gathering silently outside Good Bloke, they'd barely glanced her way. Except for the blond girl, the one she'd seen talking with Bec, who gave Di and her salon a good, long look. But then Justin had opened up, and the blonde turned quickly away and marched into Good Bloke along with the others.

Di had immediately rung up and canceled the next two appointments, sent Maddy and Kim home for the day. She was shaky enough to want a cig, although it was five years since she quit. She stayed on, busied herself with admin tasks as best she could while she kept an eye on the bust. Should she ring Chris the lawyer? No. Justin would do that soon enough. But still she waited, watched Andy and the Stooges being taken away. Then finally Justin, handcuffed, with the older cop next to him, not even holding his arm, walked to the lift.

She could feel Justin aware of her there, but he didn't look her way—gallantry, maybe, keeping her out of it. But Mac-Donald, who was now holding the Fitness First bag, turned her way and knew exactly where she was in the salon. He caught her eye, shrugged sadly, said, "Sorry, love," or something. He and Justin disappeared into the lift. The doors closed.

She let the lift go, then said to herself, *Fucking jesus, just go!* and ran down the stairs. Got there as Justin and Mac-Donald were stepping onto the footpath, into the roar of New South Head Road. So casual that you wouldn't even notice it was a bust unless you looked closely. She ran around, stood in front of them. MacDonald paused, for the first time unsure, and annoyed.

"Ring Chris?" she said.

Justin nodded quickly. "It's federal. Not state. Tell him I'll be in Goulburn Street. *Federal.*"

"Got it."

MacDonald had recomposed himself. "Now, now, now. Better leave this alone, Diane. That's right, isn't it? *Diane?* We know you, don't we?"

That rattled her.

He leaned over, beaming kindly now, and whispered, "So bugger off, dearie, or we'll fuck you from here to Christmas."

She took a step back, said to Justin, "Ring Tony?" His re-covery sponsor. Justin pulled a look, nodded.

She watched them get into the dull green car in the side lane—she knew shit about cars, but it was so obviously a cop car. Up the street she could see the blond cop at the driver's seat of another car, dull blue—also obviously police—chatting with Bec in the passenger seat. Was Bec being questioned? Was she one of them? Another young male cop came out of the food court carrying takeaway coffees, handed a cup to the blonde, one to Bec, and off they drove, laughing. Yes, one of them.

Ten minutes earlier, upstairs, in the Good Bloke office. Mac-Donald, Dave, and another cop, all sitting around Justin's desk.

Mac smiled, nodded slowly. "Went well, boys, no doubt about it," speaking softly so not to be heard in reception, where a handcuffed and mournful Justin was waiting with a junior constable. "They pinched the Koreans half an hour ago. Pounds of piss, goods in custody. Gone for a row of shit-houses." He looked directly at Dave. "And *you*," he went on, grinning broadly now, "you've done well, Dave. *Bloody* well. Best I've seen. Best anyone's seen. All that time and effort. It's been noted at the highest echelon, you get me?" Then, looking more closely at Dave, "You alright?"

"Yeah, first rate boss, no worries."

Mac stood up. "Show's over now. Consider yourself back home. You won't be needed in court, they've got enough. But obviously, don't let any of those cunts see you, not just yet."

Dave nodded.

The other cop said, "They'll know what's up when Dave doesn't show up in remand."

MacDonald shrugged. "No matter." To Dave he said, "You've seen enough of the inside of Long Bay, eh?"

Dave nodded again, grinned uncertainly.

Mac walked to the door, patted Dave's shoulder as he passed. "Give us a minute while I take this prick out here away. You blokes follow up later. No rush," and he was gone.

Dave and the young cop looked at each other. Mac had conspicuously *not* asked Dave to front up the sandwich bag still stuck in his pocket. Mac never overlooked anything. His idea of a reward? *No rush,* he'd said.

The cop grinned at Dave. "So?"

Di arrived back upstairs, saw the lights still on in Good Bloke, shadows moving around in there. She went quietly into New Beginnings, stopped the fountain, turned out the main lights, sat there at her stool, and called Tony the sponsor. She finished, looked up to see Dave step out of Good Bloke, then a detective. Dave's hands were free.

Dave pulled the door shut until it clicked, turned to the cop and nodded. Job done.

The cop was about Dave's size, his age, even his build. He and Dave walked to the lift and the cop pressed the button. Dave rolled his shoulders. He said something and the cop guffawed.

Di stared. Dave and the cop still joshing with one another

while they waited. Old friends. Dave's voice sounded different. The laugh too. The shakiness gone.

The door opened and the cop stepped in.

Dave suddenly looked back down the hall, straight into New Beginnings. He saw her there staring back at him. His smile went. They held the look. This time Dave let it out, let it show. Maybe he just couldn't hide it: he was drowning. She had nothing to throw him.

He walked into the lift, his head down.

Acknowledgments

Many thanks to Ann Dombroski for her editorial insights, and to all the talented writers who contributed to this collection. Thanks also to Johnny Temple and his team at Akashic Books, and to the city of Sydney.

ABOUT THE CONTRIBUTORS

JOHN DALE was born in Sydney. He is the author of seven books, including a memoir, *Wild Life*; a campus novel, *Leaving Suzie Pye*; a novella, *Plenty*; a true-crime biography, *Huckstepp*; and three crime novels: *Dark Angel*, *The Dogs Are Barking*, and *Detective Work*. He lives in Sydney with his wife and son.

MARK DAPIN is the author of the highly praised military-police novel *R&R*. His debut novel, *King of the Cross*, won a Ned Kelly Award; his next, *Spirit House*, was long-listed for the Miles Franklin Literary Award. His short fiction has appeared in *Meanjin*, *Best Australian Short Stories*, and *Penthouse*. He lives in Sydney, where he makes a living as a journalist and screenwriter, including for the recent *Wolf Creek 2* TV series.

Tony Mott

PETER DOYLE is the author of four novels and two collections of archival forensic photographs, *City of Shadows* and *Crooks Like Us*. He also writes about popular culture and music history, and has guest-curated a number of museum exhibitions, including *Pulp Confidential* and *Suburban Noir*. He is an active musician (slide and steel guitar) and works as an associate professor of media at Macquarie University, Sydney. His most recent novel is *The Big Whatever*.

ROBERT DREWE'S novels, short stories, and memoirs—*Whipbird*, *The Drowner*, *Our Sunshine*, *The Shark Net*, *The Bay of Contented Men*, and *The Bodysurfers*—have won national and international prizes, been widely translated, and adapted for film, television, radio, and theater around the world. *Our Sunshine* became the international film *Ned Kelly*, starring Heath Ledger, while *The Shark Net* and *The Bodysurfers* were adapted for ABC and BBC television miniseries.

Ciaran Gilling

TOM GILLING is a writer and journalist. Two of his novels, *The Sooterkin* and *The Adventures of Miles and Isabel*, were chosen by the *New York Times* as Notable Books of the Year. He has also cowritten several true-crime books.

JULIE KOH is the author of *Capital Misfits* and *Portable Curiosities,* which was short-listed for the Readings Prize for New Australian Fiction, the Steele Rudd Award, and a NSW Premier's Literary Award. She is a 2017 *Sydney Morning Herald* Best Young Australian Novelist and a member of Kanganoulipo. Her fiction has appeared in *Best Australian Stories* (2014–2017) and *Best Australian Comedy Writing.* "The Patternmaker" is the result of a collaboration with designer Rioko Tega.

Hugh Stewart

ELEANOR LIMPRECHT is the author of two novels, *What Was Left* (short-listed for the 2014 ALS Gold Medal) and *Long Bay.* Her third novel, *The Passengers,* was published by Allen & Unwin in 2018. She writes contemporary and historical fiction, essays, book reviews, and short fiction. Her short stories have been included in *Best Australian Stories, Sleepers Almanac,* and *Kill Your Darlings.*

Sarah Rowan Dahl

GABRIELLE LORD'S first novel, *Fortress,* was adapted into a film starring Rachel Ward, and *Whipping Boy* was made into a movie for television. She has now published sixteen adult novels. Her YA series of seventeen books, Conspiracy 365, is an international success and a TV series. Her recent releases include the first book in a YA trilogy—48 Hours—called *The Vanishing,* and the adult novel *The Woman Who Loved God.*

Borys Raudko

PHILIP MCLAREN is the author of: *Sweet Water, Stolen Land* (winner of the prestigious David Unaipon Award), *Scream Black Murder* (short-listed for the Ned Kelly Award), *Lightning Mine, There'll Be New Dreams, Utopia* (winner of France's Auteurs d'Ailleurs Award) and *West of Eden.* His work is translated and taught in universities across Europe, the US, and Australia. Both his parents are Kamilaroi First Nation Australians from Coonabarabran. McLaren was born in Redfern, Sydney.

Joanne Saad

P.M. NEWTON traveled to Mali after thirteen years in the NSW police to write about music; and India to study Buddhist philosophy. An award-winning author of two crime novels, *The Old School* and *Beams Falling,* her short fiction and essays have appeared in *The Intervention Anthology, The Great Unknown, Seizure, Review of Australian Fiction,* ABC's *The Drum,* and *Anne Summers Reports.*

Peter Rae & Fairfax

PETER POLITES'S first book, *Down the Hume,* was published by Hachette in 2017. It is part queer, part noir, and all Western Sydney.

TSC Tempest

LEIGH REDHEAD has worked as a deckhand, masseuse, exotic dancer, waitress, teacher, and apprentice chef. She is also the author of an award-winning crime series featuring stripper-turned-private-investigator Simone Kirsch: *Peepshow, Rubdown, Cherry Pie,* and *Thrill City.* Leigh is currently completing a PhD on Australian noir fiction and a noir novel set in an alternative community in rural Australia.

Tanya Lake

MANDY SAYER is an award-winning novelist and nonfiction writer. She lives in Sydney's red-light district with her husband and two dogs. For more information, visit: mandysayer.com.

KIRSTEN TRANTER is the author of three novels, most recently *Hold,* long-listed for the 2017 Miles Franklin Award. Her first novel, *The Legacy,* was a *Kirkus Reviews* debut novel of the year, short-listed for the ALS Gold Medal and the ABIA literary fiction award, and long-listed for the Miles Franklin Award. She is a cofounder of the Stella Prize. Raised in Sydney, she now lives in the San Francisco Bay Area.